Mental Cruelty

A Novel for Divorced Men

Lee Kronert

WestBow
PRESS

A DIVISION OF THOMAS NELSON

WestBow Press books may be ordered through booksellers or by contacting:

WestBow Press
A Division of Thomas Nelson
1663 Liberty Drive
Bloomington, IN 47403
www.westbowpress.com
1-(866) 928-1240

Because of the dynamic nature of the Internet, any web addresses or links contained in this book may have changed since publication and may no longer be valid. The views expressed in this work are solely those of the author and do not necessarily reflect the views of the publisher, and the publisher hereby disclaims any responsibility for them.

Any people depicted in stock imagery provided by Thinkstock are models, and such images are being used for illustrative purposes only.

Certain stock imagery © Thinkstock.

ISBN: 978-1-4497-6787-7 (sc)
ISBN: 978-1-4497-6788-4 (hc)
ISBN: 978-1-4497-6786-0 (e)

Library of Congress Control Number: 2012917252

Printed in the United States of America

WestBow Press rev. date: 7/10/2013

Introduction

"ALRIGHT," THE JUDGE BEGAN, "This is Spencer versus Spencer. I'm told that there is a settlement."

I sat in my chair and calmly listened. Beside me sat my attorney, Kevin Vail. He wore a beige sport jacket which dulled some of the redness of his hair. His freckled face showed a suggestion of boredom. He reached and tugged on his earring, not glancing at me at all. Across from us sat my wife, Janine, and her attorney, a tall, stern- looking man named Ben Hill who had a reputation for ruthlessness and always getting what his clients wanted. He stood and answered the judge:

"Yes, Your Honor." He spoke authoritatively. "I've handed you the amended complaint. I've explained to my client that this oral stipulation will be set forth in a transcript."

Lawyer talk. In other words, whatever was said now would be written out later.

"That transcript will be annexed to the judgment of divorce..," Attorney Hill continued.

My mind was racing with all kinds of thoughts.

How differently I would have done things had I known what I knew now. I made so many mistakes. There were many oversights and I must confess to a lack of sufficient effort on my part to do what would have been best for me and for the kids.

I sat now in front of a Judge thoroughly disgusted with myself.

Look at the facts:

Janine wanted this divorce. Why didn't I demand that she could have what she wanted as long as she first got a job and proved to me that she would at least attempt to support herself financially? Instead, I will be paying for everything. Why didn't I make a better effort to fairly assess the equity of the division of our personal property? Why did I so easily agree that she would be the one to remain in our new house? I'm the one who always kept it clean; why did I trust that Janine would suddenly become a reliable caretaker?

Sitting beside my lawyer, my mind wandered to how I just knew that my wife had stashed our money away in some hidden account and that for some reason I had either been too lazy or simply too stupid to try to find out where. In a few minutes every dollar she'd stolen would be hers and it would be too late for me to do a thing about it.

I suppose the only excuse I can give is that I've never been divorced before. This was all new to me. What did I know about deception, greed, manipulation, and back-stabbing the person you once claimed to love? This was my first divorce. Yep, divorce. I work three different jobs, love my kids, and believe in my heart that I really tried to make my marriage work. Yet here I stood in divorce court in front of a judge, two attorneys, and a court stenographer, about to be divorced. Twenty-five years of marriage, plus an additional four years of dating, and in five minutes I would be single. I wasn't the least bit unhappy; in fact, I was surprised by how completely unemotional I felt as I listened to my wife's lawyer ramble on in words I'd never heard before and would probably never hear again. Twenty-five years...

When I'd met Janine Cunningham she was 10 years my junior, so for many months back then I did my best to discourage a relationship. The only problem was that she showed up at my house daily during the summer and she was enjoyable to spend time with. Oh, and did I mention that she was also very attractive? I should have resisted her advances, but my willpower was weak. After all, I was already past my twenties, unmarried and rapidly running out of my drawing pool of potential mates, and I really did want to meet someone special and spend the rest of my life with her.

"The other issues have been mainly concerning the children," Ben Hill droned on in a monotonous tone.

Issues about the children....

I had a great role model growing up. My father lived for his four boys. When we were really young, we couldn't wait for Dad to get home from work. It wasn't because we missed him or anything like that, but because every day he would bring us each a small piece of dark chocolate that he kept in his lunch box. He was always thinking about us. Throughout our childhood, Dad displayed often to all four of his boys just how special we were to him. Mom was the same way. We were always cherished and made to be loved. I always remember thinking, "Someday, when I'm a dad, I'm going to love my children the same way!"

Well, as life would have it, I was honored by God to be a father... and I've always made the most of it! As I stood before the judge at my divorce hearing I thought about my children. Sydney, my eldest, was at college this very moment sitting in an education class. She is studying to be a high school Science teacher. Garrett, my middle child, is a junior in high school. Lilly and Layla, the twin babies of the family, are only in the seventh grade. All four of them were safely at school, their eyes, hearts and young minds spared the embarrassment and accompanying failure visible at these divorce proceedings. Good kids. They love their parents. They love God, and they were raised to know that the Bible is the true and eternal word of God. In the book of Malachi it is written: "God hates divorce!" So do I! And I'm pretty certain that my children feel the same way.

What has it been like for them all these years?

Chapter 1

I THINK I WAS four years old.

I remember leaning up against the wall of a garage building that was adjacent to the home my parents rented. I had a year old brother, Richie, who kept mysteriously turning up with little red marks all over his arms and legs. Mom and Dad were alarmed at first fearing some sort of circulation problem, until my aunt Marie commented once, "Looks like someone's been pinching him!" Well, how can anyone hold a four-year-old, who had never been consulted on the topic of having a new addition to the family, responsible for actions typical of a selfish and insecure child? Besides, I was always sensitive to the time Richie needed to heal between attacks!

On this summer day as I stood against the wall, I experienced a unique revelation. It was at that moment that I realized that I, Lenny Spencer, was a living, breathing, existing something, which my mother later informed me was a human being. It was my moment of initial awareness.

So now that I knew that I am a separate, unique, and distinct something, the question quickly became: What do I do with this thing that is me? Feed it, bathe it, and brush its teeth, of course. Yet, the big question was then and remains today: What am I...and who made me? – And why?

My early childhood was all about family. My mother had two sisters and a brother who along with their children made up the bulk of our social circle. We rarely visited with my Dad's side of the family. There was really nothing unusual or noteworthy about these early childhood years except that, well, I was kind of a different child.

To be perfectly blunt: I was somewhat effeminate.

I cried easily, other boys at school bullied me, and Dad was always angry at me for not fighting back. One summer afternoon my mother had to come out to the backyard to rescue me from a bumblebee. I was a sissy about everything. But that all changed in the second grade.

We had just bought a house and moved to a new town. The very first day we lived there, an eight year old girl came to the back door. She wanted me to step outside so she could beat me up! I hid in my new room the entire day.

My second grade teacher was Mrs. Smith. She introduced me to the class and then for the rest of the week an incredible thing happened: no one picked on me! For recess everyday we did the same event. The entire class ran from the outside door about forty yards to a fence, turned around and ran back. That was recess. Every day. Every *single* day. And every day, Larry Mayes won the race. Yet no one in the class felt dejected or handicapped or really anything negative: Except me. For the first time in my life I was no longer satisfied with being this separate, unique and distinct me. I wanted to be like Larry Mayes! The fastest! Looked up to! A winner! So the effeminate little boy who was picked on all the time started to train. All during the winter, while other children watched black-and-white TV, and drank Yoo-Hoo, I would run outside from my house to a telephone pole down the street and back, increasing my speed, gaining confidence, and preparing myself for the ultimate confrontation. I even gave myself a nickname, "White Lightning." I could barely wait for the winter's thaw.

I don't remember the exact date but I will always remember the day. Mrs. Smith took us outside for our first run of the new spring. When she shouted, "go!" it was the most alive I had ever felt in my young life! For the first twenty or thirty yards, Larry Mayes and I were running neck-and-neck. Unbelievably, with a sudden burst of speed, I actually touched the fence before Larry did. Wow! I was half-way home to victory. On my way back towards where Mrs. Smith stood waiting, I noted the surprise and disbelief on the faces of the other students. They could not believe it either! But this momentary mental lapse was just the pause in focus that Larry Mayes needed to overtake me. I lost the race, but I was never more proud of myself as I sat in class the rest of that day. I was an athlete. It was the best thing a young boy could be, and I was one! I never really noted the change in me that took place that day, until years later when I reflected back on it, but it was an unmistakable turning point in my life. The sissy was gone. No longer effeminate, I made friends, played sports, and did well in school!

I suppose that standing in this courtroom on the threshold of a divorce was yet another major turning point in my life. What do I do now?

"The complaint," Attorney Hill resumed, "specifies minimal grounds, that being the agreement of the parties, that they would minimize this. They are both nice people. It's just that they've got other things to do with their lives and it doesn't really involve the other one into the future. What they have in common are the children."

Divorce: How does it happen?

I met Janine Cunningham when I coached her during summer soccer. Yes, I was her soccer coach! At the time I was still a relatively young man and lots of the girls on the team flirted with me. I really thought nothing of it. Janine was different. She was my best player, scored the most goals, and the most emotionally mature of my players. We got along well and became friends. And that's all we were: friends! But as the summer season wore on our relationship changed. We played tennis together a few times and once she brought over a chicken and broccoli meal that she cooked especially for me. She started to stop by my house nearly every day. One night I crossed the line of coaching and kissed her. Wow! Before long we were both in love. Four years later we married.

Two people make a solemn agreement to spend the rest of their lives together. It starts out so romantic and exciting. You both look at each other in a very special way. You talk together effortlessly. All day long you think about one another, you look forward to being together again. The intimacy between you is an incredible high. Is there anything better? You realize that this is what you were created to experience: To love someone. To be so connected that you share one heart, one mind, one body. All your hopes and dreams can be summed up in the unity of you and your mate. What an idea by an awesome God. I remember thinking: I am set for life!

While dating on one fourth of July, I got my first glimpse of disharmony. We sat on a blanket with my parents and my brothers while we watched the fireworks. We talked. We ate. We laughed. An hour later, when we were back at my parent's house, Janine started crying. She cried for over an hour. She refused to tell me why. I did my best to console her, but it was to be of no avail. No matter how many times I asked her what the problem was, she turned away from me, seemingly ignoring my concern. Then it suddenly dawned on me: I'm the reason why she is crying! I didn't know what, or why, or how, but I was growing certain that I had done something to hurt her. To hurt her badly, I realized, as I watched her tears turn to sobs. I knew too at that very moment, that her knight in shining armor had just fallen off his horse. And worse yet, that try as I may I would never sit in my sparkling attire in her eyes ever again. I knew it then. And I turned out to be right.

One thing I want the readers of this novel to remember is that they are only hearing one side of the story: my side. It would be fascinating for me to read what Janine herself could remember about that July night. To this day, I don't know what exactly hurt her that night, but I've got a good idea.

David Phelps has a song called, "End of the Beginning," where he shares the message of Jesus and the Bible. The insinuation is that although the first stage of salvation is completed, there is very much more to come. Well, for Janine and I, the end of the beginning was here. I never could figure out exactly what changed so drastically between us, but try as we may, we never did recapture our beginning. The once-upon-a-time knight in shining armor had become a troll! Oh, not all at once, mind you, but slowly and persistently over the years, a former friend and lover became a stranger and the enemy. I still do not completely understand it.

We were walking through the woods in New Jersey the next spring when I caught another glimpse of trouble. We were discussing our plans for the summer.

"I'm going to play on two softball teams," I stated matter-of-factly.

Janine stopped dead in her tracks, "Then why am I coming home for the summer?! I'm not going to just sit there and watch you play." She stated firmly.

Honestly, I was a bit taken aback by the brashness of her opinion on this issue. What is so bad about a guy playing softball? I always played softball during the summer. That's what I do! And quite frankly, I felt a bit resentful to be told that this may not be.

"Do you want to spend time with me, or would you rather play softball?"

Tough question.

If the truth be known, every female relationship partner I've ever had, has had to deal with a rival. I love sports! Whether it is football, basketball, soccer, volleyball, tennis or softball, I enjoy talking about sports, reading about sports, watching sports, and especially playing sports. The Lord did not bless me to be a gifted athlete. I am five-foot-seven inches tall, and today I weigh about 170 pounds. I made myself as athletic as I could possibly be. Whatever little athletic success I have experienced was due to my speed, my determination to win, my heart, my love of competition, and mostly my self-image. You see: I always convinced myself that I was a lot better then I really was. An example that comes to mind is a time when I told Janine how I was guarding a friend in a basketball game because he was my size. She gave me a weird look.

"He's not your size," she exclaimed, "He's at least 4-6 inches taller then you!"

In my mind I thought we were about the same size. It used to drive Janine crazy!

"You are not a home run hitter." She would try to explain to me after I would fly out three times in a league softball game. "Whoever told you that you that you were so good?"

Dad did. He told me all the time.

In the early sixties there was really only one sport that mattered in America: baseball. Hitting, fielding, throwing, stealing bases; there was nothing better for a boy to do with his time. My friend Rob lived down the street and I think baseball is the only thing we ever talked about. A couple of us used to jump on our bikes, bringing our gloves, bats, and a ball and ride to the nearest field. During the summer, we played baseball everyday. And if it wasn't baseball we would play with the larger softball or hit a whiffle ball against my house. We made up our own leagues, kept statistics on every player and shared our latest league standings with each other. We talked about Mickey Mantle, Roger Maris, Yogi Berra, Hank Aaron, Willie Mays, Ernie Banks, and Dale Long. Dale Long? Well, Rob was a diehard Chicago Cubs fan.

Then came little league….

In 1960 the population explosion in America was probably at its peak. Dad was very excited about his oldest son playing in the town league. It seemed to me like there were hundreds of us who showed up at the tryouts. The parents in charge timed our running speed, watched us throw, catch, and slide, and they were especially interested in how well we hit that darn baseball. Let me be blunt: I sucked! For some reason the boy who played nearly everyday with his friends just couldn't handle the pressure of an organized tryout. I was never so nervous in my life. In today's world, any child who showed up to play gets on a team, regardless of how poorly they may play. But back in 1960, with more 9-years-olds then at any time in Unites States' history, not every child made the team. I was exhibit A. Too many boys were better players than me and there were certainly not enough roster spots for everyone. But fear not, the Little League leadership had a back-up plan. It was called the clinic. Dad broke the bad news.

"There are too many players for all the boys to be on a team," he started by manipulating the truth, "so you are going to go and practice once a week at the clinic." He stammered on, "That will make you an even better ballplayer then you already are!"

The clinic? I had never heard of such a thing before, but one thing was certain: it wasn't good! Tears came to my eyes. In my young mind I knew exactly what this meant: I wasn't good enough to make a team. Dad sensed my emotional disappointment.

"All the coaches," he lied, "told me that they thought you were a good player. You just need to work on your hitting and fielding."

My hitting and my fielding?! Is that all? What else is there?

"They told me that you are blinking when the pitch is thrown at you, and when you have to catch the ball."

That was the first time in my life that I was told that I had a blinking issue. But in my mind I began to formulate exactly where I stood. I was a good player, (Dad told me so), but this darn blinking phenomenon was unsettling to the Little League leadership. Suddenly, I wasn't upset any longer. Instead, a sense of failure was replaced by a renewed sense of commitment. Simply put: I would go to the clinic and get better!

Later that night, as I was getting ready for bed, I heard Dad talking to Mom in the kitchen, "No," he was explaining, "the coaches thought that he was really good. He was one of the best players there. But he blinks too much." Dad paused. To this day I can still see the lump that formed in his throat. "He's a ballplayer, Hon. They were just concerned about the blinking."

I realized two things at that moment. One, Dad was not telling Mom the entire truth. Secondly, as well as a nine-year-old can trust his limited perception, I knew that my father truly believed that I was something special. To my Dad, all his boys were the best, not because that was the reality, but simply because Dad believed it in his heart. I think the Bible calls it unconditional love.

Unconditional Love:

That's what God had in mind when he binds a man and woman in holy matrimony. The apostle Paul refers to the union of marriage as a mystery.

When I married Janine, to be perfectly honest, I wasn't sure that this was the right thing to do. We had been dating for four years and I was already in my mid-thirties, so I went through with it. I certainly loved her, but the question was whether I could live peacefully with Janine Cunningham. I knew that she would be high maintenance and difficult to please, but after all, I dreamed about having children, a home, and a workable relationship. Looking back, I must agree with Meatloaf, "That two out of three ain't bad!"

We got along fabulously those years we were in college. I was down in South Carolina and she was in Delaware. For four years we lived 500 miles apart but saw each other as often as we could. We drove cars, took planes, buses and trains to make every effort to see one another. Perhaps it was the distance and lack of real time spent together that sustained us. I don't know. But while we were dating in those early years we got along fine. Movies, plays, baseball games, you name it; we had fun! But when we were together more often, like over summer vacation, there were road bumps. We still had lots of fun over vacation but there were now arguments and lots of heated discussions.

We were in Spartanburg, South Carolina at the Chiropractic College that I had graduated from just a few months earlier, when a discussion of the impending wedding came up.

"I really don't think that we should go through with this." I showed my concern. "We're not getting along like we used to. Maybe we should just postpone the wedding for awhile until we're sure."

Janine appeared momentarily stunned before she uttered the statement she would grow to regret for the next twenty-five years: "No, the invitations are out, so let's just go through with it."

Well, I suppose that was that! In three weeks, we were married. Pastor Dave stood before us and read, "Therefore shall a man leave his father and mother, and shall cleave unto his wife; and they shall be one flesh."

Now I never went to a Seminary school, but I know that this concept of one flesh means more than just the sexual act. You see: at every wedding between a man and woman a real life, honest-to-God miracle takes place. God takes two separate people and then as only He can do, He turns them into one! You can stare at the bride and groom all you want and you won't see it. There's no spiritual dust that falls from the ceiling nor does a bolt of white light suddenly twirl around the outside of the couple. That's the thing. You can't see it, smell it, hear it, or feel it- but a miracle has just taken place. On our wedding day, Janine and I were part of a miracle. God miraculously joined us together forever. So what happened to the forever part?

Ephesians chapter five in the Bible is pretty clear about how a man is to love his wife. A husband is to love his wife as Christ loved the church. Well, let's think about that: Whether the reader is a believer of the Bible or not, the guideline set forth makes a lot of sense. Everybody has heard the story of Jesus; some believe it, and some do not. According to the Bible, Jesus loved the Church so much that he was willing to be brutalized and murdered for it. Ephesians says that "He gave himself up for it." Now that is quite a sacrifice if you ask me. So as Janine's husband, my duty, my responsibility, my pledge is to be willing to lay down my life for her. Pretty heavy stuff!

Ephesians says that Jesus might present it to himself a glorious church, not having spot or wrinkle, or any such thing, but that it should be holy and without blemish. In other words, Jesus was committed to loving his people unconditionally. He was going to do whatever he could to make it the most awesome thing that this world had ever seen. Ever been to church? Dealt with all the different types of people? Glorious? Holy? Without spot or wrinkle? Give me a break! If you want to meet people with issues and problems, join your local church. Well, for all the good things I loved about Janine, there were also things that I just couldn't seem to deal with.

Janine was energetic, athletic, loved animals, kept a clean house and was an awesome cook. We used to read the same book together and later talk about it and analyze the author's intent. On the other hand, she could be so moody, bossy or irritable when these discussions were contentious. But none of that cancels the Bible's command to me as her husband to love her unconditionally. I was to love this flawed woman unconditionally, and build her up, so that she would know that I saw her as glorious, holy, spotless, and without blemish. Needless to say over the course of the next twenty or so years, I failed to do so.

So what exactly happened? Well, let's start with the honeymoon. Or better yet, let's go back even further:

I am going to risk transparency now because I am about to confess a character flaw that had its roots long before I ever even met Janine. Here goes: I find women attractive. Okay, so what man doesn't? Back in the early seventies, when I was an undergraduate at St. Francis College in Loretto, PA, a whole group of us used to stand atop the steps of the Sullivan building and wait for the girls to come by. We referred to this male spectator sport as ogling. We even had a rating system of one to ten, with a score of ten being the best and highest. Obviously, there were debates, disagreements, and occasionally ratings were ridiculed if a particular score was considered overly generous. It was meant to be fun and it was a great way to pass the time on one of the few warm Western Pennsylvania days. There was one particular young woman who caught my eye and since she was a freshman, I dubbed her as my rookie of the year. I quickly learned that her name was Betty King and that she, like I, hailed from New Jersey. I had never spoken to her, knew nothing about her, and yet decided that she was the girl I wanted. Does the reader think that I am a self-centered, superficial, shallow package of testosterone, in search of his own pleasure with no regard to or any concept of what it takes to be in a relationship? Bingo! Hey, I was nineteen years old. I liked what I saw. What I needed now was a plan!

During the fall of my sophomore year, I decided to pledge a fraternity. On one particular Thursday evening, the fraternity pledge master informed us that there was going to be a social tomorrow night and all the pledges were to bring a date. Talk about pressure! Where was I going to find a date in twenty-four hours? Suddenly, as I stood in the pledge line, a light went on and a scheme began to unfold.

When we got back to the dorm I phoned a girl who I knew was a friend of Betty King. Her name was Kathy.

"Hi Kathy, this is Lenny." I cut to the chase, "Listen, I need a date tomorrow night for the fraternity social," I spoke not knowing where I was heading. I paused for effect and then went on. "You have any ideas for me?"

"Well, there's Candy Pierce."

My plan was beginning to materialize. "Tell me about her," I responded, pretending to be interested. I listened to my friend Kathy patiently, knowing that all along I was not going to agree with her first choice.

"Who else?" I asked.

"Well," she continued, thinking aloud, "There's Betty King."

Paydirt!

"Who's that?" I asked. Duh, like I didn't already know.

Kathy told me a little about Betty, where she was from, and where I might have already seen her around campus. When I heard enough, I decided to end the charade.

"Ok, I'll take her."

"Let me ask." Kathy had me hold on. This was the moment of truth. I had ogled Betty King for over eight weeks now and dreamed of taking her out. Now I stood on the threshold, waiting to receive a favorable reply.

"Lenny?" Kathy returned to the phone, "She said she'll go!"

Well, since this book is not about Betty King, let me summarize the next two years: We had many great times together and many disagreements with respect to the nuances of just what makes a healthy relationship. You see: I wanted Betty because she was beautiful and fun to be with. What I didn't want was to have to explain why I wanted to be with the guys sometimes, or why I didn't call enough, or say, "I love you" enough, or focus everything in my life around my relationship with her. I must confess: I didn't treat Betty very well. There was no abusive behavior, but looking back I certainly could have shown both her and the relationship a lot more respect. Two years later, Betty King came to her senses and dumped me. The only question that ever really nagged at me afterwards was what in the world did she ever see in me in the first place?

The point of this little transgression from my story is this: I chose my college girlfriend based solely upon her looks. Yet I came to realize that as much as I found women attractive and desired them physically, I really can't say that I grew to like any of them. There was something about their attitudes, their demanding spirits, and their unrealistic expectations of the man they expected me to be, that always rattled my cage.

Janine was no different.

But I need to backtrack for just a minute because the end of my relationship with Betty King did have a profound moment. Perhaps I could even call it a defining moment in my life. The last time we were ever together we discussed the reasons for our unfortunate break-up. Here's what I remember: Betty shared with me ten faults that I had. Ten! Funny, to this day, I cannot recall a single one of my ten supposed flaws, but I remember the number: Ten! Betty told me that there were ten things wrong with me. I told all my buddies about it afterward and to this day they will still laugh and tease me about my ten problems. It really wasn't until many years later that Janine told me that I had some issues that I needed to deal with. You guessed it: Ten faults. So let's get back to the finding other women attractive issue. First of all, no, this was not one of the ten things on the Betty King fault list. Sure it annoyed Betty at times when my attention strayed but she never took it personally. Janine did. Boy! Did she ever!

Remember my memory of the July fourth night when Janine cried and cried and never explained to me why? Well, the same thing happened the very next Fourth of July celebration night. She was mad and I was clueless as to the cause. At times, during that summer, I would be distracted momentarily by an attractive young woman and instantly a lively conversation would turn into dead silence. Usually she was wrong. I was not checking out other girls, it was just her jealously creating imaginative scenarios in her mind. Honestly, it took me awhile to put all the pieces together, but when I did, the puzzle was always the same. Finally, towards the end of the summer, it was all released like the great flood of Noah's day.

We rented a beach house with my family in late August. In a couple of weeks Janine would be returning to the University of Delaware for her junior year, and I would go back to South Carolina where I attended Sherman College of Straight Chiropractic. This was supposed to be the last hurrah of summer. Romance, sun, waves and the New Jersey boardwalk were to be our due. Instead, it was pure hell! Apparently, Janine had had enough of my visual recreation and told me in no uncertain terms how much she hated it and felt unloved by my disgusting habit.

I looked at girls. That was it. My glances were brief and I never kept my eyes riveted to their body parts. All I ever did was look.

"You look at every girl who walks by." She said this, stepping onto the boardwalk, her eyes blaring with anger.

"You don't even care how old they are. You just check them out and you don't seem to care that I am walking beside you."

I was speechless.

"What is the matter with me?" She wailed, "What do they have that I don't have?"

I can answer that without hesitation. The other women that I supposedly looked at had nothing to notice that was better than Janine. Janine had it all physically. Breasts, butt, long hair, legs, a flat belly- you name it. My girl was put together! That's the rub in all of this. The issue is not that I was looking for something better, but that I was simply looking at, and it really had nothing to do with my feelings or desire for Janine. Of course, she would never believe that. Over the years, Janine Cunningham/ Spencer would always interpret what she thought my ogling as proof of my dissatisfaction and lack of desire for her physically. Was it ridiculous for her to think so? Absolutely! Yet try to explain that to someone who could never believe otherwise. Two things: One, I understand why she felt the hurt as a result of my mildly wayward eye, but two; I always knew that her interpretation was wrong. I loved her and only her.

I talked about love and what it means for a man to love a woman as outlined by Ephesians chapter five. Let's make a point of clarification right now. I'm the writer of this story. I was there. These pages contain my memories, my appraisals, and my thoughts at the time, and my perception of the reality of my relationship with Janine. I am not Janine. I never understood her side of the story, let alone explain it. Let her write her own book!

Chapter 2

WE HAD PLANNED FOR over two years to travel to the Caribbean on our honeymoon: Punta Cana, Jamaica, and the Bahamas. It was going to be a dream- come- true. We planned to tan at the beaches, body surf, and kayak. As a matter of fact, during our three week honeymoon we enjoyed everything we had set out to do. The only thing that was not part of our original plan was all the fights: Lots of them. We fought over which foods to buy, where to shop, how long to stay in each area, when we were going to workout during the day, and of course I was still being chastised for noticing an occasional female as she passed by. But the biggest disagreement that Janine and I had during the honeymoon was over my desire to visit a high school friend who had moved to Jamaica. Whew! Big mistake!

George Marks was one of my best friends in High School. He and his family had moved to Springfield, New Jersey in the beginning of his sophomore year. I was a year older and a grade ahead of George. Through a mutual friend, Dale Yablonski, we quickly became friends and fellow adventurers. George was everything that I was not. He was always in a good mood and always up to something mischievous, but more importantly, George was a genuine ladies' man. All the girls loved him! He was of slender build, with long brown hair that often fell over one or both of his eyes. George and I ran track together in high school and if the truth be known, had we spent a bit more time training and less time finding ways to hide from the coaches, we probably would have had more success.

Actually, George did pretty well in the meets. I was the one who just couldn't seem to get over the hump when it came to athletic competition. Still bothers me a little today.

The thing I'm reminded most about when I think of my friend George is that he helped to make me more confident when it came to approaching members of the opposite sex. Quite frankly, at seventeen years old, girls made me very nervous. George used to just walk right up and talk to them as if it was the most normal thing in the world. I needed a Cyrano De Bergerac.

Until Suzie.

The New Jersey town, Springfield, that I grew up in was about eighty percent Jewish. There were two synagogues, and every Saturday morning the sidewalks were covered by the feet of walking yarmulkes. Suzie was an attractive Jewish girl who was two years younger than me, and George always insisted that Jewish girls were loose.

"They don't believe in Jesus." He would explain to me. "So since they're not worried about going to hell, they'll do things with us."

Us? What kind of things?

At seventeen, I was about as naive about sex and girls as anyone you could ever meet. I liked their breasts and wanted to see their breasts, but I had no clue about those other female body parts.

One afternoon George was telling me how he and this girl he knew had spent over three hours in the town cemetery. I smiled and agreed how great that must have been to be alone with a girl that long, but what I was actually thinking was: What in the world can you do with a girl for three hours?

Back to Suzie.

When I first met Suzie she was my friend Benjie's girlfriend. They were both Jewish so everything was cool. Only, as the school year was ending, Benjie informed all of us that his parents were making him work as a camp counselor a few hours away. All of us were disappointed to realize that it would be a summer without Benjie.

Benjie pulled me aside the night before he had to leave for camp, "Listen Lenny, you're my best friend and I want to ask you a big favor." Benjie paused for effect. "I want you to keep your eye on Suzie, make sure that she doesn't go out with anyone else. Can you do that for me?"

When you're seventeen, life seems more dramatic than it really is, so I quickly assured my good friend that I could be trusted to be an excellent watchdog. And looking back I suppose I did a good job, considering that Suzie didn't date anyone else, except for me, of course. But she was so pretty, and funny, and smart; who could blame a guy, or for that matter a bodyguard for falling for his assignment? Perhaps I took my job too seriously, got too close, and when the tide of love changed, the sheer force of the waves was too strong for either of us to resist. Okay, maybe that is overstating it a bit, but seventeen year old hormones are stronger than honor and trust. Simply put: I blew my assignment.

One night in early August Suzie had a party at her house. George and I went together. Within five minutes, he was off looking for his latest female conquest. I knew who I was looking for.

"Hi!" Suzie actually walked up to me first.

"Hi," Was all I could think of to reply.

For the last six weeks, during my friend Benjie's absence, I found myself spending a lot of time with Suzie at the Springfield pool. A group of us always sat together listening to music, laughing, flirting and simply getting to be comfortable with members of the opposite sex. We played volleyball every day. It seemed like Suzie and I were always on the same team and I was always hitting the ball to her more often then any of my teammates. I knew that I was starting to like her and that she seemed to like me too, but what about Benjie? She never talked about him. I certainly didn't talk about him. What a mess this was becoming.

"Do you want to go sit over by the tree?" Suzie asked me. And then she reached for my hand. Oh my God, I was in trouble now!

"You know a lot of people," I stated awkwardly, desperate to say anything that didn't make me sound like a total fool.

She looked into my eyes and smiled.

At that moment there was only one thing on earth that I wanted and needed to do. No, not run for my life; I just wanted to kiss her. My mind was swirling with clever things to say, romantic things that would just make her want her lips pressed to mine. But all I could come up with was, "Can I kiss you?"

So we did. We kissed and we kissed some more and for the first time in my life I knew that I had found something better than playing sports.

Then as I was kissing Suzie the words of my friend George came to my mind: "Jewish girls are loose."

I had one arm around her back while my other arm dangled by my side. I suddenly wanted more than anything to touch one of her breasts. Nervously, I brought my hand up to her chest and I did it! Wow! I left my hand there and Suzie made no attempt to move it. She liked it, I thought. Guess George was right. These Jewish girls really did let us do things to them.

As soon as I got home that night, I went right up to my room and sat at my desk to write a letter to Benjie. I wrote:

"I feel like a rat! I know you asked me to keep Suzie away from other guys, but I couldn't stay away from her myself. I am such a lousy rat! Cheese is the only thing I deserve to eat. I just couldn't help it, Benjie. We were always together at the pool and it just sort of happened. I know we may never be friends again. I am so sorry for what I did. I am such a rat!"

I mailed the letter the following morning. In the meantime, I called Suzie and we got together with friends everyday that next week. I actually had a girlfriend and it was the most wonderful thing in my life. I never even gave my friend Benjie a thought. Until his letter arrived. He wrote:

"Lenny, don't feel so bad about what happened between you and Suzie. It's my own fault for putting you in such a position. I'm the one who should apologize. It's going to be hard for me, but you and I will always remain friends. You're not a rat. Enjoy her. She's yours."

His final words have always, even to this day, had a profound meaning to my life. "She's yours." And it was somehow true. Over the next year and a half, I belonged to Suzie and she belonged to me. We were a couple. We did things together. We talked on the phone nearly every night. We kissed a lot. I don't really know how to explain it, but Suzie was mine!

Teenage dating is a wildly exciting time in a young man's life. There's this unexplainable understanding, an agreement if you will, that you pledge not to date anyone else. The thought of dating someone else never even enters your mind. Your girlfriend is your partner; you do things together. And if someone else ever tries to muscle in on your territory, you experience this new unpleasant emotion called jealousy. Looking back at my time with Suzie, it's as though it represented my first experience with practicing what marriage would someday be like. Only, teenage dating involved none of the legal titles, or financial issues, or nurturing of children that marriage certainly entails. I'm not saying it was easy. But it was less stressful. As Allen Iverson would say, "It's just practice."

The Bible in 1 Corinthians chapter 7 tells us that it is good for a man to have a wife. Sexual desires are strong, but marriage is strong enough to contain them. The apostle Paul wrote that "the marriage bed must be a place of mutuality. The husband is to please his wife and the wife is to please her husband. The marriage bed is not a place to stand up for your rights." The Bible goes on to talk about how the husband owns his wife's body and that the wife also owns her husband's body. This concept always reminds me of Benjie's words from years ago. "She's yours." Through the miracle of the union of marriage God has allowed us to stamp our seal of ownership upon our chosen mates. They belong to us. And just like the owner of a brand new vehicle takes great care of his possession, so too should we honor, cherish and care for what is now ours!

My car is in my name. My house is in my name. Now I can choose to sell them and forfeit my ownership, but my car would never wander out of the garage on its own and find a new owner. It's mine! I decide to do with what is mine. The Bible assures me that likewise, in a very real sense, my wife is also mine. She belongs to me. Only, let's face it: she's not a possession like a car, or a house, or a set of golf clubs. And unlike the ludicrous notion of a wandering automobile, a wife does have the free will to leave her husband should she decide to do so. Janine chose to leave. Why? Well, I can't really claim to understand her motives, but I do know that her decision was preceded by many years of flare-ups, accusations, tears, and depression. As I already mentioned, our honeymoon had its share.

When we found George Marks' house in Kingston, Jamaica, no one was home. There was a note on the door telling us to make ourselves comfortable and that they would be back soon. Janine sat on the couch in the living room and said nothing.

"Look, "I began apologetically, "we'll only stay for a couple of hours, okay?"

That opened her up.

"Why are even here?" She cried out. "This is supposed to be our honeymoon. Why do we have to visit one of your old friends?"

"I haven't seen George in over fifteen years!" I explained my side.

"We're here in Jamaica, and who knows when we'll ever be back again? What's the big deal? It's only for a couple of hours."

"The big deal, "she hissed," is that I am your life now. You should be willing to give up old friends and this past of yours that you seem to love so much."

"What are you talking about?"

She was becoming livid.

"You know exactly what I'm talking about! You haven't seen this guy in fifteen years! What do you care about his life now? I want you to care more about me than old friends you never see, never have any contact with, and will probably never see again. Why can't I be first in your life?"

I hated when Janine talked like this. Of course she was the most important thing in my life. We were planning a future together. Old friends are just that. They are no more than old friends. Why was it that every decision I made was somehow a choice between, or better yet, regarded as a preference over her? She always saw things that way. How come Janine could never seem to understand that just because she was the most important person in my life, it did not mean that she was the only person in my life? George and I had a history together. My goodness, here I am sitting in my old high school friend's living room right now! What was the big deal?

"Nothing to you is a big deal." Janine resumed, apparently reading my very thoughts. "You don't care about what I think, or how I feel, and you certainly do not value my opinion on anything."

Again I said, "What are you talking about?"

"Marriage is important to me. It matters." She started to explain to me. "I want you to be my life. God has made us one. This marriage should be the most important thing in the world to you. But instead, you refuse to let go of your past, as if it were the most important thing."

What nonsense!

"That is not true!"

"It is!" Janine resumed her tirade. "What are we doing here, "She made a sweeping motion with her arms, "on our honeymoon? This is our special time together, and it is supposed to be about us and only us!"

She began to cry.

Just then the front door opened and George and his wife entered the house. Janine quickly recovered, and acted as though her visit here was the most natural and enjoyable thing in the world. Actually, the four of us had a great evening of food, sharing memories, and catching up on our lives. Janine was great. She was funny, lively, and especially affectionate to me while in their company. She was always good that way. Janine had a knack for hiding any emotional damage when we were with other people. I liked that about her. Of course, through the years I learned too that her loving demeanor lasted only until we were alone again. Then she had an equally astounding knack for resuming an argument right where it left off, and with the same fervor. I wasn't too fond of this knack of hers!

Alright, time to dissect and analyze just what took place. From my perspective, the opportunity to visit an old friend could not be wasted. I mean, it was George Marks! We share a huge amount of memories. Janine and I were on our honeymoon, starting our entire lives together, so what are a few hours? In fact, how many couples get to honeymoon for more than a week? I just didn't think that time spent together should be an issue. What was the big deal?

Now, let's consider her perspective.

A honeymoon is a social custom where the happily married newlyweds can get away by themselves and simply spend time loving one another's company. It's a celebration of one of the most important decisions in life! It is not about the past, in fact if anything, it designates a very real separation from the past, pointing to a new and brighter future. The Bible says that the man is to cleave to his wife, leave his father and mother behind, and give up himself for his chosen mate. To Janine's way of thinking, I was breaking an unconditional understanding. Instead of cleaving to her, I refused to let go of who I used to be, where I used to be, and who I used to be there with. I understand how she felt. I recognized her fear and concern. I just didn't think that it was warranted. We stayed at George's house for two hours. Two Hours! I know I sound like a broken record, but what's the big deal!

Sadly, my honeymoon does not evoke warm and fuzzy memories of an awesome time spent with my lover. Quite frankly, I have rarely in the past twenty-five years reflected upon it at all. Yes, it was fun. I'm glad we went. But it was not the most special three weeks of my life. It was a social custom that all newlyweds perform. We went through the motions and then flew back to New Jersey to meet face-to-face with the greatest challenge of our lives: Marriage! Following the honeymoon, I was not exactly optimistic.

Chapter 3

I ALWAYS HOPED TO get married. I really did! When I was in my early twenties I used to fantasize about being with a beautiful woman, having healthy, intelligent, athletic children, owning a home and being successful at something. I believed that somewhere out there I had a soul-mate. In fact, I still do believe it. The vocal group, The Moody Blues, sing a song called, "I Know You're Out There Somewhere". Deep inside of me, I have always imagined and prayed that I would find that one special person whom God created just for me. Now on this side of twenty-five years of marriage and a divorce, I continue to trust that my soul-mate is out there somewhere.

Janine.

Looking back, I wonder if I ever really considered her my soul-mate. During her younger years Janine Cunningham was certainly a fine, young woman. She had a caring spirit, an appropriate sense of humor, enthusiasm for life, was adventurous, and even quite an athlete. I was always proud to tell people that she was a member of the track team at the University of Delaware. Janine is a slender five-foot-five brunette who was blessed physically. Her shapely frame and long brown hair actually made her quite stunning to look at. But one of the things I really found myself attracted to was her speed! I remember standing on our dead end street, talking with my Dad, while Janine prepared to race my brother, John.

"Watch this, Dad," I said as I pointed towards my new girlfriend.

Janine fired past John.

"Wow!" John exclaimed as he stood amazed at his defeat.

"I think I'm going to marry her." I told Dad.

Dad smiled and shook his head affirmatively.

"I would too!" He answered, laughing softly. "Where else are you going to find a set of legs like that?"

By this time I had already completed my first year of Chiropractic College. We were taught a lot about the human body that first year, including the theory of genetics. When my father and I watched Janine run, the unspoken was understood by two males who love sports. I envisioned the athletic potential of my future children. My Dad was probably contemplating retirement and watching his grandsons play ball. Do guys really think like this? I often wondered whether subconsciously I married Janine because I wanted to have children. I love kids! Especially my own! Sydney, Garrett and the twins are the best thing that ever happened to me. That question would occasionally come to mind during a real down time in our relationship. Did I want to be a father more than I desired to be a husband? Normally, I would come to this conclusion: No, I did not subconsciously use Janine to sire offspring. I loved my wife. I care about her. I wanted to be a good, caring, and loving husband. I just didn't know how.

So what kind of an excuse is that to shout out to anyone who will listen? There are lots of things in life that I don't know how to do. My father was a mechanic. I have to pay to have my oil changed! Decisions about how to fix things around the house is a no-brainer: Call someone to come over and do it for me! I can't distinguish one type of flower from another, nor do I know what kind of tree I'm looking at. The point is: There are many things that I don't know a thing about, or how they work, or how to deal with. Unfortunately, marriage ended up in the category of knowing a lot, but obviously not enough. There are a few things though that I consider myself very knowledgeable about: Sports, the Bible, chiropractic, and Math. That's about it! As for Janine Spencer, I was always trying to learn more about her, but even with my on the job training I ran into countless obstacles that convinced me of my relational ineptitude. Truthfully, I never did figure her out.

My life has really been in two stages: The years before Jesus came into my life, and the last twenty-three years since. During the first stage of my life, I admit that my relationship failures were a result of my own selfish, self-centered nature. I lived for myself. Right and wrong were understood, but blurred to my conscience. This is probably why I treated Betty King so badly during my college years. That's why she informed me of my ten faults. I did not believe in a God, and whatever little I may have considered possible concerning a Divine Being, was certainly nothing personal. It was my life, to do as I pleased, and I was determined to live it however I wanted.

I was raised Catholic. Now Catholicism may be a wonderful religion for some, but in my house it was essentially a meaningless exercise in futility. I made my Holy Communion at seven, was confirmed at thirteen, and never once got through a complete reciting of the Rosary. I knew the Hail Mary, Lord's Prayer, and even the Apostles' Creed by heart, and I can still recite them today. The only difference is that in the first stage of my life they had no meaning. Today, the Lord's Prayer and the Apostles' Creed especially, are packed with meaningful and spiritual significance.

There were a few spiritual moments that I can vividly recall. In my late twenties I was a math teacher in Lambertville, New Jersey. One night I stood looking out my kitchen window up at the dark sky. I don't recall the cause of my mood that evening, but I know that I was at a crossroads for some emotional and spiritual reason.

"God," I spoke aloud, although I was alone in my apartment. "I've heard a lot about Jesus and how he's supposedly the answer to everything but," I was truly sharing my heart, "I'm just not ready to commit. I think that someday I will, but not today. I'm just not ready to change my life yet."

As a result, my life did not change. Due to my lack of Biblical knowledge, I thought that it was up to me to change first, before an unknown God could accept me. What I was perhaps really saying that night was this: I don't want to be a goody-two-shoes, who tries to do everything right and who has to follow all these rules for living. Of course, having never read the Bible, I had no clue as to what these rules might be, so instead, I came up with my own self-improvement plan for personal salvation.

Believe it or not, my upgraded agenda for a new and more fulfilling life was crudely based upon not the Ten Commandments of the Bible, but rather upon correcting the Ten Faults as outlined by Betty King years before. Now I didn't know any of the Ten Commandments at the time, but that was alright because I had no real memory of my ten faults either. I suppose I never was a good listener! It was the notion that I had these ten faults that motivated my resolve to change. My goal for change was simple: I was going to become a beautiful person. That's right: Beautiful! I wanted to be more loving, caring, generous, humble, a friend to the unloved, hardworking, and just an all-around great guy!

So I started reading books on all types of topics: war, psychology, spirituality, and philosophy. I taught myself how to draw! I took horseback riding lessons, and I even joined the ski club. I was on my way to becoming a new me. I even decided that I would not date until I had learned how to treat women better, kinder, and with more respect. I went three years without a date!

One day, while in between classes where I taught high school, I walked into another teacher's room to tell him something. There was a young girl sitting in the room alone doing her class work.

"Are you in here all alone?" I asked.

She smiled sweetly and replied:

"No, I'm not in here alone. Jesus is with me."

Okay.....

Well, I didn't see Jesus anywhere in the room, so I playfully told the young girl so.

"He's here!" She responded joyfully. Then she lightly tapped her chest where her heart would be. "He's right in here. He's with me always. Everywhere I go!"

I left the room with such an uneasy feeling in my stomach. How sad that this young teenage girl was already so brainwashed about this Jesus stuff. She really thought that everything in life was going to turn out just fine because she believed that Jesus lived inside of her. I remember thinking that Jesus was a crutch that she and so many like her lean on instead of facing life's difficulties head-on and growing from it. Would she ever learn to take care of herself in this cruel world? Would she risk adventure, try new things, think for herself, or would she always just smile and say yes to whatever this Jesus told her to do?

Years later, when Janine and I first started to date, I used to drive up from South Carolina to visit her at the University of Delaware. One day while she was out of her dorm room I noticed writings on one of her walls. They were written by Janine in her calligraphy style and they seemed like words of wisdom and strong faith. Oh no, I remember thinking. These are from the Bible. When Janine returned I asked her.

"You're not one of those re-born Christians, are you?"

Janine told me that indeed she was.

To save money on phone calls from South Carolina to Delaware, Janine and I called each other after eleven o'clock at night. There were no cell phone family plans in those days. We talked about everything back then: Our future plans, traveling the country, our personal goals, and often the conversation turned to Jesus. I always politely listened and inserted my personal opinions on the matter, but generally the topic would wear itself out and we would go onto another subject. Yet afterwards, as I was out going for a run, or riding my bicycle, my thoughts would return to the phone call from the night before. And my reaction was always the same: Who is this Jesus guy anyways?

As the relational tension grew between Janine and me, the subject of Jesus rarely came up. Once during Easter we drove from South Carolina to Key West for spring break. There were certainly some memorable moments, but overall, it was not a fun trip. We were fighting more than ever before and looking back, I believe that we were even starting to dislike each other. On the long drive back to South Carolina, we hardly spoke. When we finally got back to Spartanburg, Janine told me that she was through trying to make this relationship work. We agreed to break-up. I remember that we were both a bit shaken by the reality that we were finished as a couple. I took Janine to the airport, and as I watched her plane take-off, I wondered sadly if I would ever see her again.

During the ensuing days I made no attempt to phone, write, or try to contact her in any way. It was useless. It was over, so deal with it!

For some reason my college gave us another week off soon after the Easter spring break, so I drove back up to New Jersey. Coincidentally, Janine also came home that weekend. She phoned my parent's house and asked if she could come over to see me. I don't really remember what I thought at the time, but I did quickly agree to see her again.

When she came to the house she was the same old Janine. It was as though the break-up had never happened. I was certainly confused, but I said nothing. All I knew was that she was back and that was fine with me. The most important thing that I remember about that night is the talk we had about the possibility of resuming our relationship. She told me that I needed to think more about the relationship, put more effort into making it work, and that if I did my part, things could improve. I had my doubts. Janine told me that if we were really going to work things out then I had some things about myself that had to be fixed. Yep, you guessed it: Ten faults!

Here's the thing I learned that changed my life.

After Betty King first told me about these ten faults of mine I had made an effort to change. I was determined to become a beautiful person. Now here I was thirteen years later being informed by Janine, the one person who knew me best, that despite my commitment to change, nothing was really any different. I was stunned. So I quickly came to this startling revelation: Lenny Spencer did not have whatever it took to change the person he was: Selfish, self-centered, lustful, procrastinator, double-minded, obnoxious, wanting my own way, and clueless as to how to be different. It was becoming obvious: I needed help. When you allow yourself to have two different young women get close enough to know you for who you really are, and both of them draw the same conclusions, well, they say that the definition of insanity is doing things that never worked before the same way over and over again! Something had to give. I tried to be a beautiful swan, but apparently I was still the ugly duckling. All that effort to be kinder, more loving, humble, and generous had fizzled like a dud firecracker. So now what do I do? Where do I find help and who can help me?

Who can help me?

As I was leaving the college parking lot on a Friday, I discovered that someone had laid a pamphlet entitled, Power for Living, on the backseat of my car. I brought it into the house and left on the desk in my room. Over the weekend I glanced at it from time-to-time, but it wasn't until Sunday evening that I actually picked it up and read. The tiny pamphlet contained people's experiences of spiritual rebirth, mostly famous people. The only one I can remember is Julius Erving, in his own words sharing his personal change and acceptance of Jesus as his Lord and Savior. Julius Erving: Dr. J! What an awesome basketball player.

And then, like a bolt of lightning, or better yet, as if God Himself had snapped up a window blind, I knew that everything I had heard about this Jesus was true.

"Of course!" I whispered.

Of course it would take God Himself to clean up this mess we all get ourselves into. We all need to be rescued. Think about the people who take drugs, alcoholics, people who rape, steal, intimidate others, extort, and even murder! How easy to recognize their need to be rescued from the consequences of their horrendous lives. Boy, do those losers need to be forgiven! Their sinful actions are so blatant, so obvious, so out there for all to see. Man, I'm glad I'm not like.....

But wait, I am!

The truth hit me like a ton of bricks. As I learned to say later: "But for the grace of God goes I". I had two loving parents, food and a roof over my head, certain talents and skills, and although I wasn't what the girls would call handsome, I wasn't ugly either! I had so much going for me, yet I still couldn't get this thing we call life right. I could spend all day listing my failures, but instead, I would rather focus on my greatest triumph.

There is an awesome mind-boggling verse in the Bible that states, "I was chosen in Christ before the foundation of the world to be holy and blameless in your sight". Can you believe that? Before the foundation of the world! What does that mean? Could it be that before the oceans, before the sun and moon and stars, before the mountains and streams, before birds, fish, and all the animals; before all of that I was on His mind! Wow!

It was true. It was all incredibly true. The One who made everything, including Lenny Spencer, considered me worthy of dying for in order to save me. Picture it: From His majestic throne, God sees it all. All the hurt, all the pain, all the murder, deceit, maliciousness, loneliness, bereavement, sorrow and lustfulness, and incredibly, He decides to do something about it!

Picture It!

God throws off His robe, gets up from His throne, and clothes Himself in humanity. He becomes one of us. A human! A person who sees, feels, cries, hurts, desires, and hopes. God becomes a man: A man on earth with a specific mission. To pay the price Himself for all who trust Him to do so. What an awesome true story!

This decision to believe the story of Jesus represents my greatest triumph, the single most important decision I ever made. Yet even now as a born-again Christian, I still couldn't seem to fix and completely heal this relationship with Janine. She was certainly happy to learn of my spiritual conversion, but what she was really looking for was the fruit! In other words, if you are the Christian man that you say you are, love me like the Bible commands.

Here's the kick:

Janine breaks up with me and then shows up at my parent's house to reconcile. Ten weeks later we're engaged. Now why would two people with a very recent history of not getting along well, suddenly decide, 'yep, this must be the person I want to spend the rest of my life with', and choose to marry? What were we thinking? Through the years I've spent time every day in the Word of God and I suppose that I can claim to know a bit about scripture. So I am very familiar with what God says about marriage and more importantly, that He expects couples to remain together for a lifetime. But consider this: WHAT IF YOU MARRY THE WRONG PERSON? I am not making excuses. What if you marry someone who is just not your type and discord is inevitable. Friends who are happily-married, who enjoy being with their mates, and who respect and share decision-making about children, finances, and day-to-day living; what do they know about living with someone you don't get along with? The answer is: Nothing! They can quote the Bible. So can I. They can tell you that love is an action word, a choice. I know that rhetoric too. But unless you've been there, and experienced how painful it is to be unevenly yoked, please spare me your well-intended advice. You don't have a clue!

It was November. Janine and I had already been married for eight years. We were arguing one day about me spending too many hours at my chiropractic office. Then she dropped the bombshell that would be repeated many times over the next twelve years.

"I don't love you anymore!"

I just looked at her. How does a husband respond to his wife when she tells him that?

"I don't love you." Janine repeated. "I tried, Lenny, but this is just not working."

I kept my cool and responded calmly.

"So what do we do now?"

Janine shook her head sadly.

"I don't know."

As I stood before the Judge on the day of my divorce there was one thing I was certain of: I would never marry again!

Chapter 4

THE COURTROOM WAS SILENT but for the monotonous drone of Janine's lawyer, Ben Hill.

"If the agreement goes through and is accepted, Mr. Spencer would withdraw his answer to the amended verified complaint and allow us to proceed, as if by default on that complaint. The complaint specifies minimal grounds, that being the agreement of the parties, that they would minimize this. They are both nice people."

Basically, what Janine's lawyer is saying is that I agree to drop my complaint about his client's ludicrous claims of mental cruelty as grounds for the divorce. Mental Cruelty! What a farce! No, better yet, what an outright lie!

As I stole a glance at Janine, seated at the table to the right of me, I couldn't help but wonder: Whatever became of the young woman I had fallen in love with? Where on God's earth had she disappeared to? The woman divorcing me certainly looked like Janine, and had the memories of our unique history together, but she was not really her. No way was this woman sitting across from me the same woman I married. She had changed a lot. Actually, it was more like the original Janine had been destroyed, obliterated, no longer in existence. She would probably agree, but for all the wrong reasons. Janine would insist that I had destroyed her, that I was to blame for her life turning out the way it did. Deeply imbedded in her psyche, I believe that she even developed a need to prove to herself that I was the cause of her depression, her unhappiness, and ultimately for the divorce. So she made up lies about me to convince herself that divorce was justified and that God was on her side, albeit, contrary to His own unalterable word.

We flew back from the Caribbean and landed in Newark, New Jersey on a Sunday. My brother John picked us up at the airport and drove us to my parent's house. Following an outdoor lunch, we drove Janine's Dodge Dart to nearby Scotch Plains, New Jersey where we would begin our lives as a married couple.

I was going to spend the summer working for my brother putting in underground lawn sprinkler systems. Even though I had graduated from Chiropractic College, I as yet had not taken my state licensing exam. Janine got a summer job at a bank. For me, summer also meant playing softball in the town league. On one particular day as I arrived home from work and anxious to resume playing since returning from our honeymoon, Janine made a simple request.

"My Mom needs a ride home from work." Janine told me a story about her mother's car issues. "Can you pick her up at six o'clock?"

My softball game was scheduled for six-thirty.

"I can't. I've got to get to my game."

Janine was not about to let this go. It occurred to me to ask her a question that I considered proper and reasonable under the circumstances.

"Why can't you get her?"

Let the tirade begin!

"I worked all day," she started, "shopped at the Mall to buy you the spikes you so desperately needed, then went to the grocery store so that you could eat dinner. The dinner, in fact," she pointed towards the kitchen, "that I'm slaving over right now for your sake."

I was confused. Am I eating the entire meal alone?

"I don't have time for dinner." I explained. "I've got a game." Then I attempted to appeal to her sense of understanding. "I haven't played in over three weeks. I really want to be there on time tonight. Can't you get her? She's your mother!"

That was not the right thing to say.

What Janine did next is what I have referred to over the years as flipping out. I did pick up her mother, and I did get to the game by the second inning. Needless to say, Janine did not attend my game that night. But when I got home, following the game, she was waiting, and all hell broke loose!

All of the emotional release valves reared their ugly heads. There was yelling, crying, hand-waving, body crumbling to the ground, and throwing of objects. Certainly, I should have readily agreed to the small task she asked. I can understand her complaint about that. But should it have caused this type of reaction? Eventually, Janine stalked out of the house and stomped into the night air. I followed. I knew that it was my job, or better yet, my obligation to go after her, console her, apologize, promise to never do it again, and persuade her to return home. Even in the streets, Janine continued to complain and yell about my husbandly shortcomings for all the neighbors to hear.

On this particular evening there was only the two of us and the neighborhood that had to listen to these frequent tirades. For many years afterwards, I mentally visualized our children as they listened to their mother scream and yell at their father. For their sake, and with their fragile psyches in mind, I did not fight back. Subjecting them within earshot of one parent's emotional outbursts was bad enough. They didn't need to hear two!

So I took it.

For their delicate sakes I did not fight back in front of them. It was different when Janine and I were alone. Looking back, I feel extremely vindicated by my choice. My four children are well-adjusted, responsible, happy, do well in school, and have an appropriate circle of friends. But I wonder: How well will they deal with the significant relationships in their future?

In mid-July, I was preparing for the New Jersey State Chiropractic Exam for licensure. I studied hard. While I put in lawn sprinkler systems, I worked with a tape recorder and headphones. I had made my own tapes filled with test information and I listened to them over and over again. I was ready, but I still felt that it was a good idea to attend a three-day review class down in South Jersey. The review class instructors were more familiar with the content of the state exam. They were privy to the types of questions asked. I informed Janine about my decision and even invited her to come along.

"Three days!" She exclaimed. "You're telling me that you're going away for three days! Didn't you promise me once that you would spend every night with me?" She was on a roll. "You said that when we got married you wanted to sleep with me every night. A month later, and you're already breaking your word."

I spent four years and thousands of dollars going to a chiropractic college. Receiving a diploma is an accomplishment, but a license to practice is the goal. State exams are given every six months. If you fail, you wait another six months for a re-take. I believe that going to a three day review seminar is a wise decision. Janine was not like-minded.

For the next two days I was given what would become a precursor to all major confrontations: the silent treatment! Successful couples deal with their disagreements by sharing their perception and feelings about a certain situation. Our relationship did not work that way. Reason: My perception was never respected. Janine utilized the silent treatment to let me know that there was a problem. The next step was for me to ask her exactly what the problem was. Then in no uncertain terms, my responsibility for the problem was analyzed, dissected, and presented to me in a clear, concise, and logical manner. Stage three was now up to me to agree with her assessment, own up to being the cause, and then to explain how I would remedy the problem. Rarely did the assessment include a diagnosis that involved fault on both parts. Only one of us was at fault. Only one of us was to blame. And only one of us was expected to take full responsibility.

Three days before the review classes were to begin, I approached Janine as I had been taught to do.

"I understand that you don't agree." I reintroduced the subject. "Everybody takes these review classes." I have a tendency to over dramatize when I wish to strengthen my case. "I'll be back in three days. I need to do this, Janine. Please trust that I know what I' m doing."

"Oh, I see it all very clearly." She shot back. "Whatever you need to do for chiropractic is a priority. Me on the other hand, I'm to wait here at your beck and call. I'm like a box on a shelf. When it's wife time, you can always go to the shelf and open the box and use me because it's convenient. It's wife time! When you don't want the wife around, close up the box and put it back on the shelf for a later time when it fits your schedule." She was getting angry. "Well, I do not wish to exist at your convenience.

I'm a person! I expect to be loved for who I am. I am supposed to be your partner, your best friend, and I should be your priority! You don't want a wife. I don't know what you want me to be. Some people should never get married. I think you're one of those people!"

"What does that mean?" I replied offensively.

"I know you need to pass the exam." Janine retorted. "And I realize that a review would be great. I'm not stupid! But you decided to do this. You decided that you would need to be away for three days." Tears welled up in her eyes. "Do I get any input? You're married now, Lenny. I just want my husband to include me in the decision making!"

"I asked you to come along."

"Yeah, after the fact." She pointed out. Suddenly the expression on her face changed.

"How long did you know about this review class?"

Uh-oh: Time to fess up. Irene Gold Associates had mailed me a flyer about the chiropractic state exam review nearly six weeks ago. I didn't tell Janine about it because I knew that the notion of my going away for a few days would upset her. I planned on telling her when the time was right. Only, let's face it: With a woman like Janine there is no right time! Here's the deal: A married couple should be able to openly share their desires and communicate freely. In other words, there should be no secrets. The only problem was that every time I had an idea or a suggestion that we do something, Janine almost always shot it down! She always had her well-thought-out, logical reasons why my idea wasn't good, nevertheless, her reply was usually no. What bothered me most was that I never felt my input, or my opinion on a matter, held as much weight as hers. She made decisions while I had to ask permission. I'm sorry, but that is not a marriage relationship! When I forced the issue for her to see things my way, Janine often resorted to emotional antics such as crying, yelling, or most often pointing out how I would never think to make such a request if I really loved her. That was the one I heard all the time. How I didn't love her. Now I am not a psychologist by any means, but I call that control! In Janine's case, it was control by hysteria. If she doesn't get her way, act up, and refocus the issue on a person's character, instead of upon the issue itself. I never learned how to deal with that. I loved Janine. I wanted to be a good husband, make her happy, prioritize her, but at the same time I needed to be respected for who I was. Unfortunately, and in my opinion, undeservedly, the desired respect was never granted.

"I got something in the mail about six weeks ago." I finally admitted.

"Six weeks!" She practically screamed at the top of her lungs. "And you don't even tell me about it until now? What if we had plans? What if I wanted to do something next week; would you change your plans to accommodate me? No, of course not," She answered her own question, "I know what's important to Lenny Spencer. Chiropractic! How can I compete with your beloved work! God, but I hate you at times!"

That was the first time she uttered those words: I hate you! Throughout our married life together I would have that phrase hurled at me countless times. Now there were certainly times that Janine annoyed me and caused me to momentarily dislike her, but I never felt hatred for her. I felt sorry for her. But I never hated her. Every time she informed me of her hatred for me my response was always the same: I remained silent and stared blankly at her. Her venomous pronouncement rendered me speechless.

"Lenny, you've got to talk to me. I am your wife. You need to tell me what you are thinking. I deserve to know."

I agreed with her. A husband has an obligation to share all his thoughts and decisions with his wife. Yet I always lived with this nagging regret: I didn't trust Janine. She was too domineering, controlling, and in my experience with her, creatively deceptive in her dealings with me. I tried to tell her how I felt, but my explanations were always met with further scorn and ridicule. Eventually, I just stopped trying.

"Why do you push me away?" She resumed. "I need to know what you are thinking, what decisions you are making, and my God, Lenny; I need to know who you are!"

Then she slumped to the ground with her back against the living room wall. With her face in her hands she shook her head dramatically. I stood staring at her in disbelief. No matter how many times I witnessed these emotional outbursts, I never got used to them, nor did I ever accept them as something distraught people normally do. How could I not have seen this coming? The whole time that I watched and listened to her, the same thought kept returning to me: Why did this woman have to happen to me? All I ever really wanted was to marry someone normal. I just wanted to have a partner in life, someone who loved and respected me, and most of all, who accepted me for who I am. I didn't want someone who was always pointing out my faults, blaming me for their unhappiness, trying to mold me into the marriage partner they wanted , instead of just accepting me for being me. I may be clay in the hands of the Biblical potter, but I certainly did not relish being molded by another clay pot! Who does?

Dropping her hands to the floor Janine continued her verbal attack.

"You've got to talk to me, Lenny. This relationship will never survive if you don't begin to share your life with me. I need for you to think about me when you make decisions, consider how it will affect me, include me, at least try to receive my input before you decide. You always step out on your own, like you're still a bachelor who doesn't want to answer to anyone but himself. If you don't talk, you are going to lose me; I swear to God! You call yourself a Christian, yet you behave ungodly in this marriage. We are supposed to be one, Lenny. Not two separate people doing their own thing, but united together and making decisions together. God is not happy with you."

This was the first time that Janine served as a mediator between God and me. It would not be the last! Throughout our marriage she told me often just what God thought about me or a particular circumstance, or how the Lord supported her side of a discussion completely. She often called me a supposed Christian. I must admit that these instances rarely bothered me for this simple reason: I didn't believe that Janine had a special hotline to God to tell me things that He disapproved of. I knew that if God wanted to show me some truth about myself, that he knew where to find me. Of course, I was forced to consider the role a wife and husband play together in hearing from God. Was it possible that I wasn't listening? Or was Janine simply delusional or manipulative?

In Genesis God creates man. The man's name, as everyone knows, is Adam. But God makes a very interesting observation: "It is not good for the man to be alone." Now I am not a theologian, nor am I bold enough to espouse that the theory I'm about to share is absolute truth, but consider this: If God created Adam in order to have a full and complete relationship with him, what's the problem, and why does creation need the woman? What's not good? Or better yet, what is not good enough? Adam was to know and be known by God. Could it just be that the marriage relationship, a man and a woman together, spiritually linked as one, somehow complete each other, and together can see God more fully as one, then as two separate ones? Interesting… Marriage therefore enhances our relationship with God. So if I fail to recognize a truth that is necessary to my relationship with my Lord, perhaps someone else, like my wife, could reveal information that I on my own do not see. Or more precisely, how about if my wife, by the nature of her special spiritual union with me is the only person who can clearly point out my shortcomings. Logically, this marriage relationship theory sort of supports Janine's right to call on the Lord as her source of confirmation with respect to how I, her husband, live.

Except that:

God doesn't criticize or ridicule. He doesn't attack our character. There is no list of shortcomings that he reveals to remind the accused of past iniquities. He's not that way. God always loves. He respects us. He never gives up on us. God doesn't force Himself on us or ever fly off the handle in anger. There is no scoreboard to tally our sins. He searches for the best in us. And He always does the right thing.

So when God says that man alone is not good enough, well, that must be true. Man and woman are meant to be united as one. I don't care how many couples don't make it. God said so! That's enough for me. Married couples are to fit together like two perfect puzzle pieces, strengthening the other's weaknesses and balancing each other to form a whole that can have the best possible relationship with this Creator. I always knew that Janine was wrong about me. But I also must confess that I have missed the mark myself in many areas and at many crucial times. I could have been a better husband. A part of me believes that a high-maintenance spouse like Janine is impossible to get along with, while another part of me admits my own failure to salvage a marriage that God had intended to last forever.

By our first Christmas time together I knew that our relationship was over. I can't recall all the many little events or spats between summer and the start of winter, but I do remember the afternoon we went Christmas tree shopping with my parents. Janine was all upset because an old college friend had phoned me.

A few weeks ago Janine had overheard me on the phone and my buddy was relaying information about a party he had gone to. Let's just say it wasn't exactly a church party! He told me about how he and the other guys attended a little bar in Philly where the dancing girls, well; we all know what some dancing girls do!

"From now on," she demanded, "I want to be here when your friends call. Don't you see what a terrible influence they are?"

So when another friend called while Janine was not at home, I did what any person would have done. I talked to him. The fellow was a former roommate of mine at Chiropractic College. Of course I'm going to talk to him! When I shared our phone call later she hit the roof!

On the drive over to the farm, my mother did all the talking. Janine and I had not spoken to one another for a couple of days. This latest silent treatment ended as we walked together among the Christmas trees.

"Which one do you like?" I asked in an attempt to begin some kind of conversation.

She stopped and whirled towards me in anger.

"Oh, are you talking to me now?"

Someone explain this to me. Janine is the one who initially stops talking for reasons that I'm not even aware of, but then turns around and blames me for not talking to her. Give me a break! In my opinion, silence between married partners has never solved anything. What I really want to know is 'what did I do?', and let's talk about it. Sounds easy, doesn't it? I wish.

"I was always ready to talk." I pronounced harshly. "I don't even know what we're fighting about! Tell me what...."

"No!" Janine hissed. "I am not going to tell you what you do wrong. I'm sick of always being the one who has to explain everything. When are you going to start thinking about how you are, what you say and do, and how you treat me? I shouldn't have to lay out everything for you! You're a big boy. You figure it out!"

Figure out what?

"I'm always the bad guy." She resumed. "Don't you ever examine your life? Don't you ever want to see how you are, how oblivious you are to me, my feelings, my needs."

What in the world is she talking about?

"Forget it!" Was all I could think to say.

My parents helped Janine pick out a tree while I stood off by myself thinking about my life with her. In my own mind, I knew then that it was hopeless. Six months of marriage and I was ready to throw in the towel. I couldn't stand all the constant interrogations, false accusations, and hysterical behavior. I wanted out! Yet I knew that it was impossible. Divorce was not an option in my mind. When you're married; you're married for life. Take the good, the bad, and the ugly! I had received a life sentence with no hope of parole.

When we got home that night Janine asked me one of the most outlandish things I'd ever heard:

"Do you want to set up and decorate the tree?"

My mind cried out no! The last thing I want to do is decorate a tree with you. I want us to love each other, talk, share our lives, make love, and plan our future together. I just want for us to get along like we used to. I want it to be like it used to be when we travelled nine-and-a-half hours just to see each other for a weekend, or talked on the phone late at night. What in God's name happened? How did we get here?

While my mind searched for answers that would never come, my body started to move towards the Christmas tree that leaned against the dining room wall. I remember that I thrust my hand through the pine needles and grasped the stalk of the tree to lift it slightly off the ground. Then as if I had no control over my own vocal chords I walked towards Janine and said:

"Where do you want it?"

Chapter 5

IT WAS BLUE.

Janine walked around the bedroom staring at the little stick as if it were a magical wand. But I must admit: It was pretty exciting to see the blue coloring on that tiny stick! I was going to be a father. It was a dream –come- true. And maybe, just maybe this new addition to our family would strengthen the bonds of matrimony.

Janine had a tough time the first trimester. I was teaching middle school math and she was working at a bank. I had obtained my New Jersey chiropractic license, but I was still looking for a doctor in the area to practice with. I was hardly ready to start my own business, and I needed more experience in working with and adjusting patients, so I thought that starting out as an associate doctor was the most sensible option. In the meantime, I resumed my teaching career in order to pay the bills. I really had no desire to teach anymore, and informed Janine that as soon as I got a chiropractic position my teaching career would be over. Looking back, I recall now that she made no response to my declaration with regard to my chosen vocation.

We worked in the same town but a few miles apart so we drove together each day. I still have fond memories of that time in our married life. Living on two salaries was pretty awesome! There were no financial issues that school year. In the morning I would drop Janine off at her job, and pick her up later that afternoon. During her first trimester she told me that when she was on break, she slept in the back room. Once we got home she napped again. I took care of her. I made dinner, cleaned, got things that she needed, and sat by the bed as we mused of the coming existence of our very real child growing inside of her. Actually, that trimester of fatigue was a good time in our marriage. We were going to be parents. There was a truce. Maybe married life with children wouldn't be so bad after all.

And then a former student called.

Thomas was in my tenth-grade math class years back before I left for Chiropractic College. He was a good kid. He phoned and then invited Janine and me to a Met baseball game sometime in April. Sounded like a good idea to me. Only problem was, a week later, I had forgotten to tell Janine about Thomas' offer. Big mistake! Thomas phoned again at a time that I was not at home. Janine took the call and was startled to learn of these baseball plans made and agreed upon without her prior knowledge. Doesn't sound like a big deal, does it? I'm sure she was pleasant to Thomas over the phone. She was not very pleasant to me when I got home.

It was the worst I had ever seen her!

After five minutes of her yelling and screaming, I told her I was leaving. I'd simply had enough. I had forgotten to tell her! Big deal! I didn't like being married; I didn't want to be married, so with no real plan of what to do next, I informed her that I was going to stay at my parents' house until we decided what we were going to do about this horrible relationship. Here's the one thing I remember vividly about that day: As I sat in my car, prepared to drive away, I heard someone screaming at the top of their lungs. Startled, I looked up towards my house and saw Janine's face in the bedroom window. She was shouting at me over and over again:

"I hate you! I hate you! I hate you!"

I stayed at my parents' house for two weeks. I did not see nor talk to Janine during that time. Actually, it was one of the most relaxing, peaceful times in our marriage. No one was complaining about me, yelling at me, calling me names, or attempting to control my every movement. It was like the old days. I was free to live and do as I pleased. Yet two thoughts nagged at me: One was that the old days, as I recall, weren't all that great to begin with, and secondly, there was now a fetus in this world which had my design on it. The thought that kept returning to me was this: The child is going to need a father. It's real father!

One night Janine phoned:

"Lenny," she was trying to sound nonchalant, "I have a doctor's appointment tomorrow. Can you take me?"

Well, I took her the following day. I was waiting in the reception room when she came out and I remember that her face was positively glowing. I stood to greet her and to discover what in the world had happened in there.

"I listened to the heartbeat!" Janine breathed excitedly. "It was amazing! I heard our child's heartbeat!"

Well, that excited me too! We talked about how awesome her being pregnant was during the ride home. Yes, home. Later the next day, I returned to my parents' house to pick up my things and went back to where I belonged: With Janine. To this day, neither of us has ever mentioned the time that I left for nearly two weeks. It was if it had never happened. But I always remembered it because it served as a reminder of the reality of our marriage. I was actually happier without her, than I was with her. Now that is a sad commentary on my personal union of marriage. And through the years, I occasionally fantasize of a life without her. I knew it was impossible, but a part of me yearned to be freed of this stifling relationship that was choking joy from my life. Still, I remained because it was the right and godly thing to do. I recall coming to this conclusion: I may never be happy in my marriage to Janine, but I had it within my power to still be happy! So I decided that no matter what, no matter how bad it got, or how much verbal abuse I was forced to endure, I was going to choose to be happy. Now I've sat through sermons and read books and articles about how difficult it is to enjoy life when your marriage is in trouble, but I made a pledge to myself to rise above the pain, endure the torment, and accept the inevitable regret, and still find joy in my life.

I found that joy in God.

Jesus died for my sins. On that day back in January of 1984, a great exchange was made between the Lord and me. He took all the muck and mire of my life in exchange for all His holiness and righteousness. What a deal! You see: no matter how things turned out here on earth between Janine and I, the promise of eternal bliss was real and mine for the taking. I can feel good about that! That should make any Christian happy.

I found joy in my work.

I love being a straight chiropractor. Chiropractic is a philosophy, science and art. Now I may be partial, but it's the most logical approach to health that I have ever heard. The human body knows how to run itself. The very first time I listened to someone explain that within each of us lies an inborn wisdom, a vital immaterial force that maintains us in health, I was sold! When I was taught that a chiropractic adjustment to the spine restores, or if you will, re-unites the material and immaterial parts of man, my immediate response was: Of course! Think of it this way: People come to your place of business. You promote health in their bodies. They pay you for it! And the best part is realizing that every single person who comes into your office is leaving healthier than when they got there. Who couldn't be happy doing that? I found great joy and happiness in my work.

I found joy in my children.

I started working for a well-established chiropractor soon after Janine and I got back together. I taught school until 3 o'clock and then worked as a chiropractor from four until eight. Normally, I arrived home about eight-forty-five. One day I returned home to the news that the contractions had begun. Janine was able to sleep a little that night, but the next day was probably the longest day of her life. The contractions were irregular and rather severe. I did what little I could to comfort her.

We went to the hospital late on the afternoon of September first. They sent us home and told us to return if the contractions became more intense. They did. We stayed at Janine's parents' house because they lived close to the hospital. I remember that I ate Chinese food while Janine writhed in pain on the bed upstairs.

We returned to the hospital later that night. Janine was apparently dilating too slowly for the nurses and obstetrician, because they repeatedly asked if she wanted them to break her water. She told them no, and in no uncertain terms let them know that this birth was going to be natural. Good girl! Janine was not pleasant to anyone in the delivery room. Contractions, back labor, and perhaps the fear of dying, or better yet, the welcoming of death made her a bit cranky. One nurse brought a paper bag towards her face to help regulate her breathing. Janine slapped the bag out of her hands.

Then I got to see something that I will remember for the rest of my life. The Bible says that we are 'fearfully and wonderfully made'. I saw my baby's little head pop out first and then quickly, whoosh! The rest of the body followed. I didn't see what I had hoped to see, but nevertheless, I was absolutely thrilled to be the father of a little girl. Now I know that becoming a father is not exactly earth-shattering news, since it happens every day, but it never happened to me before! I am a father! I must have repeated that in my head a hundred times. The other thing that stayed with me was how proud I was of Janine. What a trooper! She did it! As I sat on a chair beside Janine's bed, watching my wife hold our baby girl to her breast, I was probably happier than I had ever been in my entire life. We named her Sydney. She was beautiful! Lots of dark hair, fair features, and bright blue eyes made me realize looking at her, that she would always be Daddy's little girl! I knew at that moment that I would love and cherish her for the remainder of my days on earth. I may be part of a lousy marriage, but praise God; I was father to a beautiful girl whom God had entrusted to me. Wow! Entrusted to do what?

Well, let's think about it:

God creates this incredibly complex world for us to live in. He forms the first man from the dust and the first woman from the rib of the first man. After that, it's all up to us! Who can understand the mind of God? That He would invite us, mere flawed humans, to join Him in the reproduction of more humans is mind-boggling. My microscopic sperm meets a female egg, and from there cell-division takes it the rest of the way! I studied the human body in depth while at chiropractic school, but let's face it: Knowing about all the parts is a lot different than making all the parts and setting life in motion. All I did was make my small contribution to the process of life, but the power of the universe knew where to put the eye sockets, arms and legs, encased the brain inside the skull to protect it from harm or injury, connected the bones with tendons, ligaments, and muscles, and gave this mesh of cells life! I think about this and I wonder: What in God's name is the evolutionist thinking? Anyway, God gave Janine and me a gift, and has now entrusted us to care for her.

I did a lot of daydreaming that first day of Sydney's life.

Loving sports as I do, I imagined my daughter as a teenager, racing across the soccer field, playing softball, and nailing three-pointers from beyond the arc. She would be a good student, graduate at the top of her class, and be very popular. But most of all, she would love her Dad! Talk about gaining a new perspective on life! It was like getting a second chance at being, seeing old things as if they were brand new, examining life again in all its wonder through the eyes of a child. The strangest thought that occurred to me was this: She's only a day old. I don't really know her, and she certainly doesn't know that I even exist, yet I can look at her and love her completely and be unable to imagine my life without her. A day ago I didn't know her. If someone invented a time-machine and offered me a ride into the past, I would say no thanks, there is nothing back there worth returning to if it means giving up what I have now.

We took Sydney home from the hospital two days later. She was too tiny to fit in the car seat we had bought. So Janine sat in the backseat and held her in her arms. I drove slowly and carefully home. As I cautiously navigated the turns, I kept thinking how unbelievable it was that a trained hospital staff actually trusted Janine and I to care for this infant on our own. We would be responsible for nurturing, protecting, cleaning, sanitizing, teaching, and loving this baby! She belonged to us. Incredible! What did I know about taking care of a baby? Nothing, true, but I was never more ready to undertake an assignment, or more anxious to get started. I knew nothing save for one thing: I was going to be good at it!

And in my heart of hearts I know that through the years I was just that. I loved my kids! My children have always been a great source of joy to me. Whenever the marriage hit a low point, I knew that there was happiness to be found spending time with my kids. Whether at a dance recital, or a ballgame, or simply shooting baskets in the driveway with the kids, I forgot entirely about the sad state of my relationship with Janine. It was blanked out! I was totally absorbed by the present moment of enjoying them. Now, of course, there were unpleasant instances of illnesses, broken spirits, and the required discipline to raise a child in the admonition of the Lord, but the vast majority of the time spent with the kids was a total blessing from God.

Despite the divorce and all the pain and suffering that accompanied it, I can't say that I was ever unhappy. I had Jesus as my savior, meaningful work, and three of the most beautiful children God has ever created. I always chose happiness, and I always took responsibility on my own to be happy. Life is a gift. Choosing happiness over despair is one way that I could express my gratitude.

"Thank you God for all you've done for me." I would pray often. "Thank you for my health, talents and skills, and all the many opportunities afforded me. Thank you for the family that raised and provided for me, and thank you too, for the family entrusted to my care today. Please Lord," I asked daily. "Bless my children and protect them physically, emotionally, mentally, psychologically, spiritually, sexually, financially, socially, and economically. And Lord," I would include the Biblical prayer of Jaebez, "Bless me, and enlarge my sphere of influence. Keep me from evil that it may not harm me." And I always knew too that, "God heard Lenny Spencer and gave me the desires of my heart."

My life was proof of that.

Chapter 6

THEY SAY THAT DIVORCE is a lot like death.

I suppose what people mean when they say that, is when someone you love dies, they are obviously no longer there for you anymore. A void is created by their absence. You feel hurt, bewilderment, regret, and you believe that life will never be the same without them. You miss them terribly. So when somebody you care about dies, you sometimes look the heavens and shake your fist and cry out to God. Why? We just can't understand why God would allow this to happen. For many couples the pain of divorce is the same as somebody dying. There is bewilderment. How did such a thing ever happen? People knew that there were serious issues, but did it need to end in divorce? Some never saw it coming. Just as an untimely death stuns us, so may a divorce.

Growing up in Springfield, New Jersey, life during the era of the Viet Nam War and protesting hippies was actually a relatively easy time to be a teenager. Certainly, there were occasions when the world reminded us that life can be chaotic and dangerous. For example, there was the Six-day war in Israel. Coming from a town that was predominately Jewish, this was a big deal in Springfield. Lots of people were on edge in the Jewish community. I recall that many of my fellow high school buddies boldly declared their desire to leave town immediately and fight for Israel. Personally, I didn't get it! I would never get all riled up if Italy went to war. And besides, I didn't even understand what the fuss was all about over there anyway. Many years later, as an adult and a born-again Christian, I was attending a Bible study when the Pastor started talking about the Jews as God's people.

"What?" I interrupted him. "The Jews are God's people?" I had never heard of such a thing before. My thoughts wandered back to Springfield, to Benjie and Suzie, and to all the Jewish friends I had grown up with. "Explain that to me." I asked him.

He did.

Pastor told me all about Abraham, Isaac, and twelve tribes of Jacob. The story of Joseph and the captivity of the Jews in Egypt for four hundred years became more real to me, as did the subsequent tale of Moses freeing them from slavery and leading his people through the Red Sea. The Ten Commandments was an awesome movie, but the true story was far more enlightening! Pastor told us the story of King David and then explained how the Bible predicted that the Messiah, Jesus, would come from the line of David. At the end of his brief summation, I shook my head and smiled.

"What is it Lenny?" He smiled back at me.

"All those years that I grew up in a Jewish town as a relatively intelligent human being," I mused, "and, I never even knew what being Jewish was! My friends were Jewish; my girlfriend was Jewish, and nobody ever explained to me what being a Jew meant. And for that matter I never even asked. I'm smiling," I explained, "because when the Six-Day War was going on I never understood what it was all about, or why my Jewish friends were so militant. I didn't know. Worse," I sighed, "I never asked. How could I be so ignorant of God and the world around me?"

On April 4th, 1968, Martin Luther King was assassinated. It was only days later that the riots began in Newark, New Jersey.

Springfield was only a few miles from Newark, where looting, burning, gunfire, and destruction were fierce for a number of days. Mom would not allow any of her boys out of the house except to attend school. During the riots she drove us to school because, as she repeated often, her children would not be struck by a stray bullet! A stray bullet? Was she kidding me? I was seventeen- years- old, but Mom was not taking any chances. These were perilous times and my mother was going to protect her boys! Years later, we would laugh and tease her about her exaggerated concern, yet today, as the father of three children of my own, I understand completely. No matter how ridiculous or absurd the degree of protection, I would do it too if it meant safety for my children. I'm a father now. I no longer view life as the seventeen-year-old who was once confined to his home.

Later that summer I got a job at a local pharmacy. As the delivery boy, I was also responsible for taking telegrams to families in the area whose child had been killed in Viet Nam. I only had to do this twice all summer. But I remember both times.

The pharmacy delivered many telegrams for a variety of reasons. It was only when the telegram contained news of a fallen soldier that I was privy to its contents. Perhaps this was done to make me sensitive to the nature of this particular delivery. All I remember is that I hated being the bearer of such horrible news.

I always turned off the radio in the car. Then I tried to think about something else to get my mind off the telegram. I would park the car, leave it running for a quick getaway, and walk nervously up the sidewalk to the house of the soon-to-be bereaving. I rang the doorbell and waited. My imagination was filled by thoughts of what the person about to answer the door was doing before I arrived. Were they gardening, reading a book, enjoying a meal, or perhaps talking on the phone and telling a friend how proud they were of their son's decision to fight for his country? In a few seconds that would be shattered by the paper I held in my hand. Parents are not supposed to bury their own children. Both times it was a woman who answered the door: Probably the soldier's mother. Each time, I handed the woman the telegram and quickly turned and left. On the ride back to the pharmacy, or for that matter the rest of the day, my mind kept returning to the woman, her family, friends of the soldier, his teachers, and I wondered: What are they feeling now that the finality of death had touched their lives? I was seventeen. Sure, there was death all around me. Viet Nam, the riots in Newark, the Jews and Palestinians; death was everywhere! But they were not people that I knew personally, talked to, shared time with, or intimately cared about. No one as yet had died in my family, neighborhood, or close circle of friends. I knew of death but I was untouched by it.

Until June 4th, 1969...

It was a Wednesday night, two days before the Senior Prom. My friend Bobby and I played basketball until dusk, and on our way back to my car his sister, Martha, came running over to us. It was dark so I could barely make out the expression on her face, but I sensed that something had happened.

"Mr. Jankowski is dead!" She told us.

I grew up with a great group of friends. There were about ten or twelve of us and we did lots of fun things together. We never drank or did drugs, but we still managed to have some wild times! Rob Jankowski was part of the group and a friend since my family first moved to Springfield. His Dad, Jon Jankowski, was one of those special fathers who adored his children and was actively involved with everything they did. Rob was the best athlete among our group of friends. As a sophomore he was the quarterback of the football team, a key contributor to our school's division champion basketball team and at this time the shortstop for the baseball team. Mr. Jankowski was at every game for every sport. He was also one of those fathers who made the time and effort to instruct his son on the nuances of the game. Often, I witnessed Rob and his Dad practicing together. Mr. Jankowski was always on the pitching mound while Rob batted. I remember watching them one particular day. Occasionally, Mr. Jankowski would stroll off the mound and offer either instruction or encouragement before tossing the next pitch. Even back then, there was something about the father-child relationship that intrigued me, aroused my interest, and perhaps added fuel to my own future desires to be a good Dad myself.

The last time I ever saw Mr. Jankowski alive was at the baseball game earlier that day. He was standing right behind home plate, beyond the cage. I never did see him dead. He was only forty-six years old. Forty-six! I'm older than that! The reason why I never saw Mr. Jankowski's dead body is because I could not attend the wake or the funeral. Oh, I had the time and the opportunity; I just didn't have the heart for it. It was like I purposely shut down my mind and pretended that nothing had really happened. I had known Mr. Jankowski for years. We spoke many times, especially about sports. But I really didn't know him intimately, so it was not like I, personally, had lost a loved one. Mr. Jankowski was not the issue. Rob was.

Rob Jankowski and I were friends seemingly forever. He used to live down the street from me and we played baseball, basketball, and football every chance we could. After Mr. Jankowski moved his family to a newer section of town, Rob and I lost contact for a short period of time. As teenagers we were reunited and became even closer friends. Rob was two years younger than me and a far better athlete. As a youngster, I was a bit jealous of Rob's athletic abilities, yet as the years rolled by I grew to simply accept the reality of his sports superiority. We were, and will be forever, the best of friends. When his father died, I couldn't imagine what my pal was going through. I hurt so badly for him, so much so that when the pain reached a certain point, I fought its very existence in my heart. I don't like emotional pain, so as a young teenager, I chose not to accept its reality. Instead, I focused my thoughts on the upcoming prom. The rest of the gang did the same.

I took Suzie to the prom that Friday night. While we ate, danced, and had a great time, Rob was at a wake for his father, standing in a line next to his mother, brother, and sister. The next day a group of us drove down to the Jersey Shore for some fun on the beach and later on the boardwalk. Rob attended his father's funeral that day. Try as I may not to think about it, or allow it to spoil our fun, my thoughts returned often to my friend. Why? Why? Why? To this day I fail to understand how that could have happened. I'm sure Rob does too!

One month later, on the Fourth of July, we were all at a party. Rob asked me if I could take him home. Suzie sat next to me in the front seat while Rob climbed in the back. As we were driving past the baseball field, Rob suddenly shouted out, "Stop the car!"

I did.

Suzie and I looked at each other when we heard the back door open. She shrugged her shoulders.

"What is this all about?"

"I don't know."

I knew.

We both watched Rob walk across the field and towards the baseball diamond. It was obvious to me that he was going down to behind the backstop to talk to his deceased Dad. My stomach dropped when I realized what he was there to do. Minutes later, he got back into the car and I took him home. To this day neither of us has brought up the memory of that night. We may have never talked about it, but I certainly from time-to-time give it thought.

Divorce is like death.

Your partner for the last twenty-five years is no longer there. When I get home from work the house is empty. No one is there to ask me about my day, or to relay some news about the latest exploits of the children. There is no smell of food cooking. You're alone. Your former partner, lover, best friend, and confidant is no longer a part of your life. Many times through the years I wondered about the Jankowski family. What's it like to be sixteen- years- old and know that Dad is not at work? He's not coming home, not tonight, not ever. I used to picture Rob and his family at that first Thanksgiving, Christmas, and Easter, and even years later when it was his graduation night, or his wedding to Gail. What was it like to know that the one special man you honored and respected and looked up to most would not be present to encourage, and applaud the milestones of your life? Thinking about it still makes me mad today. It's just not fair!

I wonder if anybody will think about me and how I am coping with my divorce.

When I see Rob today, I see him as a successful businessman, father of three grown up children, and a very spirited, happy man. He's been married to the same woman for thirty years. Apparently, he has turned out fine. So I wonder as I stand in the courtroom on the day of my divorce: how will I turn out? Will I honestly be able to tell inquirers that I am fine? Rob recovered from the death of his father. How long before I see the bounce in my step restored?

My mind raced with memories as I stood before the Judge. Mechanics Drive came to mind because that was the spot where I kissed Janine for the first time. I was ten years older than she, so I knew that if I kissed her it meant that this was going to be a special relationship. This kiss was not about the pleasure of kissing a young beautiful woman. This just might be for keeps!

"I know this is crazy," I said as I held her, my back against my car "but all I really want to do is kiss you!"

And so we did. Twice.

Janine was leaving for the University of Delaware the next day. We made tentative plans for me to visit over the Labor Day weekend. Then she left.

I visited Janine three weekends before I left for Chiropractic College myself in South Carolina. We were in love! There is a saying that the moment you are born, you begin to die. I can relate to that.

I look at my children and what I see is growth, energy, and a future filled with hopes and dreams. They're living! They're not dying! Their bodies are becoming stronger; their minds are expanding with knowledge, and their hearts pumping with vitality.

Janine and I were like that once.

We were growing together as one. The chemistry between us was electrifying. Our relationship was always gaining strength, our two minds becoming one of a new solidarity as we grew in knowledge of one another's hopes, dreams, and needs. It was like we shared one heart, beating furiously with energy, supplying all the cells of our love for one another and nourishing our time together with a zest that made both of us feel as if we had suddenly been re-born to life as it was supposed to be! Together, we were anything but dying.

Looking back, I can vividly see where the seeds of death were planted. Sure, we got along fabulously in those early days of romance, but things were done and said back then that caused damage later on. Thinking about it, I am reminded of one of Jesus' parables about the wheat and the tares. Wheat was planted intentionally to grow and be used as food. Yet one day the farmer looked out his window and saw weeds growing alongside and throughout his field of wheat. What he said was this:

"Where did the weeds come from?"

Ever wonder that yourself?

Here we are, Janine and I, having the time of our lives. We write, phone, visit as often as possible, make plans, and then one day you look out your window and there are weeds! Everywhere! We're the same people, but the weeds are choking us, placing a serious strain on our relationship, transforming the petty into major arguments, and causing doubt. It's not working like it used to. We're told by pastors, friends, magazine articles, and marriage counselors that love is an action word, and that we need to decide to love, to do something to restore and bring back to life that which is broken.

And we try.

But let's face it: The relationship is dying.

Mr. Jankowski died of a heart attack. It was sudden, lethal, and totally unexpected. He never saw it coming. Sometimes, that's how death takes us out. Quickly. From out of nowhere. Unexpectedly.

The death of my marriage wasn't like that. This was more like a slowly growing cancer, eating away at our relationship one cell at a time, crowding itself in the center of our finances, our conversations, our disagreements concerning child-rearing, and even in the bedroom. The weeds were multiplying from sources unknown and neither of us knew how or where to begin to stop it. Eventually, it was the days of wheat that were few and far between as the weeds soon became the norm, the expected, the defining landscape of who we had become as a couple.

Chapter 7

"It's good for a man to have a wife...Sexual drives are strong... The marriage bed is not a place to stand up for your rights....Abstaining from sex is permissible for a period of time if you both agree to it...." I Corinthians, Chapter 7.

Some people say that once you're married your sex life is as good as over! After Sydney was born, for the next eight months there was no sex between Janine and I. Sometime in the spring, I persuaded Janine to comply with the sexual act. I believe that the next time we had sex was somewhere around the end of summer. Now let's face it: It's pretty sad if a man can accurately remember each time he had sex with his wife during the year. But that's how it was.

"After a woman has a baby," Janine explained to me, "the desire is not as strong as it used to be. My whole internal body chemistry has been discombobulated by my pregnancy. I know it will change. You'll see."

I didn't like that answer at all.

"But what about me?" I reasoned back. "I'm a man with sexual desires that are not being met! You're my wife. You're the only one I can have sex with. What am I supposed to do?"

"Be patient."

"I've been patient." I retorted. "We've had sex twice the entire year! I just don't understand what is so horrible about having sex with me. You used to like it!"

I'm sad to note that nothing changed.

Our second child, Garrett, was born three years later.

"Looks like you got it right this time." My brother Johnny remarked in his best Bill Cosby impersonation.

A son!

I won't lie to you. There's something special about having a boy. This was going to be my athlete; this kid was going to excel where his father had failed.

My Dad asked me: "Did you want a boy this time?"

"I didn't really care." I lied. "Just as long as it was healthy."

I cared.

For many months following Garrett's birth, Janine and I made love a grand total of zero times! Not once! I asked and I begged. I no longer accepted the internal body chemistry excuse because I knew that her refusal to submit had more to do with her need to control me. Following this excruciating year-and-a-half of, sorry, but I have a headache period in our marriage, the return of sex remained an event that took place rarely, and only if I jumped through the right hoops. For the rest of our marriage, the granting of sex was strictly performance based. In other words, if I did everything I was supposed to according to her code of acceptance, maybe, just maybe tonight could be the night! One mistake, one involuntary slip of disobedience on my part and the show was over. Not only did this mean that there would not be sex tonight, but it usually put me back at square one. I would have to perform a whole new array of marital duties before facing the next sexual parole board.

We went to Myrtle Beach one Easter Break. We took our two children and had a wonderful family vacation. I must have done something right, because on the last night of the vacation Janine and I made love and I didn't even ask permission! It just happened. Now I remember this for one very significant reason: Our twins, Lilly and Layla, were born the following winter. And I know the precise date of conception because that was the only time between our vacation and even well beyond their birth, that we had sex. My brother, Johnny, used to tease me by holding up three fingers whenever the subject of sex was discussed.

"Three times!" He joked, hinting at Janine's three pregnancies. "At least I know you've had sex three times!"

I remember one particular evening during the summer when my lack of sexual pleasure was most acute. I had bought a tent, and when we were not traveling, I would set it up in the backyard and the kids and I would sleep in it. Janine chose not to join us, preferring to sleep in her own bed. When the kids were asleep, I sat up and stared at her bedroom window. The light was still on. I wanted to have sex so badly that I just couldn't stand it any longer. Quietly, I got out of bed, and carefully zipped opened the door of the tent so as not to disturb the kids. Shutting the door behind me, I made my way into the house. I went right to our bedroom.

"We have not had sex since forever!" I began as I stood before Janine, who was lying there reading a magazine. "This is ridiculous! You're my wife, and there is no one in the entire world for me to have sex with, except you. I need sex!"

"I need love!" She shot back, putting the magazine down at her side. "You don't love me. All you want from me is sex and a running partner!"

We worked out and ran a lot together.

"That's not true!" I fired back. "I love you and I do my best to be a good husband for you. Is it so awful to expect a little something in return for my dedication to you?"

"Something in return for what?"

I could sense the familiar smell of defeat.

"Look," I was getting angry, "I'm a man and I want to have sex with my wife just like any other normal guy on the planet. Married couples have sex! I'm tired of all this, 'you don't love me', nonsense that you spout all the time. I do love you, and I desire to make love to you. I'm tired of your moods," I was on a roll so I decided to give it to her with both barrels blazing, "tired of your unfounded accusations, and I'm especially tired of you dangling sex in front of me like a carrot in front of a horse. I don't deserve this kind of treatment. No man does!"

"You don't deserve anything from me!"

That was her only response. Janine then dramatically pulled up the covers and thumped loudly on the bed. She turned and buried her head into her pillow. Well, so much for that discussion between two mature adults. I walked back outside to rejoin the children. The next morning we cooked eggs outside the tent. The kids and I enjoyed our special backyard camping adventure. Janine never did join us, even in the morning. Me? I just went on with my sexless life as though last night's conversation had never taken place.

But I did come to acknowledge this disappointing reality: I was alone. Not only didn't I have a true sex partner, but I had to accept that Janine was neither a friend nor partner of any kind to me in any capacity. I was stuck. As I examined the current state of my life, I had to admit that all I was doing was spinning my wheels, and going nowhere with this person who once claimed to love me. If this is marriage, then I want out! Yet I quickly realized that there was no escape. I was stuck and I would have to live the rest of my life in a loveless, sexless relationship with someone who verbally abused me, insulted me in public, and treated me as if I owed her something for causing her unhappiness. There's no other word for it: Stuck! Thank God I had the children to give my life meaning. I guess I really wasn't alone, so long as I had them.

That's when the daydreams began.

My little fantasy world took all sorts of forms. Usually, they were very creative, yet potentially realistic scenarios that just could possibly happen if all the stars were perfectly aligned. The general premise was as follows: Janine would ask for a divorce and I would be free! The kids would wind up with me and we would live happily ever after. I would be financially secure, and I could search for true love once again. These daydreams would enter my mind while driving in the car, or walking the dogs, or especially lying in bed at night besides a woman who wanted nothing to do with me. Unfortunately, I never acted out on these daydreams because I considered divorce wrong. Now if Janine took the initiative to seek a divorce, that would be a different story.

I used to imagine that I would receive an anonymous phone call from some irate woman informing me that her husband was having an affair with my wife. The Bible says that adultery is a legitimate reason for me to divorce Janine. I dreamed of discovering a legitimate means of escape. Without grounds, I would never have asked Janine for a divorce, so all I could really hope for was that someday she would become so fed up that she would demand a divorce from me. That would place the onus of blame squarely on her shoulders. I would not be the bad guy, nor would the kids see me as the cause of their disillusionment. My only hope was to wait.

Instead, Janine and I found ourselves as part of a Bible study. We met every Sunday night. There were about twenty of us, all of us members of the same church. We often talked about marriage, its godly intent, and the need to make our own marriages better. There was food afterwards and plenty of fellowship.

Janine and I were the stars of the Bible study. On many occasions the other couples were forced to forget their own issues and focus their concern on ours. We went at it right in front of them. Janine would make some kind of outrageous comment about me and the fire was lit. Once, the discussion centered on the cultural roles of the man and woman.

"Lenny only does the things he likes around the house." Janine chimed in.

I retaliated immediately.

"What are you talking about?" I interrupted her. "Do you think I like doing all the dishes, cleaning the counters, throwing out the garbage, vacuuming, walking the dogs, feeding the dogs, shoveling the driveway, picking up the entire house, and cleaning the toilets?" This topic always annoyed me. "There's not a thing around the house that I don't do! I work all day at school, and then at the office, and when I get home I walk into a pig sty! You don't lift a finger to help out. How dare you accuse me of not doing my part!"

The room was silent.

"That's not what I'm talking about." Janine countered. "I have to tell you a dozen times to fix things around the house. How long has the kitchen sink had a leak? You don't call the plumber, and I need to remind you constantly about things that need to be done! You always tell me the same thing." She was turning red. "I'll get to it later. Only, later never comes. You're supposed to be the man of the house."

What usually happens next still floors me to this day.

"You know, Lenny," one of the other men says, "if you need some help, I'll come over and show you how to fix that leak."

I'm dumbstruck.

I mean, he's just being nice; I understand that. But did anyone hear a single word I said? I just told them how I clean our house single-handedly, and how Janine does absolutely nothing to help. I want to shout out: ask the kids! They'll tell you the truth. For the life of me, I don't understand why they always stick up for her. Sometimes I want to shake them, and enlighten them to the reality of who Janine really is! I work three jobs. Janine has all the money, and I try to please her every chance I get. And instead of some show of appreciation, or better yet, respect, all I receive for my effort to be a caring husband is ridicule, insults, outlandish accusations, and a cold body lying next to me in bed. I don't deserve this kind of treatment. I crave to have just one person see the truth, see how in fact I do love my wife, and call Janine on the carpet to 'cut the crap', and return affection to her deserving husband. Yet as the years go by, not a friend of hers, not a single pastor, or family member, steps forward to challenge her erroneous opinion of me. And I just can't believe it!

"Why do I have to be the one to call the plumber?" I respond, knowing that I sound like a prideful and foolish man who just wants to win a standstill. Our group discussion goes in a new direction and the flare-up with Janine is filed and forgotten as it usually is.

We ride home in silence. Another Sunday night of learning about the precepts and principles of marriage leaves us no better off than when we first started. It's hopeless! We both know it, yet we continue to go through the motions of reconciliation. The kids sit in the back of our conversion van and watch a movie, oblivious to the very real possibility that Mom and Dad are on a destructive path to divorce. I often think about them while I drive. This whole ordeal is not fair to them either. One unreasonable, selfish, self-centered person is taking an entire family down the tubes! Everybody loses. What does she want from us?

What do you want from me, Lord? You've known me my entire life. Since the time I was a young teenager I have dreamed of having a special partner. I dated in high school, college, and up until the time I met Janine when I was thirty-two-years-old. I never seem to be able to find my soul-mate. You know all of this, Lord; you know that all I ever wanted was a normal relationship with a normal woman. Other people do it. Why not me?

When I start thinking and feeling like this I always stop, because I don't want God to think I'm complaining. I love and appreciate the life he's given to me. Honestly, I wouldn't trade places with any one on earth, and I wouldn't change a thing about anything that's happened. I don't regret marrying Janine. I really don't. There are four good reasons why: Sydney, Garrett, Lilly and Layla. Janine and I are the only two people capable of producing those four. My sperm and her egg were the only ingredients the Lord had to form these four beautiful children. No, I wouldn't trade a thing if it meant trading their existence for something that seems more appealing or fulfilling. They are my treasure, my reward for remaining faithful, my anchor of hope and joy in a world that often separates and destroys. Just thinking about them causes me to break into prayer:

"Let me live, Lord. I pray that you will allow me to see them graduate college, pursue fruitful careers, marry, give me grandchildren, and know that their lives are led by a desire to please you. I want to die before any of them die. They need me, Father. They need my guidance, my model of Christianity, and the knowledge that there is a man in this world who considers their lives a precious gift to him. Let me live for as long as they truly need me. Let it be my gift to them. I may not be happily married, but I am certainly blessed."

You see, I learned long ago a very important lesson about life; it is not about me. The world doesn't revolve round Lenny Spencer. I'm just glad I belong to God. I'm grateful for my talents and opportunities, yet I know too that my blessings are not to be hoarded, but shared. God has blessed me for a reason. And that reason is to be of service to others. Even in the Middle School setting where young undisciplined boys and girls disrespect me, I need to remind myself that I am here for them, to represent something that is good, something that is different from what they see in a world that so often tells them that they have the right to do whatever feels good. Now I'm not claiming to be better than anybody else. My failed marriage is proof of that. All I'm saying is this: I'm a school teacher for a reason. I believe that God helped me get a job in the school system. But he didn't do it just for me. It's not about me!

So if I believe that my blessings have been granted for the benefit of others, the obvious question is this: What about Janine? Have I been a blessing to her?

Jesus tells us in his word that we can't claim to love a God we can't see, if we choose not to love the people that we do see. Not loving others is unacceptable to God. Knowing that, I must confess that there was many times that I just flat-out couldn't stand Janine Spencer. But I knew better. There are principles of love, and they are to be put into action no matter how people behave. That includes Janine. So here's how I understand it:

If she treats me badly, I'm to love her. If she withholds a sexual relationship from me, even though she knows full well the extent of the pain it causes me, I'm to love her. When she calls me names, laughs at my shortcomings, questions my manhood, or threatens me with some sort of relational punishment, I'm to love her.

The truth is: it was too hard for me. There were periods of time where I gritted my teeth, and took it on the chin in the name of love. Yet there were many other stretches where I just couldn't do it. But I always reminded myself to praise God and to be grateful even when my life was the pits. I figured if I can praise Him from the depths of despair, then I can certainly praise Him when I rise to the top. And I decided, too, that someday I would overcome this dreadful marriage and be completely happy with my life. In my mind, the question was never if, but when I would see my life restored. I had no plans. I only held out hope.

Chapter 8

"THE PAYMENT OF $700 per week, as allocated, $350 maintenance, $350 child support, is for a period of 78 months or sooner remarriage of Mrs. Spencer."

Yep, seven-hundred dollars a week for the next six-and-a-half years! I'll be old by the time my money will be all mine. In the meantime, the immediate future looks to be a financial struggle, an exercise in living month- to- month, and dependent upon my will to hustle and build my chiropractic business. Seven hundred dollars a week! Thirty-six thousand four hundred dollars a year, for doing absolutely nothing! Janine was the one who wanted the divorce, yet I'm the one who has to pay for it. I mean, if you want to be single, then shouldn't you be responsible to work, and support yourself? My wife has a degree as a certified accountant. When the children were older, she agreed to become a self-employed accountant and work on a part-time basis. According to her tax records, she claimed to make a grand total of $735 for the entire year. Compare that to my annual income of eighty-five thousand and the New York State alimony-child-support formula leaves me in financial distress. I've seen her appointment book and I know that $735 isn't anywhere near an accurate account of her income. What a perfect way for her to set herself up for a big alimony payout. She's a perfectly healthy girl who has the capability of working a full time job like a normal person, but she claims that she never wants to return to it because she doesn't enjoy it. A year after the divorce, I reviewed my alimony-child-support-custody issues with a new attorney and discovered what I already feared: There is not a thing I can do about it! Financially, I was screwed!

Janine got the house and everything in it. I'm even expected to pay her lawyer for a divorce I never wanted!

"The parties have agreed to a joint-custodial situation. They have not had a significant issue with sharing the children basically even."

The kids would stay with me every other week. We agreed to split custody fifty-fifty. I was fine with the whole custodial arrangement except that it didn't seem right for me to have to pay her when I had the kids just as much as she did. Not only that, but the reality was that when the kids needed clothes, or new spikes, or cash to attend activities, only one of us provided the financial means. Guess who that was?

Yet as the lawyers relay the details to the Judge, I'm not overly concerned about my future financial difficulties. All I know is that in just a few minutes I will be free of Janine Spencer! Well, legally free. I held no illusions that it would be the last time I would have to deal with her. This was not going to be an easy divorce either. Yet I must confess that I was looking forward to the end just as much as I suppose she was. Twenty-five years of marriage over at the pounding of a gavel.

My wandering mind was suddenly startled by the voice of my attorney.

"At this juncture Mr. Spencer and I will leave. We'll formally withdraw our appearance and allow Mrs. Spencer to obtain the divorce on a default basis. Thank you, Your Honor."

We left.

I'm a divorced man.

The miracle of a God-woven union was broken by the State of New York. 'Let no man separate' was blown to smithereens in less than twenty minutes. I walked out to my car with my attorney, we shook hands, and it was over. Oh, there would still be a hefty bill coming in the mail, but besides that I would probably never see him again. Kevin always assured me that I would be alright someday. The Judge gave me a month to leave the house Janine and I had had built just four years earlier. I looked forward to being away from her, but it still didn't seem right. I thought once again of the children. All four of them were in school as I drove from the County Courthouse to head home. Janine would arrive home later, yet no longer my wife, my partner, or even my friend. It was over. Over twenty years of marriage, plus additional years of courtship, over just like that! I was single and alone.

During the drive back, I remembered a time before we were married, when we met in Ocean City, Maryland. Janine, who was coming from Delaware, arrived about an hour later than I did. Unbeknownst to her, I had grown a beard over the four weeks since I had last seen her. So when she entered the room, she stopped and smiled, seemingly acclimating herself to my new appearance. But I knew that it was more than that. Her eyes had that special look of love reserved solely for the most important person in her life. That was me. Janine, at that moment loved me more than anybody else. I remember that look. It was honoring, uplifting, and a sort of salute to the magnificence of our early relationship. Today in the courtroom, she didn't look at me at all. I suppose that in her mind, it was all a big mistake. There really wasn't anything special about me. In fact, just the opposite turned out to be true. I was her greatest disappointment. As I drove though, the memory of that day quickly faded, replaced by the soothing reality that I was still a young man with a lot of living to do and God-willing, a lot of time left to do it. I wondered to myself: Is there someone out there somewhere for me? And if there is, will I find her? No, I quickly decided, there's not, and even if my fantasies could become reality, there was no way I would ever get married again!

I suddenly remembered the day we got engaged.

It was a beautiful day.

Janine and I had already purchased an engagement ring that she had picked out for herself. For a month or so I kept it in my dresser at home. Today would be the day. We went to a Park in New Jersey called Surprise Lake and it was there that I proposed. Since we both already knew about the ring and our plans to get married, it wasn't exactly a prime romantic moment. I must confess: I wasn't sure about this, but I guess there was no turning back now.

The next thing was to tell our parents.

My parents and brothers were genuinely thrilled and congratulated us heartily. Janine's parents had begrudgingly accepted our ten-year age difference and welcomed me into the family. Let me say this: My years of marriage to Janine may have been difficult, but my relationship with my new mother and father in-law was a sheer blessing. I may not have been to their initial liking as a mate for their daughter, but they loved me and their four grandchildren completely, unconditionally, and without reserve. People tell jokes about their mother-in-law all the time, about the butting in and the poor treatment of the son-in-law, but nothing could be further from the truth for me. I got lucky. I had great in-laws. The sad truth is that even before our divorce was final, I knew that I would miss them. You've heard it said that a divorce is an event that involves far more than the two culprits who instigated it. A lot of people are affected. My divorce is no different. Never again would I be a welcomed part of holiday dinners or discussions with Janine's brothers and their wives about the latest exploits of the children. On Janine's side I had, or I suppose I should say used to have, five nephews, two nieces, two brother-in-laws, two sister-in-laws, not to mention Janine's parents and her darling grandfather. I would no longer be part of their lives. One of the reasons why I chose the teaching profession is my love of kids. So I always took the time and energy to interact with my niece and nephews. No more. Uncle Lenny no longer exists.

The last time I saw them was over a year ago at Sydney's high school graduation party. Janine and I worked hard all summer to get the yard and house ready for the party. Things were not good between us, but we were able to pool our efforts and work together for Sydney's sake. My family came up from New Jersey, Virginia, and Florida, while Janine's family came from the Pittsburgh and Utica, New York areas. I played touch football with my nephews and my own boys, and spent a good amount of time with the Cunninghams and my other in-laws that day. Our marriage was certainly in trouble, but the final decision to divorce was still a few months away. I enjoyed having both sides of my children's family there for the graduation party. Little did I know that it would be the last time that I would ever see Janine's family again.

Life is interesting. You think you have all the time in the world to be with loved ones, only tomorrow promises nothing to anyone. Janine and I agreed to divorce that following October. She told me that she had had enough, that she could not go on like this any longer. This time I agreed to let her have her divorce.

I think that this was the eighth time she asked me for a divorce. My memory is not very clear on each request, but I certainly remember the first time:

It was quite a night!

We were arguing as usual, this time about my desire to take the family to the Jersey Shore for a week. My parents and brothers rented a place on the beach every summer. The first two years, Janine, the kids and I joined them. We had a great time swimming, fishing, tanning, and going to the Boardwalk both years. The kids loved it! Yet for reasons known only to Janine I suppose, my family would not return to the Jersey Shore again. She claimed that she preferred to do something different. I had no problem with that. Only, that doing something different never materialized and the kids and I were left to wonder why.

There were other whys that I wondered about. Like why did an intelligent, fair-minded person like me allow Janine to call the shots? Why did I stand for it? Why didn't I just pack the kids in the car and tell her that, 'look, we're going to the beach, if you want to come, get in, and if you don't, see you next week' ? What was it that stopped me? The beach thing is just one example. There were numerous things the kids and I wanted to do, or places we wanted to go, but we didn't because Janine said no. We used to visit our parents once a year. Why, only once? Because Janine said so! Why didn't I stand up to her rigid control of my life, and for that matter, the missed opportunities for my children? What was I afraid of? Was it selfish of me to want to spend time with the parents who raised me and the brothers I loved?

"We haven't been to New Jersey since Thanksgiving!" I explained one summer. "Why can't we go?"

Listen to her answer:

"Oh, does Lenny need time with his Mommy? Has it been too long for you to be away from home? I always thought that this was your home. Why do you have to run home to momma? You're such a momma's boy!"

Excuse me?

Wanting to go visit my parents, brothers, nephews, and niece makes me some kind of momma's boy? Give me a break! But this was Janine's controlling style. She would side-step the issue and attacked my character. Usually, she employed ridicule, or some type of mocking tactic to reduce my argument to the immature and selfish desires of a self-indulgent child.

Yet I must admit: Most of the time these tactics worked! Somehow, Janine's psychological hold on me forced me to consider the possibility that her ludicrous claims could be true. Maybe I did need to grow up. Perhaps I was a bit too selfish about wanting to see my New Jersey family and after all, I'm married now so let's just cut the cord and be done with it. Believe it or not, I often found myself apologizing to her because of my selfish behavior and promising that it would never happen again. Yet later on, when the dust from the battle had settled, I would return to my senses and resent her even more. On occasion the resentment was self-directed. 'What a coward you are!' I would think. And then at my lowest point, I would wonder about the children. Something that all of them and Dad had wanted to do was denied by their mother. Mom always got her way. Mom was the boss. Dad? He always backed down. He always gave in. He wouldn't stand up to Mom. And I suppose, finally: What is the matter with Dad?

So I must ask myself again: Why did I stand for it?

I did it for them.

In my mind, it was better for the children if I took all the lumps in order to spare them another night of hearing their mother shout and scream at their Dad. When Janine was hot about a particular issue, she would corner me somewhere in the house, and not release me until she had had her say. Walk away? She would follow me until the ends of the earth! Another problem was: there was no end to her say! She would accuse, re-accuse, and repeat the same accusation a number of times. Old arguments and issues from the past would somehow enter the fray, and with a new look, reinforce the legitimacy of her side of the argument. I hated these times! Oh, not because I felt bad or defeated by Janine's shrewd logic, but because of the children. I knew they could hear her. 'What were they doing', I often wondered. I would be half-listening to Janine ramble on incessantly and at the same time form a mental picture of my kids, sitting on their beds, jolted by the screams, and fearful that their world is falling apart. I don't think Janine cared one way or the other about what they saw or heard. She was too selfish to care, too wrapped up in her own self-centered view of what she needed as a wife to care about the children who loved and adored both of us.

I rarely yelled back. I wanted my kids to know that one of their parents was stable, that one of the people who brought them into this world refused to stoop to the level of degrading behavior that they saw from the other.

Following a violent discussion, I would always make it a point to join each of the children with whatever activity they were presently involved in. I was my usual casual self, smiling, happy, indulging their interests, while all the time praying that their psyches were somehow untouched. My easy-going demeanor during these post-war episodes was my way of assuring them that everything was going to be alright. Dad is unscathed by Mom's harsh treatment of him, and things are not as bad as they seem. Usually, after a few minutes, we were laughing and acting as though nothing out of the ordinary had happened tonight. Mom was just letting off some steam. That's how some people deal with their issues. Husbands and wives fight sometimes. Mom and Dad still love each other. You'll see! For me, it was all about maintaining peace, giving the children some sense of family stability, and reassuring them that their father would always be there to shield and protect them from the things their minds were too young to understand.

Looking back, it is certainly painful to reminisce about a period in my life when I allowed another person to bully and control me. It was not a pleasant experience, and it is with regret that I recall the treatment I permitted. Obviously, I should have been a stronger man and told Janine to knock it off! But I didn't. I accepted the tirades as though they were my due. I took it on the chin for the team, somehow believing that at all costs I needed to be the glue to hold this family together. I think I feared that if I argued back, the debate would become more heated and the result would be a divorce. I didn't want a divorce. Not while the kids were still so young. There were always these convictions in my mind that if Janine and I could just get past this most current issue, things would settle down and be alright. We would stay together and our staying together was best for the kids.

I was wrong!

One heated argument was followed by another. The pattern became predictable. There was peace for awhile, a truce for a period of time, but it was always short-lived. Today, my assessment of damages done to the children is this: They seem very happy. All four of them are doing well in school, popular, lots of friends, playing sports, no involvement with alcohol or drugs, and showing no signs of being emotionally, mentally, or psychologically affected by living through a divorce. Mission accomplished!

By the grace of God, (and I prayed for their protection daily), they have come through the fire apparently unscathed. At times I will tell myself, "It was worth it, all of it". I would die for them! And I would suffer abuse if it means that they could better live a happy and healthy life. It will be interesting in the future to see just how our divorce will affect their ability to function in a relationship of their own. Sydney has a boyfriend. They have been dating for over two years.

One day after the divorce was final Sydney and I were in the car together. The subject of her parents' divorce came up.

"So what if Mom decides to get married someday?" I asked, curious as to how she would respond.

"Well," She answered. "I certainly wouldn't approve of it. It would be too weird! What Mom did," she continued in a different direction even though I hadn't asked, "was wrong. Two people should be married for life. I've accepted your divorce, but I still don't think it is right. And I think," she was on a roll now, "that the dating that Mom is doing is really stupid! I mean, what's the point? If she asked me to be in her wedding, I would refuse."

"Do you remember the night we went to the Chinese restaurant and you said that we should have gotten divorced a long time ago?"

Sydney was surprised when I related that memory.

"No," she said, half-smiling, "I don't remember saying that at all, but if I did; I've changed my mind. I never wanted you to get divorced."

We rode in silence for a full minute.

"Hey," I broke the mood, "what if I get married?"

She shook her head.

"You're too old to get married!"

Well, on that summer day when Janine asked me for a divorce for the first time, I broke free of the argument we were having about my joining my family at the beach, and went into the basement to do a load of clothing. I was just putting the dirty clothes in the washer when Janine called down to me:

"I want a divorce!"

Now I suppose that if I were the God-honoring man that I purported myself to be, my initial reaction would have been one of outright protest. Instead, I pumped my fist into the air, and thought to myself: Finally! After all, I had dreamed of this day. Freedom, freedom, freedom! The Governor was granting me a pardon. It was truly a triumphant moment!

About an hour later I was riding my bike on the Allegany River Trail, when I was suddenly consumed by this thought: Divorce is wrong and I just can't do it! I felt like I could hear the voice of the Lord explaining to me that He was the author of this marriage and that if it were to be dissipated then He would be the one to do it. I knew that God wanted us to stay together.

"I will help you". I sensed his small still voice assure me.

So I resolved to keep the dying embers of this marriage burning. I would stoke whatever little heat was left until the flame returned. It was noble; it was heartfelt, and a strong state of commitment flooded my being. I refused to accept the death of our relationship. I would make it work, even if I had to do it all alone. I would do it for the children and I would do it for my Lord!

The first step in my plan for reconciliation was to find some help. Putting my bike back in the car, I drove over to the house of a Christian family that we were friends with and that I trusted.

Sally and Carl Miller are a happily-married couple who both loved the Lord. When I arrived, Sally Miller answered the door.

"Janine wants a divorce." I quickly let her know the reason for my surprise visit. "I don't! I need your help. Will you talk to her and try to get her to change her mind?"

What a night it was!

While our four children joined theirs out at the backyard gazebo, the four of us talked about the problems Janine and I were having with our marriage. There was lots of crying, angry accusations, and downright hysteria. After a couple of hours of this I was beginning to already regret my new commitment to staying married. Eventually, the women went off on their own while Carl and I sat on the swing set.

"She holds out on me sexually all the time." I shared with Carl. "I'll ask, but then I have to meet a whole slew of standards before she'll even consider it."

"Why do you want to remain in the marriage?"

Wow! Great question!

"I'll be honest with you, Carl." I began. "Janine is a high-maintenance marriage partner. We both want to be the man in the family! I probably want out just as badly as she does, but out on the bike trail today I knew it was the wrong thing to do, a terrible thing to do to the kids, and most importantly, against the commands of God. Our children are so young." I pronounced with feeling. Sydney, the oldest, was only twelve; the twins were only six. "They couldn't handle this right now. They love both of us and a divorce would destroy them! I can't let this happen."

"Well," Carl interrupted, "I can appreciate your concern for the kids, and I think it's very commendable, but," he sighed, "marriage is about a man and a woman linked together for life. It's a commitment, an unconditional promise made in the presence of God. I'm just wondering how you feel about that?"

How do I feel about that or what do I think about that? I had no doubts about how I felt. I wanted to run away from Janine Spencer as fast as my legs could carry me! But I knew that God wasn't really interested in how I felt; He wanted to see what I thought. So I answered Carl by telling him what I think. It was like taking a test in school. The teacher disperses information and then through rote memory I write out the proper and correct response. Well, in this case, the Bible was my teacher and I responded accordingly.

"God hates divorce." I started by quoting the Book of Malachi. "He doesn't call it sin, but He hates it because He knows its destructive repercussions. Janine and I made an agreement, took an oath, a pledge to love one another in good times and bad. I aim to honor that promise. I know it won't be easy, but I am willing to do whatever is necessary to save my marriage. I am a man of God, and I need to act like it!"

When the four of us reunited at the swing set our conversation was noticeably more relaxed, less strained, and peaceful. We continued to talk until about two in the morning. The children didn't seem to mind. It was a warm night so they played board games with the Miller children. On the ride home the car was silent.

For the next few days things were a bit strained around the house, but certainly tamer than they had been. A week later the kids and I were back at school and life at the Spencer home was pretty much back to normal. Janine's first request for a divorce was stymied and I must confess that I was somewhat relieved. Maybe we needed to come to this particular crossroad in our marriage to begin restoration as a couple. We had hit rock-bottom so now there was no place to go but up! Perhaps Janine and I could make it after all.

Wrong!

I had a day off from school so we decided to take the kids to a museum in Niagara Falls, New York. Before we left, Janine was leaning forward reading something that lay on the kitchen table. I came up behind her and put my hands on her waist. I moved my hands up-and-down along her hips. Suddenly she whirled around to face me.

"What?"

"You know what!" She spit back. "You were feeling my waist to see how fat I am. Do I meet your standards? Am I just the way you like your women?"

"What are you talking about?"

"Don't play stupid!" Janine hissed. "You know very well what you were doing." Then she spread her arms out to her sides as if to present her body to me in full view. "Well, how do I look? Do I pass inspection? Am I good enough for the great Lenny Spencer?"

This was probably one of the saddest moments in our marriage. Sad, because it was one of the first times I caught a glimpse of how desperately unstable Janine truly was. Now I don't know a thing about mental illness, but there was something here that didn't quite meet the eye. This was abnormal behavior. Later in January I was riding with my brother, Rich, and so I shared Janine's antics that day.

"She's crazy, Rich."

"Yeah," my brother smiled, "crazy like a fox!"

Back on that day at the museum we had anything but a fun outing. Janine kept to herself, cried, even shook while she cried, and made the trip generally miserable for all of us. As I watched Janine sulk, cry, and act like she was about to die of depression, I wondered: Do her children see her? And what do they think?

During one summer, we took a vacation to Panama City. An old high school friend of mine gave us his time-share for a week. We were psyched! Since we were driving down to Florida we decided that we may as well spend an additional week at the beach too. Janine had heard about a place called Chadwick Beach so we went there prior to Panama City. This had all the makings of being a great family vacation.

While on the beach at Chadwick, Janine was floating on a raft in the ocean. I was tanning on the sand. A group of young people settled their blankets a few yards behind us, and were tossing a football around. Girls and boys playing catch. I lay there watching them. Within minutes Janine stomped out of the water and glared at me. What now, I wondered?

"You're unbelievable!" She verbally assaulted me. "We're supposed to be on a family vacation and you're staring at these young girls. Do you think they'd be interested in you?" I sensed she was beginning to lose it. "Look at you: short, bald, old, and fat! Are you ever going to grow up?"

Wait a second.

Now I won't argue that I am short, (five-foot-seven-inches), old, (50 at this time), or bald, (I shave my head daily), but fat? I thought I looked pretty good! Seriously, Janine's propensity to make a mountain out of a molehill was a very annoying trait. 'Not now', I remember thinking. We're on vacation. Let's just enjoy ourselves. Please, no issues this week.

Forget it!

The remainder of the week at Chadwick Beach was in shambles. All Janine wanted to do was for me to address all my issues, girl-watching among them. Me? I wanted to enjoy my two week vacation in Florida with my wife and children. It was eighty degrees outside! Would I rather swim, play ball in the sand, take the kids for ice cream, or stand underneath a hot sun and rehash the miseries of our marriage? But to Janine, the issues between us needed to be discussed right at that moment no matter what else we could be doing. I hated that about her. I really did. Young people were playing football and I watched them. No, I was not lusting after the young women, nor was I staring inappropriately at any body parts. I can't begin to tell you how sick I was of all this nonsense!

A few days later, after some of her anger had calmed a bit, we drove up to Tampa to watch a parade. We were sitting on the curb, enjoying the day, when all of a sudden Janine turned to me and attacked!

"Do you remember the time that you told me that my breasts were too small?"

That's not exactly what I said.

It was eighteen years ago and we were in bed together down in South

Carolina. Janine looked really good and I wanted to tell her so. What I actually said was this:

"You are very beautiful. If you had bigger breasts you could be a playboy bunny!"

Alright, it was insensitive on my part. But I meant no harm. I thought I was paying her a compliment. I thought that she understood that I was impressed with her body and that she was right up there with the most beautiful women in the world. Janine's breasts are fine. I wasn't criticizing their size, shape or anything about them. They just didn't resemble those fake silicone breasts of the playboy bunnies. That's all I meant by it. Geez, I had no idea that my comment bothered her at the time, let alone still festered eighteen years later. Besides, I don't like those fake playboy breasts anyway!

Eighteen years later, she was boiling mad!

"Do you know how insulting that was?" She said to me as we sat with the kids on the curb watching the parade go by. "You have never liked my body. That's why you're always looking for something better, with bigger breasts or a fuller butt. You have never been satisfied with me."

I said it years ago! I was being reprimanded for it now! Now either she really is a crazy, insecure woman who has been deeply scarred by remarks made by her insensitive husband, or my brother Rich was right:

"Crazy like a fox!"

I needed to explore this in my mind.

Janine is obviously a very unhappy woman. She does not love her husband and blames me for being the cause of her unhappy and unfulfilled life. She constantly accuses me of not loving her and that I am searching to find someone else that I could love more than I do her. Now, none of this is true, and deep down I have a strong suspicion that Janine and I both know it. So if I'm right that we both know that these wild accusations about my issues are really just fabrications, the obvious question becomes: What is her motive?

Why would someone bring up an issue from eighteen years ago to start a fight today? Either she has been thinking about the incident for years and only now found the strength to bring it up, or she purposely creates reasons to show me what a lousy husband and boyfriend I have been. Think about it: I said what I said about her breasts, but she married me anyway! Shouldn't it have been an issue then too? Why wait until years later to bring up her pain at my callous insensitivity? What exactly was she trying to do?

It took me a lot of years to arrive at this conclusion, but sitting on the curb that day in Tampa, Florida, I think I was beginning to recognize the horrible truth:

Fact: There was a ten year age difference between us.

Fact: Janine was young when we married.

Fact: She doesn't love me anymore, and has told me so as far back as the early 1990's.

Now for a supposition: I'm guessing that early in the marriage Janine Spencer came to the painful realization that she was stuck with a man she no longer loved. Possibly never loved, owing her involvement with me to the fascination of a teenage girl with and older man. It was purely infatuation, not love. As she grew to become a woman, the infatuation wore off, but unlike a successful relationship, there was no love to provide a foundation in its place. It became apparent to Janine Spencer that Lenny Spencer was always going to be a boy in a man's body. She wanted a man! She wanted out but she needed a plan.

Thinking about it, I began to understand her deception.

She was not going to be the one to blame. I know Janine well enough to be sure that she could not face the reality of her own sinful thoughts. She's a Christian, knows what the Bible says about commitment in marriage, and would have to deflect the truth of her lack of commitment to someone else: Me! I had to be the bad guy, the cause of all marital disharmony, because if she took any responsibility at all for this failure then she would look bad. That she could never permit. Janine believed wholeheartedly that she was more than capable of being the Christian wife and mother that Proverbs 31 describes. No way could any of this be her fault. To save face, and to maintain the pretense of her own perfection, Janine needed a scapegoat. Someone else had to be to blame for her unhappiness, her failures, and her emptiness in married life. There was no way that she, Janine Spencer, could be at fault for this failed marriage in any way, shape or form. No, it had to fall on me. And the horrible truth that I was coming to realize was that her twisted mind had to prove just that to me!

Yep. She needed me to accept total blame, and not only accept it, but believe that it was true. So through the years she began to work on me, to confuse me, make me believe that black was really white. And you know what? It worked! Yes, for a long while I trusted her opinion, relied upon her intuition, and regarded my wife as an honest, high-integrity, strong-willed and righteous woman who only demanded what the Lord Himself expected. Certainly as human beings we are flawed; that's why Christ came, but I was forced to wonder often if Janine ever recognized that she too had flaws, or that she too was in need of a savior. Now I'm not being cynical. She was never wrong, never at fault, never to blame, always the good wife and mother, at least in her own mind.

So here's what I figured out:

Janine started arguments, fostered debates, and created relationship issues that in reality didn't exist. Did she do this just to start a fight because she had nothing better to do? No, she did this for my sake so that I would recognize my faults, the difficulties for anybody living with me, and with full intent of making me accept total responsibility for the sorry state of our marriage.

The breast issue in Tampa was one such example. There were many others.

There was Barry Manilow.

Yes, I admit it: I am a Barry Manilow fan! Now I don't belong to any of his fan clubs, but let's face it; the guy is good! I also enjoy the Rolling Stones, Beatles, The Who, and many other rock bands, but, well, Barry is different. When I'm working around the house I put on a CD, and on many occasions, Barry was the music of choice. For years, Janine would be giving me the silent treatment, or glaring at me for reasons unknown, and I would be completely baffled by its cause.

"What did I do now?" I would finally break down and ask her.

Here was her famous line:

"If you don't know, then I'm not telling you!"

That was another disturbing part of the game she played with me. Through silence, stares, and body language Janine would go well out of her way to make me see that I had somehow made her angry. The point of the game, I suppose, was for me to realize that I was a bad husband once again, and that she had a legitimate right to be upset with me. Next, it was my responsibility to guess why she was angry, and usually I remained clueless even days later. Still, Janine was not going to tell me.

"Why do I always have to be the one to point out all your issues? I'm tired of being the one who has to explain every detail of your behavior. Think about your life! Think about the things you do and why you do them. I'm not your mother, Lenny, so why should I always have to tell you everything?"

Ah, maybe because you're the one who's mad?

Eventually, she would come around and share the cause of her distress. Sometimes that took days or even weeks. With Barry Manilow, it apparently took years before she told me the problem.

"Who do these songs remind you of?" She one day asked out of the blue.

I said the first thing that popped into my head.

"What songs?"

"You know what songs! Don't play games with me!"

At the time I was doing the dishes and listening to Barry Manilow sing 'Even Now'. Obviously, Janine was referring to Barry's music.

"All of his songs," she began, "are about a lost love, or someone from the past dealing with a broken heart. You always listen to these same songs. What is so important about those songs to you?"

How do I answer that kind of question? My response was quite simple and to the point.

"I like his songs."

"No," she shook her head dramatically, "there's more to it than that. It is not normal for a man to listen to the same songs over and over again unless they mean something very special to him. Who do they remind you of? Why do you keep listening to them and how do they make you feel?"

How do they make me feel? They're songs! I like them and I enjoy singing along with Barry. Where is she going with this?

"Think about them." She resumed. "The song you're listening to right now is about a lost lover. The other ones like, 'This One's For You Wherever You Are', 'If Ever I Should Love Again', 'Looks Like We Made It': They're all the same! These are songs for people who miss someone, who look sadly back at their past, as if they're not over it yet; it still hurts and no relationship since has soothed the pain."

No relationship since has soothed the pain? Was this speech rehearsed?

I put down the dish I was washing and stared at her.

"I like his music. I like the melodies and I enjoy singing along with him. His music makes me feel good, not sad over some lost lover that you seem to have invented in your mind."

Wrong thing to say!

"How dare you accuse me of imagining things! I know that you're not happy with me. You hate me but you just won't admit it! It's obvious. You listen to these songs of his over and over again because they hold some meaning for you. It certainly doesn't matter to you that you're married now. You live in the past. Why don't you just find this old lover of yours and let me be free to live my own life. I'm sorry if I haven't filled the void she left. You never loved me anyway!"

All of this from Barry Manilow?

A few months later she really lost it.

We were at the Mall and the kids wanted to go into the music store. Janine shopped elsewhere while I stayed with the kids and browsed through the CD's. I found a Barry Manilow CD that I had never seen before. It contained two of my favorite songs: 'I Made It Through the Rain', and 'If Ever I Should Love Again'. I bought it.

Unfortunately, I only got to listen to this particular CD for two days. One night when I got home from work I went upstairs and found Janine lying on our bed crying. 'Now what', I wondered nervously. She saw me, threw off the covers, and stomped over to the CD player. She pushed the play button. The player was cued-up to the Barry Manilow song, "If Ever I Should Love Again'.

"Who is she?" Janine cried out. "Why can't you forget about her and love me? What is the matter with me?"

Now at the time my conclusion was obvious: This woman is nuts! There was no lost lover from my past and these songs brought back no memories. Yet every time I tried to explain that to her or deny her ridiculous accusations, Janine became more hysterical and more adamant that her conclusions were true. I remembered something my father once told me: 'You can't argue with a crazy woman!'

The next day I did something really stupid! I took my new Barry Manilow CD, placed it back in its case, and tossed it in the garbage. I made sure Janine saw me do this. She gave no response or indication that she even noticed my sacrifice. I thought it was the right thing to do under the circumstances. Once again, I did whatever I could to maintain the peace. Looking back, I see that my action was not a wise move. All I really did by tossing away the CD was inadvertently give credence to her belief that Barry's music was not appropriate for a married man who claims to have no one else on his mind. Worse than that, it provided Janine with yet another circumstance to reach for in our next confrontation to prove how badly I treated her. I fell for it!

A few weeks following the Barry Manilow fiasco, a light went on in my head. My brother was right; she was crazy like a fox! Janine was trying to force my hand in the divorce issue. The usual pattern was that we would fight, Janine would ask for a divorce, and I said no. My commitment was to restore and maintain, while hers was to undermine and destroy! The next stage in her plan was to get me so mentally contorted and emotionally distraught by her odd behavior that I would simply throw up my hands and surrender to her divorce requests. Or better yet, she was trying to get me to be the one to pull the trigger. It was all beginning to make sense to me.

Think about it:

From the early 1990's up until who knows how long, there was no sex, no tenderness, no romance, basically no relationship, but we didn't fight so much either. Then two things happen: First, Janine asks for a divorce, and then secondly, I recommit my effort to rescue this marriage. I thought that my resolve to make this thing work, to prove my love and dedication to her, would help remove all doubts, and she would know that I love her and only her. Wrong! While I redoubled my efforts to restore the relationship, Janine redoubled hers to make things as difficult and out of control for me as possible. She didn't want me committed to her. She didn't want me to be a good husband. And she certainly did not want this relationship to be restored. Janine only really wanted one thing: She wanted out!

The big problem was that her psychological hold on me was tightening. I knew it, but for some reason I wasn't able to do a thing about it. Janine was too smart, too clever, and dare I say, too devious to outmaneuver. She, of course, could never prove any of her ludicrous accusations, yet she cleverly presented them in a way that always placed the burden of proving innocence on me. Her arguments were often convincing and logical, except for the fact that their basis was pure fantasy. I didn't know how to turn the tables and make the truth irrefutable to her. I felt lost, defeated, alone, and destined to lose at every turn. I had never dealt with such a deceptive mind before, and really had no stomach for a retaliatory assault.

Enter Cybil McGready.

When my friend Carl Miller left the Orchard Park school district, he was replaced by a young attractive woman named, Cybil McGready. As the new music and band instructor, Cybil taught the same students that I, as an eighth-grade math teacher did. Over the years we became friends. And that's all we ever were: Friends! The major problem with our friendship was the most obvious: She was young and very attractive.

We were friends so people talked. In the Middle School where I taught for a number of years, I really never made any close friends. I had plenty of high school and college friends in my day, but now that I was married with children I simply lost interest in making new friends. So having no one else to really talk to at work, Cybil became my only friend at school.

I must also confess that I am practically computer illiterate! I don't know if I'm just afraid to learn new things or have no real interest, but nevertheless, I didn't even know how to send an e-mail until Cybil showed me. Sitting right beside me one day, Cybil took me through the nuances of the e-mail.

"Write something," she directed me, pointing at the computer screen, "and I'll show you how to send it."

"Write to who?"

"Write to me and then we'll check it on my computer to see if it got there and how to open it. Then I'll answer you back."

"Okay." I said and began to type.

I quickly typed a silly poem.

Was I being a little flirtatious? Perhaps. It was not a romantic or inappropriate poem in any manner, shape, or form; it was just an attempt at humor, nothing more. I don't even recall what it was about; that's how non-threatening and innocuous it truly was. Anyway, I now knew how to send e-mails. A new world was opened to me!

Cybil and I e-mailed back-and-forth maybe once a week or once every two weeks for the next couple of years. We were no more than two people who were glad to see each other and who stopped and talked in the school hallways. I was married, albeit unhappily married, but I wasn't looking to replace Janine with someone newer and younger. But I will admit this: After years of ridicule, insane accusations, disrespect and verbal abuse, it sure was nice to talk to an attractive woman who listened to and respected my ideas on life. I imagine Cybil knew, or at least suspected that I was going through marriage difficulties, but she never asked me about it nor pried into my affairs at any time. We were simply friends.

Cybil one day confided in me that she was interested in a music teacher from a nearby school district.

"I was out with him and his friends and they were all watching a ballgame on TV." She told me. "It was like I wasn't even there. Should I say something or just leave it be?"

"I'm probably the last person you should ask for advice on relationships!" I smiled. "But look, I've got to go to class. I'll talk to you about it later."

At the end of the day, I sat at my computer and wrote Cybil a letter, pretending to be the new boyfriend. I made the letter apologetic and sought forgiveness. Unfortunately, when it came time to send the e-mail to Cybil, I must have clicked the wrong key because my intentional attempt at humor was sent to another teacher in the district. Realizing this, I immediately went to the office phone and called the woman who had inadvertently received the fake boyfriend's e-mail.

"Hi, I'm Lenny Spencer from over at the Middle School," I probably sounded a little frantic, "I sent you an e-mail by mistake. It was intended to be a joke, and I would really appreciate it if you just deleted it without reading it."

She assured me that she would.

About a week or so later, Cybil saw me in the halls and told me that there were rumors about the two of us. I told Cybil about the wayward e-mail. After that, one of Janine's friends enlightened her concerning the rumors. Janine said nothing at the time, but a week or so later she came to the school looking for me, and spotted me talking in the hallway with Cybil.

That's when all hell broke loose!

I got home late, because as coach of the seventh -grade basketball team, we had had an away game that night. Janine was ready and waiting.

"We are going to the Millers!" She angrily informed me. "I told them all about your blond-haired girlfriend and they are waiting to talk to you."

So there we were back at the Millers, attempting once again to rescue a marriage that could not be saved.

"What exactly does she mean to you?" Carl asked me as the four of us sat on chairs in a circle.

"She's just someone I talk to, Carl."

"Do the rumors bother you?" Sally Miller interjected.

"Of course not!" I replied with conviction. "None of its true, so why would I care what people think?"

Around and around we went for hours. Finally, I agreed to the three of them that I would write Cybil a letter explaining that our relationship was inappropriate, and that I thought it best that we not be seen together anymore. I felt that the matter was settled in the minds of the other three. Their interpretation of the whole sordid ordeal was that I was wrong to be spending time with an attractive woman, first because I was married, and secondly because it did not look good to others who were watching me because of my professed faith as a Christian. Truth was, I just wanted to get away from these people, including Janine, and get on with my life. I was not guilty of anything, except perhaps being a bit flirtatious at times to an attractive woman. That I'll confess to. But the rumors of a romantic relationship between Cybil and I were blatantly untrue and unfounded. What's the matter with people anyway? Don't they have better things to do with their time?

I gave Cybil my handwritten letter the following morning. To her credit, she has honored it over the years. If we run into each other at school, we'll talk briefly. We're still glad to see each other, but mostly we're glad that the rumors have stopped and we've both gone forward with our jobs as school teachers. Cybil will be getting married soon. Me? Well, I'm recently divorced.

Looking back on this trial I recognize some very interesting viewpoints:

I knew that my wife never believed the rumors for a second. The whole charade at the Miller's house was not about restoring a wayward husband to his poor distraught wife, but was merely a new tool to use in Janine's effort to show the world how horrible a man she was stuck with . Of course, there was also this need of hers to make me see that I was the reason why this relationship didn't work, that it was because of my infidelity, whether actual or in lustful thought, that caused the demise of our marital union. I had to be to blame, and more importantly, I needed to be the one who accepted the blame in order to legitimize her right to a divorce. It was subtle, calculating, and well-thought-out on Janine's part. Yet for reasons known only to her, it was still not the right time to demand a divorce. Me? I am totally clueless at the time that I, along with Carl and Sally Miller, am being played for a sucker in Janine's game of deception.

One last note concerning Cybil McGready:

When I was finally served divorce papers by Janine there was the usual claim of mental cruelty on my part. What was also added to the decree was that I had been unfaithful to her.

"You know that that was all nonsense!" I told her. "If this lie is not removed, you'll never get your divorce."

"I never told the lawyer that you were unfaithful." Janine fired back. "I just told him that there were rumors."

"Have it removed or forget about it!"

A week later my lawyer called me and told me that the divorce papers had been changed at my request and that I needed to sign the updated form.

At his office I sat back in my chair before signing.

"This is ridiculous!" I sighed. "There has never been any mental cruelty or control on my part. In fact, if anything she's the abuser and the control freak!"

"Lenny," Kevin Vail gently persuaded me, "nobody reads this stuff anyway. The state of New York requires that there be a cause for divorce. These accusations are in all divorce decrees. Trust me; it's not a big deal. The Judge won't even look at it."

I signed.

Chapter 9

THE JUDGE GAVE ME a month to move out of our brand new house. The whole process of divorce between Janine and I had taken about twenty months. During that time neither one of us sought a new place to live. The divorce was never my idea so I certainly wasn't leaving. Living under the same roof during this period was not as stressful as one might imagine, in fact, it was a time to relax, plan, and focus my energies on the future.

I moved out of our bedroom and slept upstairs in a spare bedroom in the loft. Garrett also slept up there, so we shared a full bathroom. There was a TV, a small refrigerator and a recreation room. I was able to come and go without seeing Janine if I chose. I chose that plan often! The only reason to go downstairs was to use the kitchen and the laundry room. Of course, since we put our home up for sale, I would have to spend time throughout the house cleaning when a prospective buyer was coming. Unfortunately, if I didn't clean it, nobody else would!

So for twenty months I basically lived like a bachelor in one-third of the house while the only awareness I had of my wife were the footsteps I heard coming from downstairs. I would hear the footsteps throughout the late afternoon and especially when Janine was in the kitchen preparing dinner for the kids. I would also hear those same footsteps click along the floor below me as they headed out of the house in the early evening. I wouldn't hear them again until hours later when Janine had apparently returned. I was left alone with the kids practically every night. No problems there; I love my kids and I enjoyed having them to myself. But where was Janine for hours on end almost every night? I suppose that that's not too hard to figure out! Apparently, my wife of twenty-five years had already found a boyfriend. How ironic! Here all these years I was always accused of searching for somebody better, flirting at every opportunity, and of course there was the whole Cybil McGready thing. I've heard it said that people will often accuse others of faults that they themselves struggle with. In other words, it takes one to know one!

During this twenty month period of emotional separation my eyes were opened to the reality of Janine Spencer. I had always suspected that the discord was really not my fault, yet at the same time I held my mate's integrity in high regard. She always complained about how selfish, self-centered, egotistical, flirtatious, dishonest, and mentally promiscuous I was. Today, I can acknowledge some degree of truth to these accusations, because let's face it: we all struggle in these areas. What surprised me was witnessing first-hand the personification of these very real character flaws in my accuser herself, my soon-to-be ex-wife! How did I fail to see it all these years? Everything I was verbally assaulted for, Janine live out daily: The facade of high character, honesty, and sexual appropriateness melted before my very eyes as I watched her daily lie, pretend, and sneak-out at night to visit her new beau.

And it wasn't easy.

Just imagine that for the past twenty-five years you are the only man who touches, kisses, dates, and plans a life around four children with a woman, and suddenly another man is doing to her what you alone used to do. Tough? You bet it is! Since I was always adept at utilizing denial I got through it okay. I mean, there were certainly times when I could not get my mind to stop picturing Janine being held by , kissed by, or even making love to another man, but most of the time when she left the house I shut my mind off and behaved as though her affair didn't exist. I never followed her, nor did I ask any entrapment questions. I ignored it. I didn't want to know, and eventually I got myself to a point emotionally, where I didn't even care. This was not the Janine Spencer I knew. This apparently was the real Janine Spencer that she had deceptively kept hidden for so long. True, we were in the process of a divorce, and I had no real proof of an existing boyfriend, but I knew! There was no doubt in my mind. I knew!

Then I remembered something.

While I worked for my brother one summer putting in underground sprinkler systems, and as a chiropractor, Janine got a job as a bartender at a local upscale restaurant. She made good money on tips and often came home well after midnight. We still lived in New Jersey and Sydney was our only child at the time, so I cared for her while Mom was working. It was, as always, a bit of a stressful time in our marriage.

One night during the summer, Sydney was asleep so I decided to go visit Janine at her work place. Only when I got there she was nowhere to be found. No one knew anything of her whereabouts. It was odd, but I didn't dwell on it, figuring there must be some sort of logical explanation. I was asleep when Janine arrived home around two in the morning

I woke up when she entered the bedroom.

"I came to see you tonight." I said, slowly waking from my sleep. "But you weren't there. I asked around but nobody knew where you were." I paused. "So where were you?"

"I was at work!" She snapped. Obviously she was bothered by my question of her whereabouts. "Why were you looking for me anyway?"

She climbed into bed and roughly turned her back to me. What was she so mad about?

Janine and I were married for three years by this time, but our roots were still quite shallow. When we first started dating, we seriously considered living in South Carolina. Soon after we were married, we twice drove up to New Hampshire as I tried to obtain a teaching position there. I sat through quite a few interviews but was never hired. Washing our hands of that effort, we next started applying for teaching positions up in Western New York. We were a little familiar with the area because my brother, Rich, had lived in Nunda, New York for over ten years. I had the local Buffalo News mailed to New Jersey and sent in applications for teaching jobs. One afternoon, as Janine and I were napping, I awoke, picked up the Buffalo News, and searched the want ads. They were advertising a math position in the town of Orchard Park. While Janine was still asleep, I called.

"Hi, my name is Lenny Spencer and I'm calling in reference to your ad about an open math teaching position."

I was told that there was still indeed an opening and that they would be interviewing shortly.

"I'm very interested." I assured them.

To make a long story short, I was hired in the middle of August. That gave Janine, Sydney and I just two weeks to pack up all our things, say good-bye to our loved ones, and begin our new life three-hundred-and-sixty miles away from our old life in New Jersey. I was initially a bit apprehensive about this change of scenery. There were two reasons for my lack of enthusiasm:

Reason number one:

The chiropractic college that I graduated from took a radical stance on the scope of the practice of chiropractic. Sherman College of Straight Chiropractic stood alone in the world as the only college to limit the practice of chiropractic to its purest form. We were not sent into our communities to fix back pain, stiff necks, headaches, or to diagnose any ailment of any kind. Instead, we held to a health philosophy that the adjusting of the vertebrae of the spine promoted overall expression of health and life because it helped to remove a deadly interference to the nervous system.

The human body was created to maintain itself in health. At Sherman College we refer to this inborn wisdom as Innate Intelligence. Explained simply, the brain creates a force, vital in nature, which coordinates the functioning of the body in health. Our skull and vertebrae protect this vital message from harm. When bones are jolted out of place, interference to this health message is created. Put the bone back, and the body's potential for health is restored.

Anyway, Sherman College's decision to stand firm on the integrity of the practice of chiropractic and the right of its graduates to do so, was met with intense opposition. Many states at the time did not permit its graduates to sit the licensing exams, New York among them. So, one of my reservations with moving to New York State was the reality that I would be unable to practice my beloved profession. Janine was always jealous of my love for chiropractic. She viewed it as a competitor for my affection. Moving to New York, even though it meant not practicing chiropractic was of no concern to her. It was to me.

Secondly, I was concerned about making a drastic life-changing move of three-hundred-and-sixty miles to a place I had never heard of, with a person I could not depend upon. Janine and I were in trouble as a married couple. Our issues were intensifying daily. Understandably, I was a little apprehensive about moving away with someone whose commitment to me was tenuous at best.

One of the best things about summer in Springfield, New Jersey was the men's softball league. I have a ton of good memories playing ball with basically the same group of guys for the better part of eighteen years. The league was competitive, intense, and more fun than I can begin to describe. My last season was no different. My team, named JK Sprinklers after my brother's business, had the best record in the league. We expected to win it all this summer! I was the pitcher. Yet during the playoffs we were upset by a team that we handled easily during the regular season. When it was over, and we had failed again to win it all, I went home alone that night drenched in sorrow. My parents and brothers were still at the field so only Janine was home waiting for me.

She wasted no time pouncing on me.

"I came this close to having an affair!" She informed me. "I am so tired of you taking me for granted. This guy valued me, listened to me, and told me that he would have protected me with his life."

Well, I came to find out that there was a fellow at work who was in hot pursuit of my wife. She told me that his name was Charley.

"Have you been unfaithful?" I needed to know.

"No! Once, he forced me into a corner of the backroom and kissed me. I told him that I wanted to, but that I couldn't. I'm married." She began to cry. "That's as far as it got."

For the first time since I had known Janine I suspected that she might be lying! My premonition was completely unfounded. It was just my intuition. Yet this thought jarred my memory: Where was she the night I went to the restaurant to visit her? And when I told her about my visit, and being unable to find her, what was it that made her so mad?

Interestingly, we did move to Orchard Park, New York where I started my job as a school teacher and where I was not permitted to practice chiropractic for many years. Eventually, the State Education Department granted me licensure and I have been in my own practice ever since. I also never thought about Janine's 'I came this close to an affair', or about some guy named Charley for many years. It wasn't like it was a bad memory that my psyche needed to suppress. It just never entered my mind again. Truthfully, I had just completely forgotten about it.

It wasn't until Janine started leaving the house at night and returning hours later, that the memory of that Charley fellow resurfaced. 'You don't suppose'? All those years I believed that I was married to a woman who, albeit was high maintenance and hard to please, but who I thought was at least honest and righteous to a large degree. Wrong! I think that if a person ever wants to feel foolish, they should examine their past, especially the things they once believed, and discover just how badly mistaken they were. I did it! It's no fun.

Lying upstairs in the spare bedroom, wondering who your wife is with tonight was a type of emotional torture that I never dreamed I would experience. Twenty-five years of living together, sharing everything, planning both the short and long term, and always counting on each other to be there, when suddenly the wheel falls off and you are left spinning into space. Well, I suppose the wheel was actually pretty loose and ready to fall off for a long time now, but anticipating an event is hardly as realistic as the event actually occurring. It was hard!

Back in New Jersey, my brother John and his wife decided to buy our parent's home. My Dad was eighty-six years old and in the early stages of Alzheimer's. John bought the old house and had it completely remodeled. While the work was being done my parents were forced to relocate until the house was finished. For three months they stayed in Florida with my cousin Phyllis. Then for the next three months they lived with me. Janine and I were in the process of a divorce, but I hadn't told my family yet. It was an interesting period of time for everyone involved.

Janine was not very keen on the idea of my parents staying with us under our present state of marital separation. My Mom knew that marriage had not been good to me, so it was no surprise at all to her that I was living and sleeping in the loft. My Dad's mind was fading fast so he never noticed. It was certainly an awkward living arrangement for all of us, but the kids and I didn't miss a beat, in fact, I think all five of us enjoyed the time we had with grandma and grandpa. Janine, on the other hand, went well out of her way to be as rude and disrespectful as she possibly could. Once again, the irony was striking!

While Janine and I were still dating, she practically lived at my house during the summer vacations. She worked at a bank in the town of Summit and helped herself to food in the refrigerator at lunch time, and usually stayed until around midnight. Every day was the same. Not only did my mother feed Janine lunch and dinner daily, but when she went food-shopping she put aside non-perishable items for my girlfriend to take back to college with her. My Mom was very good to Janine.

When my Mom and Dad stayed with us for three months up in Western New York, Janine did not exactly return the favor! My mother was unable to use the phone during the day because Janine had locked the bedroom door. Only my wife had a key to open it. My Mom wanted to show her appreciation by cooking meals for us on occasion. More than once she was scolded by Janine for using some of her spices to do so. Me? I said nothing. I listened to my Mom's complaints about Janine's rude behavior and I was occasionally forced to hear my wife's side of the story too. There was stress. There was tension. But at the same time there was this ever-growing, ever-illuminating revelation. By losing Janine to divorce, I was actually losing nothing! She was nasty, selfish, mean-spirited, and hardly the type of person anyone would want to spend time with. I thought I was losing something. I was wrong. There was not a thing to feel bad about any longer.

In the movie, 'Rocky", Sylvester Stallone's character is poked fun at by the champ, Apollo Creed, during a television interview. Rocky laughs and plays along and even states that whatever Creed says about him doesn't bother him at all. Later, when Rocky is alone with his girlfriend, Adrianne, he confides to her:

"Remember when I said that stuff doesn't bother me? Well, it does!"

I know now how Rocky Balboa feels. I convinced myself that losing my life and marriage to Janine was the equivalent of losing nothing at all. I told everybody that none of this divorce stuff bothers me, in fact, I went out of my way to tell people that I couldn't wait to be free to start my life over again. But one day after church, I was talking to the pastor and he asked me how things were going with the kids and my present situation, so I had an honest moment.

"Remember when I said that stuff don't bother me?" I answered with my best Rocky Balboa impersonation. "Well, it does."

How could it not?

One day during our separation, we were bickering over some type of issue. I was getting frustrated.

"You never admit you're wrong. You think you're some kind of princess!"

Janine's reply was very telling.

"Well, someone does know how to treat me like a princess!"

That someone obviously wasn't me.

Yet somewhere out there was a man who was indeed treating my woman like a princess. Who was he? Where was he? What did he do for a living? Was he handsome? None of that mattered really. What hurt was the knowledge that he was out there somewhere and that he had a relationship going on with my wife. Imagine someone sitting across from the woman you love, sharing his experiences, his philosophy of life, accomplishments and failures, and she doing the same. Imagine that this growing fondness and increasing knowledge of each other is leading to an intense infatuation. He reaches across a dinner table somewhere and takes her hand. They gaze silently into one another's eyes, saying nothing, yet exchanging an understanding of mutual respect and admiration. Imagine that the sexual tension is intense and that both of them want more than nothing else to share their first kiss.

How do you erase these imaginations from your mind?

The only thing I could come up with was to stay busy. I taught school until three, went to the office until six, and spent lots of time with the kids before they went to bed. Weekends were the hardest! I worked at my office in the morning and then went over to nearby Delaware Park to run, walk, bike, or find someone to play tennis with. I lifted weights, read my Bible, wrote sermons, and once again spent as much time as possible with the children, playing ball, watching TV, or going out for ice cream. Often, we went to Subway, or the mall, or Pizza Hut, anything to get out of the house where I knew Janine would be primping herself, getting ready for another night out with the boyfriend.

I suppose the best thing for me to do now to counteract this painful reality was to go and get a new partner of my own.

My friend Fred said to me:

"You need a girlfriend!"

I shook my head and smiled.

"That's what got me in this mess to begin with!"

No, the last thing I wanted to do was find myself a new girlfriend. I knew that what I needed to do was to stay away from the opposite sex for awhile until my head cleared. I mean, don't get me wrong. I like women. I like the way they look, the way they move, laugh at my jokes, make me feel special, but I can live without them! Well, for awhile anyway.

My parents returned to New Jersey the first week in May. The home they purchased over forty years ago was not completely renovated as yet, but my Mom was especially antsy and wanted to be back in her familiar surroundings. My Dad, well, nothing was really familiar to him anywhere. One day while he was still with me in Western New York, I found him standing in my driveway, pacing back-and-forth with a very concerned look on his face.

"What's the matter, Dad?" I asked.

"I've got a real problem." He began. "Your mother tells me that I have Alzheimer's. That's not good, is it? What do I do about that?"

This was the first and last time that my father ever mentioned or showed any awareness to his condition.

"Well," I explained as best I could, "it's just a deterioration of the brain. You begin to lose your memory, forget things; that's all." I lied.

Alzheimer's is a silent, mentally-debilitating cancer whose roots affect not solely the mind of its victim, but spreads its tentacles throughout a family, friendships, and community. Sometimes, when I would watch my Dad, I think about Mr. Jankowski who has been dead for almost forty years now. He was at his son's baseball game one day, and later that night he was gone. It was sudden and it was final. Here one day, gone the next! Losing someone you love so unexpectedly is its own type of tragedy. Losing someone slowly, day-by-day, may not share the finality of a sudden death, but it is a tragedy nevertheless.

My poor mother.

Born Angelina Rose Colangelo in 1931, my mother was raised in a dysfunctional family setting with an alcoholic and physically abusive father. As children, she and her two sisters and brother more than once applied the force of a frying pan over their drunken father's head to calm his violent outbursts. Her mother, (my grandmother), was beaten repeatedly throughout their childhood. My grandfather died before I was born. My grandmother lived with us my entire childhood.

My Mom and Dad have been married for over fifty-five years! People talk about families having generational curses. Some obvious examples are alcoholism and poverty. Great Grandpa was a drunk, grandpa was a drunk; Dad's a drunk, so you'll probably wind up an alcoholic too. Or Great Grandpa was on welfare, Grandpa was on welfare, your father is unemployed and collecting welfare, so your future doesn't look so bright either. Interestingly, in my family there were few alcoholics, and everybody worked, but the generational curse that afflicted us was divorce!

The spread of divorce started out very slowly. First there was my Uncle Tony and next my Aunt Vera. Those divorces were followed by my cousins Phyllis, Irene, Crissy, Frank, and Donna, and in turn by my brothers, John and Rich. I followed suit. Even more curious is that I have five other cousins who avoided divorce the easy way: They never got married! On my mother's side, the family relationships are somewhat strained. 'God hates divorce', the Bible tell us. It's not hard to see why.

So here I grow up with a parental model of two people married over fifty years, and I and my brothers cannot duplicate the feat. Were my parents the ideal soul-mates? Hardly! But they accomplished something by remaining together for life, that less than half of today's couples are able to do. I must add my marriage to the list of failures. The latest statistics are not a glowing pronouncement on the sanctity of marriage. And when people fail to stay together for life, the entire family suffers. So what is the best solution? Should couples remain together in a relationship that just isn't working, arguing in front of the children, tolerating instead of loving each other, or is it better to go their separate ways and try it again, though perhaps leaving a trail of emotional damage behind.

I don't know the answer.

The only marriage I have any right to an opinion on is my own, and there is lots that I didn't understand about that! What is so impressive to me are the things that a person does for another in the name of love, even during those periods where love is the last thing they feel. I have twice watched my mother do just that.

My grandmother was a four-foot-seven-inch Italian woman who spoke broken English and who, though physically slowed by diabetic feet, was still quick to slap your face if you misbehaved. I remember once when I disobeyed her, and it wasn't until days later that she snuck up behind me and jabbed a sewing needle in the back of my ear! Ouch! She was often mean, ornery, rude, and rarely friendly to the grandchildren she lived with. In 1975 she had a stroke. Soon after, a form a dementia set in. She remained obstinate and stubborn, yet my mother cared for her needs despite her lack of caretaking training. My mother did not leave the house much over the next five years. Her sisters and brother were of little to no help, so alone she took on the burden until grandma died.

Now my father has Alzheimer's.

I try to see the whole picture.

They meet at a roller skating rink in the late 1940's. My Dad is twelve years older, fresh out of service in WWII, and he's just met the girl of his dreams. They court; they marry. I am born exactly nine months after their wedding day. Go figure! Together they have three more children, buy their own home, work, pay their bills and raise four boys who have no issues with drugs, alcohol, or brushes with the law. They attend nearly all their boys sporting events, chorus concerts, plays, and celebrate all our accomplishments from the first Holy Communion to the birth of their grandchildren. There were certainly financial concerns, discipline, broken bones, stitches, illnesses, and the hazard of coping with teenagers. But they did it, and they did it together, and I would strongly suspect that divorce was not only not an option, but likely a term that never entered their minds. Was it easier for them back then than it was for Janine and me? I doubt it! They fought, and often they ignored each other's existence. I saw it myself, firsthand. There was absolutely nothing perfect about them.

Around 2003, my Dad began to show signs that things were not right. By the time they came to stay with us in 2006, he had slid downhill considerably. My nice-guy Dad, a gentle man who reached out to help anyone in need, who sacrifice his own pleasure at times to be of service to others, had slowly turned into a selfish, demanding, and occasionally violent man whose dementia altered everything we ever knew, loved, and respected about him.

This was the man who taught me how to drive, play baseball, helped me find a summer job, worked a second job at night to pay for my college, and he was also the man my mother spent fifty-five years of her life with. But let's face it: That man was gone. Oh, there was no funeral, no obituary, no family ever gathered around his death bed to comfort him during his last living moments; the man we knew no longer existed.

Still, someone has to keep an eye on him, see to his needs, feed him, clothe him, and yes, at times scold him in order to keep him in line. That someone is my mother.

"What did I ever do to deserve this?" My mother pronounced in exasperation many times.

Answer: you married him.

Marriage is a miraculous union instituted by God that we are to honor for a lifetime. When you say, 'I do', it is supposed to be a promise to keep forever, during good times and bad. It's unconditional. It is not an ironclad contract drawn up by lawyers, to argue, dissect, and interpret during disagreements. It is not a deal! There are no conditions!

Now to me the point is this:

I wanted out of my lousy marriage as badly as Janine did. Emotionally, I believed that no one should have to live and be treated like that. And, I'm glad it's over! Yet I still can't get past the very real notion that I am a hypocrite. I don't believe in divorce, would never have asked Janine for a divorce, yet now that I am through with the pain, rejection, and emotional trauma, I'm glad to be free of her. So I suppose I believe one thing, but I don't really believe it enough to live it out in my day-to-day life. Hypocrite! When the going got tough for Janine and me, we both wanted to run for the hills. Yet I still maintain that if any one walked in my shoes during the marriage, they too would be happy to start their lives over. But that still doesn't make it right!

No one has more of a right to run for the hills than my mother! When I go to New Jersey to visit, I witness what she goes through. It's not pretty. He never leaves her alone. He asks her questions, makes demands, asks the same question again, repeats his demands; asks her the same question again for the third and fourth time. Get the picture? Yet where some people might watch Mom respond with anger, frustration, ridicule, and downright nastiness and think how unloving she is to this poor demented man, I see something else. I see commitment, dedication, acceptance, taking the oath of for better or worse seriously, and showing those around her that love is indeed an action word.

She talks often of sticking him in a nursing home because she claims she can't take it anymore. One day she phoned me up in New York. As always I asked about Dad.

"Getting nuttier every day!" She replied. "He cried a lot yesterday and I just couldn't get him to stop."

"Why?"

"Well, he told me that he hasn't seen his brother in awhile and wanted to go see him." She paused. "I told him that his brother died thirty-five years ago. That upset him. He was mad at me for not telling him that his brother was dead, and then the rest of the day he just cried and cried."

Pitiful.

"Just tell him his brother's alive!" I sympathetically instructed her. "Tell him that you'll visit next week. He won't remember. Why torment him with the truth?"

Our conversation quickly switched gears and turned to my children.

"Garrett and I played basketball at the town court," I was sharing my day, "and I'm going to see Sydney on Sunday to take her to the Buffalo Zoo."

"You do a lot with your kids." Mom mused. "You're always there for them." Then she added. "You're a good dad, just like your father."

There was a moment of silence.

"I know what a good man your father used to be. It's so sad to see him turn out like this. Life isn't fair."

It certainly isn't! Life is not Hollywood. People hurt. They deal with the pain in private where there is no paparazzi to glamorize the issues of life.

In the movie, 'The Natural', baseball hero, Roy Hobbs, meets up with his old girlfriend and they share lemonade at the local soda shop. The Glenn Close character asks Roy a very normal question, asking him about his life through the years. I agree with his response.

"Life didn't turn out the way I thought it would."

I can say amen to that!

I suppose my mother could too. I've never asked my mother what her dreams were. But we all have them. She was a stay-home mom whose life was centered around her children. She took care of us. True, she may have developed a bit of a biased impression of how wonderful we were, but she loved, protected, fed, clothed, and was always there for us. Of course, this role too can be overdone.

On the night before school, my mother used to lay out the clothes we would be wearing the next day. They were separated and placed on the ends of our beds. When school was over and it was late in the afternoon, she would stand at the top of the long street we lived on, and look for us. Once she spotted us, she hurried back into the house, hoping we didn't notice. We did: Always. And not one of us liked it!

When we were teenagers, driving cars, going out with friends late at night, Mom never went to sleep until we were safely home. Never! We would come in and be faced with her complaints about how we needed to be back earlier so she could get some sleep. I would yell back at her.

"Go to sleep! You don't need to wait up for me."

And I was right. I'm not a baby! Well, I was her baby. I know the feeling today as a father of four children of my own. Sydney, now twenty, Garrett is almost eighteen, and the twins are fourteen. The two older ones are out late at night on occasion. But you know what I do? I sleep!

"You don't have the brains that God gave a screwdriver!" She told me when I disobeyed her once.

"Oh, but you do?" I disrespectfully answered back.

"Yes, I do!"

To this day we still tease her about admitting to having the brains of a screwdriver! Could you imagine if we were all smart, good-looking, intuitive, friendly, blessed financially, and perfectly healthy? Well, we're not, and the person whom we choose as our mates is also lacking in many desired areas. Still, we have dreams.

When I was a senior at St. Francis College in Loretto, Pennsylvania, I kept a journal that I wrote in almost daily. Usually, the topics varied based upon the events of the day. One afternoon a bunch of us sat around talking humorously about what we expected from our future wives. Unfortunately, my journal was lost among my parents things, cleared out of the attic and thrown away one spring-cleaning years ago, so I don't remember exactly what I wrote later that night following our discussion of future mates, but I do recall the gist of it.

The first thing I wrote about my dream-girl was how she would appear physically. Of course! She would have a pretty face and a knockout body. But that was just a shallow description of the dream. The core of the dream was not what she looked like, but who she was! She could be trusted. She enjoyed having a good time. She would care about the needs of others. She would be my best friend! She would keep no record of past mistakes. She would love me for who I am and I would do the same in return. We would share our thoughts, hopes, goals, minds, and even the pain of failures. We would support one another no matter what, and we would forgive one another, no matter what.

I had a dream girl!

Following Suzie in high school and Betty King during my college years, I dated many other young women before I met Janine. I have a lot of good memories. Yet not one of them, Janine included, fulfilled the dream.

I'm divorced now. At least the nightmare is over! I wake up in the morning now and I'm alone in bed. The kids and I will still be a family, and will do things that families do, and although this new life will be better without the screaming and yelling, and name-calling, it will not be the dream. Someone is missing. I cannot deny that there is a void. Only one person can fill it, and though I had hoped for many years that Janine was the answer, I also spent many years knowing that she was not.

I have friends from a church I used to attend. Their names are Barry and Halley. Barry is a teacher like me, and Halley home-schooled their children. Their lives appear hectic at times, financially-challenged at times, and I often wonder just how they do it. They are best friends. He is the man and she is the woman. They are so together! They have great kids. They serve their communities in numerous functions, and most of all their commitment and dedication to one another is evident to all. How do they do it? As marriages topple around them, they manage to form a strong team, a united front together representing all that is good about love and relationships. That's what I want to do! That's what I want to be a part of. I long for a partner to truly and intimately share my life with. That's my dream and I need to do it!

As I drove away from the courthouse following my divorce, the memory of my dream girl shook my thoughts. I was not the one who terminated this union. I was not to blame! So now here I am on the other side of my life, no longer a husband, without a legal partner, and no longer bound to a relationship that had failure written all over it from the start. Yet as I took stock of my post-divorce position, I tallied that I was still a father, still a teacher who could serve as a positive influence to his students, still a chiropractor who could not only assist the body's healing process, but also touch the heart and minds of those patients who came to me, hurting physically, emotionally and psychologically, and most importantly, still a child of the Living God who I knew had a better plan for my life!

This would be my new beginning. I would not only survive, but I would flourish at my second chance! Can a man just turn off the pain of divorce like a water valve? Of course not! But I had in my possession full control of what I would face next and how I would react to it. "Woe is me" was an unacceptable path to travel down. Barry Manilow sings a song, 'I made It Through the Rain'. I would make it through my rain. I knew I would hurt for awhile, yet I knew too that time would ease the pain, and that one day I would hear that deep belly-filled laughter that only a person with great joy can express, and I would realize that that person is me!

Until then, I was alone.

PART II
Chapter 1

A FEW WEEKS AFTER my divorce, I received in the mail a copy of my final divorce papers. I skimmed through it, basically familiar with the finer points of legal judgment. Janine was granted her divorce by the State of New York. I was legally obligated to pay her $700 per week, $350 as alimony and an additional $350 for child support. Fair? Of course not! The weekly amount is a result of a formula used by the State of New York to determine equity. Now I don't know about the other people and their divorce settlements, but here's a look at mine:

Janine wanted this divorce. I had no part in it. After six years of denying her requests for divorce, I stepped back and offered no resistance. She grabbed the bull by the horn and hired the supposedly best and craftiest lawyer in the county.

"He always gets his clients what they want." Janine bragged.

Anyway, not that it matters, but here's what I think: If someone wants a divorce so badly, then they should take responsibility for their lives, including financially, for the future following the divorce. I mean, if you expect to live at a certain level or standard of comfort then you should have to work for it and earn it yourself. I believe that supposition is biblical! Janine, to my way of thinking, wants her cake and wants to eat it too. Only problem is, I have to buy the cake. She plans her divorce strategy with the notion that her life and creature comforts will be unchanged following the financial settlement. She plans do this without getting a job. And apparently, the State of New York agrees!

Let's look at the figures:

I take home approximately $1900 every two weeks as a school teacher. Subtract the two $700 checks I give to my ex-wife, and that leaves me with $500 take-home over the two week period. So for all my effort to teach young teenagers, many of whom are terribly unruly, disruptive, and potentially dangerous, I make $250 a week! That's approximately $50 a day! As a chiropractor, working part-time, I need to make enough to support myself. There is rent, electric, natural gas, cable TV, office rent, cell phone bill, car insurance, malpractice insurance, x-ray film and chemicals, car loans, food, rising gas prices, and that doesn't even include the needs of my children! I discovered after I moved out that there were many other expenses that I had not anticipated nor budgeted for, and that Janine refused to share the burden of. Our kids are involved in many extracurricular activities. That stuff costs money! Every time I asked Janine to help out with these financial needs, she makes excuses and cries poverty. Imagine: You are receiving over thirty-four thousand dollars a year, and have your own accounting business, yet you don't have the money to spend on your kids!

What about the $350 a week for child support?

Good question!

Apparently, the State of New York awards the child support amount with no concern about whether the money is actually spent on the children or not. I've been divorce for a year and a half now, so I do have some foundation to question my ex-wife's fiscal integrity. The only real source of information or proof that I have is what the kids tell me. They say that there is little or no food to eat at Mom's house. Garrett, who has his own car, stops to eat dinner at my apartment everyday! The court's decision to award her joint-custody was clearly laid out. She is supposed to feed them on the days they are with her. Now don't get me wrong, I love that Garrett prefers being with me, and eating food that I buy, and in fact, all of the kids have slept numerous weekends at my place when they were scheduled to be at their Mom's. No problem there either; I want them with me as much as possible. The only question I have is, 'what is the $350 a week for'? I mean, I'm the one who buys their gym shoes, blue jeans, pays for the majority of their school lunches, and for their other activities. I bought each of them cell phones and pay the monthly bill without assistance from Janine. You name it, and I'm the one who reaches into their pocket and comes out with the means for their needs. When Sydney needs money for college, she doesn't even bother to ask her mother. She knows. But get this: When it was time to do my taxes, Janine, who donated zero cents to her daughter's education, got the benefit of writing off Sydney as her tax exemption.

Why?

Once again, I suppose that Janine's claim that her lawyer gets what he wants for his clients may have some validity to it! The divorce settlement includes agreed upon tax write-offs. Janine claims Sydney, our oldest, while I get to claim Garrett, Lilly and Layla. Three-to-one! That sounded good to me so I agreed. When Sydney graduates college, we split the twins. Still sounds fair, doesn't it? Finally, when the two girls are the only ones left, we alternate years of declaring the youngest as our tax deduction.

I'm not a lawyer so it all sounded good to me. Unfortunately, the man I hired is a lawyer, and in my opinion, he really blew it! When I went to see my accountant, expecting a sizeable return, I was met with some surprising news:

"Only three-thousand dollars?" I asked, expecting my refund to be much larger.

"Well," he explained, "you lost about three-thousand more because you no longer have your daughter's college exemption."

"What exemption?"

"Well," he slid forward in his chair, "the federal government offers a tax break to people who are spending a good deal of money to send their kids to college. That return amount now belongs to your wife since she's the one who claims your daughter."

"Wait a second," I interrupted, "I'm the one paying for her education! Do you mean to say that Janine is getting a tax return on my money that I alone paid for?'

I already knew the answer.

"She claims Sydney." He continued. "Your lawyer should have known that."

Obviously, he didn't.

"So in other words," I resumed incredulously, "I pay for everything, but she writes it off on her taxes!"

"Yup."

Three weeks later I took advantage of a free consultation with a different lawyer. I told him about the college exemption issue, how I pay for everything, how the house is always a mess, the child support being used improperly, and anything else that reeked of a financially moral trespass.

"Can anything be made right?" I asked when he was done looking through a copy of the divorce papers.

Here's what he told me:

"There's not a thing you can do about the tax exemptions. The papers are signed and reversible only if your wife agrees to make a change."

Fat chance!

"What about child support?"

"Your obligation," he explained, "in fact, your sole financial obligation is to pay the $350 per week. After that, you are not obligated to pay a thing, not food, clothing, activities, not even medical or dental. The $350 per week is your part of the deal, and anything beyond that is above what you are legally responsible for."

"But," I answered, although the reality of my plea for help was sinking all around me, "they're my kids, and I want them to have and do the things that every kid does. She's not going to pay, so what am I supposed to do? I love them to death! I want them to play sports. They need spikes, sweatshirts, money for McDonalds; how can I deprive them just because their mother is greedy?"

He smiled and spread his arms out to his sides.

"You're a good father." He told me. "And you want the best for your kids. That's why you do it. Fair? Not at all, but you know what," he spoke with a gleam in his eye, "your children will never forget the things you do for them, and as for your wife, let her have the money. You can't do a thing about it anyway, so just go out and try to make more! Keep doing what you're doing and I know you'll never regret it. They say, 'what goes around comes around'; she'll get hers!"

Since that consultation I made a decision to do two things: One, I would no longer worry and fret over the financial inequity of my divorce, and secondly, I would make more money! Actually, a year-and-a-half into my divorce, I am at a greater peace now because I have accepted the things that I can do nothing about, and recommitted myself to those things I do have the power to change.

Another issue following my divorce was the agreement that I would be out of the house we built together by the beginning of the year. I wasted no time and found an apartment in town right before Christmas.

My brother came down from Nunda to help me move. Janine and I supposedly split the house belongings evenly. Once again, I was too lazy, cowardly, or just plain stupid to challenge her fair assessment of the merchandise. Perhaps I just wanted to get away from her as quickly as possible, so I accepted her division of property. Looking back, I think I allowed myself to be taken advantage of once again! There were so many things I could have done differently. I really wish I had. They say that here in America freedom comes with a price. I suppose the same can be said for someone who deep-down wants a divorce. I was free, but I was certainly paying a heavy price to be so!

About the house we built:

We saved and purchased five-and-a-half acres of land. I remember coming over to the construction site early one evening following yet another spat with Janine. As I walked around from one unfinished room to another, I entered into prayer. I drove back to our little apartment knowing that God had heard my prayer, knowing that he loved my family very much, but that the result of our dreams still depends on how we live and what we do with the time, skills, and opportunities given to us. I've never forgotten that day. Me and God, we're a team; actually we're an unbeatable team! Oh, not because of anything special about me, but solely and completely because of His compassion, His commitment to me, His promises that can never be broken, and because He's got a bigger plan than for me than I can ever imagine. He lets me, Lenny Spencer, be part of what He's doing! He doesn't need me, but He loves me! I'm useless to Him, yet He instills me with a sense of purpose. I have failed Him daily, but He forgives, forgets, and offers me yet another chance. The world has existed before me, and will continue to exist long after I'm gone, yet He counts me worthy to create, to provide for, to redeem, to die for, to justify and to sanctify. I've played on a lot of sports teams, but Jesus is by far the best teammate I've ever had! He listens, His loyalty knows no bounds, and He is determined to present me glorious before the Father, Jehovah!

The house:

The Judge decreed that I would have to move out, but that Janine could continue to live there. That was initially fine with me. Of course, my agreement was based on my trusting that she would be a good conscientious care-taker of our home and its premises. We had put the house up for sale during our marital separation. To date, there were still no takers. The house remains unsold for three years now. There are two main reasons for this: One, with our country on the verge of a recession, the real estate market has been slow to move sales. All potential sellers have had to deal with this. But specifically, my house is having additional difficulties selling because Janine does not maintain it. The inside of the house is dirty and messy, stuff is strewn all over the place, and the outside of the house is also poorly maintained now that the person who used to keep it clean no longer lives there! I have to come over and clean the house every time it is about to be looked at.

During one summer, I worked out in the yard every day! I dug out the lawn, planted flowers and shrubs in those areas, and spent I don't know how much on wood chips to make it look nice. These areas of our lawn were to border a new pool that we were having put in by professional installers.

"How much is this going to cost?" I asked Janine.

"Around seven-thousand dollars."

Interesting.

One of the main reasons for the new pool is because we are planning a high school graduation party for Sydney in late August. She will be attending Riley College in the fall. Private colleges can be very expensive so we did the best we could to come up with enough money to send her there. Unfortunately, we did not have enough to allow our daughter to live on campus that first year, so we agreed that since the college was only forty-five minutes away from our house, she would commute. Sydney was not too happy about this arrangement, but as a part of the Riley College Honors program she would be awarded an all-expenses paid trip in the spring to Croatia, Serbia, and Italy. With that carrot dangling in front of her, Sydney accepted the terms of agreement and commuted her first year of college.

How financially short of her living on campus were we? Oh, about seven-thousand dollars!

I thought immediately of this when Janine and I first discussed the cost of the new pool.

"Shouldn't we be putting this money towards Sydney's room and board?" I ventured.

"We agreed that she would commute for a year!" Janine replied with a degree of hostility. "Look, I want things for my life too. All our money does not go to the kids. I have a life too, you know! This pool is going to make the backyard look beautiful and can't I have a nice backyard? Besides," now Janine was attempting to show me the logic of this decision, "it will increase the value of our home if we ever decide to sell."

Anyway, the house remains unsold years later, and as for the beautiful pool that was going to increase the resale value of our home, well, you can barely see it! It is surrounded, or better yet, engulfed by weeds that have grown three-to-four feet high within the flower and shrub garden that I worked long hours on during the summer. It's disgusting! Janine still gets to live in a huge house that I worked three jobs to pay for, yet she treats it as though she were an unappreciative welfare recipient. I was told by the second lawyer that I consulted that there wasn't a thing I could do about it. Bummer!

I suppose that despite all the inequity of the divorce agreement, at least I got to have my kids with me. Originally, Janine argued that the kids could see me whenever they wanted, but that it would be best for them, psychologically, if they slept in their own beds at the house. I balked at that arrangement and insisted on joint-custody where we shared the children evenly, and where they spent nights at my house too.

"I'll concede that one." Janine caved eventually, either in an act of great empathy, or as a threat to remind me that other issues would not be so amicably resolved.

I rented a U-Haul truck and moved my things out on a Saturday. I felt torn between the anguish of leaving behind my old life, and the excited anticipation of getting away from Janine. Honestly, the only thing that bothered me was the kids. What could they possibly be thinking watching their father pack his stuff and move away? It wasn't right! No child, no matter how old, should have to witness this.

I spent the first few days alone.

My life has always been about family. When I was a kid, my mother's side of the family gathered at our house every Christmas Eve. The reason was because my grandmother lived with us. My memory is limited to the good Italian food that was always cooked by grandma. But if I really thought about it, I'll bet my mental picture of those days would be playing with my cousins and listening to my aunts and uncles sing dirty songs in Italian! I had a great childhood! I really did. We may have been a tad dysfunctional, but I grew up loved and well taken care of by my entire family.

The kids were still at the house with Janine. I drove out to the Ponderosa Steak House to enjoy a steak, fries, and a buffet. I watched a little TV before going to bed early.

On Sunday morning I walked a hundred yards down the street to a Baptist Church. I knew a few people, but I suppose I looked like one of those guys who only attend services on Christmas or Easter Sunday. Then I went back to my apartment to prepare a meal of macaroni, sausage, and salad. The kids would be over around one o'clock for dinner.

The five of us sat around the dining room table and even though we enjoyed our meal, I could sense how weird and uncomfortable it was for them to be at Dad's place for the first time. We got through it though, and since then my apartment has become their home. For a period of time it was, 'I am at Dad's house', but now it's simply, 'I'm home'!

So began the back-and-forth between houses for my beloved children. Sydney went back to college in January. The younger ones had some getting used to, but their busy lives of basketball practices, friends, school work and projects, and of course endless hours of video games, kept them well occupied during this transition phase of their young lives.

Things were beginning to settle down nicely. I enjoyed my work, joined the YMCA, nobody was complaining or yelling at me, and I now possessed the freedom to do what I wanted with my time and money. Of course, there wasn't really a lot of either to go around, but as the Bible states in Proverbs, 'better to live on the edge of a roof, then with a contentious wife'!

It was actually a very liberating period for me. No one making unreasonable demands, no one harping on my shortcomings, no one going into my car and taking things that weren't theirs, and no one to see, desire, and know that I could no longer have or call my own. It was over! Well, except for the phone calls.

Janine phoned me several times every day! Yes, the same woman who didn't want me, didn't love me, and subsequently divorced me, continued to want something from me. But what did she want?

"Lenny," she always said my name first when she called. "I'm going to take Garrett to the orthodontist. I need your credit card number."

"Lenny," she began again, "the refrigerator and freezer are broken. We need a new one or you need to call someone to fix it."

I need to call?

"Lenny, the kitchen faucet is leaking. You need to call a plumber."

"Lenny," it never stops, "the walls in the laundry room need to be painted."

"Lenny, Garrett's room is an absolute mess. You need to come over here and supervise him cleaning it."

Excuse me? His room's a mess?

"Lenny, the house insurance is due. Your half is sixty-two dollars and fifty-eight cents."

Heard enough?

Now when you first look at these countless phone calls, your initial impression may be that she is a woman used to going to her husband for certain needs or duties , and that some habits are hard to break No, that's not it. If you look closely at these requests, they all involve a need; only the need is for more money from the sugar daddy. The divorce clearly stipulates that Janine is responsible for maintenance of our home since she is the one residing there. Also, things such as medical, dental, and other health needs for the children are to be split evenly. Here's the issue that my ex-wife refuses to see:

I have a flex plan from my school job. I put aside a certain number of dollars, before taxes mind you, and that money is for dental, chiropractic, or vision care. I have this designated amount removed from my school check. It's my money! It's my money after the $700 I pay weekly to Janine. My ex-wife thinks that if my kids accrue a dental bill of say, $100, that I just put it on my credit card, send the bill to the flex plan, and get my money back a few weeks later. What Janine fails to understand is that someone is still paying the dental bill! That someone, of course, is me. I am more than willing to do my part. Only, in this case, $50 is my part. And when I request a bill for services, I ask for half of the bill, namely what I paid for! Then I mail that portion of the bill into the flex plan and receive my $50 back. Why is that so hard for her to understand? I'll tell you why: Because it means that she is responsible for the other $50! Janine wants to be divorced from me physically, emotionally, spiritually, and psychologically, but heaven forbid if she loses me financially!

"The kids are all going to need dental checkups and probably new contact lenses." She informed me, raising her voice as if to utilize the intimidation that used to work when we were married.

"I will pay my half." I replied calmly.

"These are needs, Lenny!" There was my name again. "You need to prioritize what's important."

"I will pay my half."

"I don't care what you did. You need to plan your finances better. Can't you do what's best for your children?"

Huh?

That type of critical revelation used to work. Janine would try to get me to think about how wrong or selfish I was being, or perhaps short-sighted in my appraisal of a situation, and then attempt to bring me to where she decided I need to be, using insults, or moral indignation. It wasn't working anymore! Her words, her opinions, her standards of right and wrong, or more aptly, her self-appointed role as my conscience held no power any longer. Ding-dong, the witch is dead!

I pronounced evenly, "I will pay my half!"

I hung up the phone.

Soon after the wave of phone calls, I did what I should have done right from the start: I didn't answer! Of course, there were times when she tricked me by using Lilly's cell phone or leaving a message that seemed worth calling back for, but even then I knew that all I had to do was hang-up when I had heard enough!

Another very clearly written divorce stipulation was that if Janine chose to remain in the house, then she alone was responsible for paying the mortgage and home insurance. Yet each month she would phone and ask for my half of the insurance money.

"I'm not responsible for home insurance!" I repeated more than once.

Eventually, that stopped.

The constant request for financial assistance was something I had to deal with so I wrote Janine a note and placed it in one of her weekly checks.

I wrote:

"About the refrigerator, kitchen pipes, and spending money to get the house ready for a sale: I already pay for you to live in a spacious six bedroom home with four baths on five-and-a-half acres. Meanwhile, I live in a gloomy dark apartment with one bedroom. You kept the kids' dressers, beds, and all our bedroom furnishings, because you didn't want to disrupt what they were used to. I fell for that nonsense. So now the refrigerator, the sink, and the dishwasher have gone on the blink since I left. I pay for all the kids needs, all their college expenses, and in case you weren't aware, I don't get to keep a lot of my money anymore to pay for all of this. I need your help, Janine. We agreed to split costs on things, yet every time I ask you for help, you cry about how broke you are. I just bought Garrett a laptop. Can't you reach into your pocket just once and restore the things around the house that need fixing? I have a stake in its sale also, you know! Can't you please help me and do your part?"

For the first time in weeks my cell phone stopped ringing! Well, for a while anyway.

The funny thing is; I always trusted Janine to handle the money. I worked; she stayed at home to raise the kids, and she kept the checkbook, paying all the bills. I had a business checkbook to pay for all the office overhead, but basically, Janine had primary control of our finances. We operated like this for years. When Janine went back to work part-time as an accountant and started making money too, a strange thing happened: Nothing changed financially for us. She used my teaching salary to pay the same bills she always had and I continued to take care of my business expenses. There was no extra money. None! She was working at her own business yet we had no more money now than we did before. There was always some sort of explanation as to where and how the money was being used, and me, well, I guess I just trusted her.

In the midst of our divorce, I did a little investigating. Janine kept her money in the same bank as our other accounts. Here are the facts and figures: From January to December Janine deposited $15,812 in her business account. As we began the divorce proceedings the total deposit amount dropped to $1381! Not only that: but the deposit total for February, March, April, and August through December was zero! Question: Where is the money going?

More than once before the divorce was final I spoke to my lawyer about this missing money. He said it would be too difficult, if not impossible, to locate which bank she was using as its shelter. Up to the time of the divorce we never did find out. I knew, though I could not prove, that Janine was stashing money away. Now the way I see it, as a married couple, the money that I made through the years as a teacher and chiropractor belonged equally to both of us. The same should be true for income Janine made. I repeat. I never saw a penny of this money. Yet I always wondered: Where was it?

I found out a month after the divorce. Too late, I know!

In early November Lilly and Layla both had dental appointments. Janine paid the bill out of our joint account and I mailed the receipt to my flex plan. Later that month we were officially divorced. Following that, I found my apartment and was in the process of getting all my mail sent to my new address. I remembered that the flex plan check would be coming soon so I phoned the company to inform them of my change of address.

"We sent that check out two days ago." Their answering service told me.

It was sent to the house.

"Janine," I quickly phoned my ex-wife, "there's a check in my name coming from the Health Economics Group. Don't you dare sign and cash it!"

"I haven't seen it." She replied.

A few days later I called back the flex company.

"That check was cashed on Thursday the 28th of December." I was told.

"Can you mail me a copy of the signed check?"

A couple days later my suspicions were realized. I looked at the photocopy of the back of the check, and sure enough, there it was, 'Lenny Spencer', my name signed in Janine's handwriting.

Forgery!

I called the flex company back.

"Where was this check cashed?"

I went down to the bank to register my complaint.

"This check", showing them the photocopy, "has my name on it. I'm a man. Why would you allow a woman to cash it?"

I explained that we were recently divorced and shared the whole story about the check and the dental care.

It suddenly dawned on me:

"Am I allowed to look at the records of that account?"

No, not anymore. We were divorced now, so the time for that was up. I had no legal right to access her account. Still, I wanted so badly to know when that account was opened, and how much Janine had stashed away while we were still married. I could have kicked myself for not making a better effort to uncover her deception. My lawyer claimed it was too difficult a task. My bad! After all, half of that money belonged to me!

I went to the police with the photocopied check to find out my options. There were two: Either press charges and the authorities will go to the house and arrest her, or do nothing about it for now.

I just couldn't have her arrested. She deserved whatever penalty the crime warranted, yet I was unable to bring myself to press charges against my children's mother! Think about it! She's their mother. Now I may not think much of Janine myself, but if I'm going to successfully raise four children, protect and provide for them, then one area of necessary protection and provision is making sure they have a good relationship with their mother. Let's face it: the woman is not easy for anyone to get along with, the kids included. Still, I believe that children, even older children like mine, require the stability of both parents involved in their lives, loving and nurturing them. Can you imagine how embarrassing and humiliating it would be for them to watch their mother being arrested by local police and taken away in handcuffs? No way could I put them through that, so I chose to simply warn Janine that I had the photocopied check and that I would use it against her if needed.

Although Janine continued to call my cell phone, and I continued not to answer, things were relatively peaceful between us. We didn't see each other, we didn't talk, and the joint-custody arrangement seemed to be going along fine. The kids appeared well-adjusted to their new living arrangement and were keeping busy with school and activities. They even seemed to like my apartment.

After living for almost five years in a spacious, brand-new home, the contrast of my apartment was almost humorous. Our house on five-and-a-half acres had six bedrooms, four full baths, a cathedral ceiling, a loft area and a large modern kitchen. My apartment? Well, it was really the bottom floor of a house. You entered into a small living room, then to the left of that was a room that I used as my adjusting area by day, and my bedroom at night. My bed was a fold-out futon. Across from there, sharing an adjacent wall with the living room was the kids' bedroom. Three mattresses on the floor, a television, and a single shared dresser that I was given by a friend filled the tiny room. Adjoining their room was the only bathroom. Off to the left of the adjusting room was the kitchen and attached laundry room. The apartment was approximately 750 square feet of living space. When Sydney was home from college, she slept on the couch. It was dark, gloomy, and the walls were brown-paneled, probably sometime in the sixties. The house that my working income alone paid for, and which overlooked a beautiful huge valley, contained approximately thirty-six hundred square feet of living space!

When my parents traveled up from New Jersey to see our new house, my mother pulled me aside and remarked, "You really have come up in the world."

I wonder now what she would say?

Once again, the inequity of the State of New York's divorce laws against the man is startling! She wanted the divorce. She forced it on me. I said 'no' seven times! When I had my own lawyer and shared my opposition with him, he told me this:

"She will have her divorce if she wants it!"

So Janine breaks her promise, made to me and to God, and the consequence of her failure to honor her word is a new house that she gets all to herself, built and paid for by the labor and money by someone else, namely me. On top of that, she gets to keep practically all the furniture and lawn equipment, while I, the partner who was willing to honor his marriage commitment, has to go out and buy furniture to furnish a place from the sixties! And I still have to pay her $700 per week so she can have a divorce that I was once unwilling to give her! All of this is based on a mathematical formula. I reported on my income taxes that I made close to eighty-five thousand dollars for the year. Janine reports that she made, well despite getting over fifty dollars per client and an appointment book filled with names, a grand total of seven-hundred and thirty dollars. When you put the numbers into the formula, and subtract her reported income from mine, well you get the $36,400 that I must pay her annually! How long? Eight-and-a-half years!

Anybody smell a rat?

She is a college graduate with a degree in accounting, healthy, children are all in school; so why can't this woman go out and get a job? Janine wanted this divorce! So why didn't the Judge declare that she could have what she wanted as long as she worked and supported herself? Don't get me wrong: I fully accept some financial responsibility for her. Janine stayed home for years raising our children. I appreciate that. She could have remained working and had her own career, but we decided that I would be the one to fulfill career goals while she would suspend her goals for the sake of being home with the kids. That's a partnership! That's working together. Certainly, money earned belongs to each of us when that type of agreement is made. Yet if you dissolve the partnership, is it right to expect the guy that you just fired to continue to work for you? Sure, I feel responsible to support Janine financially based upon our past living arrangement, but not at $700 per week! That's ridiculous! If you want to be single, go get a job! She could get a good job and take the heavy load off of me. Instead, her job is to collect $36,400 from me and have her own part-time business where she claims to make a measly seven-hundred dollars all year! Obviously, I think the State of New York needs to revisit and reprise the financial rewards afforded to women who are quite capable of working. I suppose that the old adage applies that, 'if you want something badly enough, be willing to work for it!'

I took a day off from work one Friday in March. I got up early, went to the YMCA, and got back home around ten in the morning.

Janine's car was in my driveway.

I found her in the kids' room. Startled by my sudden appearance, she claimed that she was searching for something that Lilly needed.

Right!

"What are you doing here?" I demanded.

"Lilly needs her pills and I don't have any at my house. I came to find some for her."

Her excuse for breaking into my apartment made no sense at all. This was a woman who rarely makes an effort to even come to town to pick-up her children. She always expects me to do the shuttling of the kids. Yet while I'm supposedly at work here she is rummaging through my house.

What exactly is she looking for?

"You are not allowed to just break into my apartment without permission!" I wanted her to understand.

"I'm here for your daughter!" She attempted to explain in that way of hers to make it seem like I was the one being unreasonable.

She quickly left.

A few months later I was going through my dresser drawers searching for an important paper. As I was looking, it struck me that one particular item was missing. The missing paper was the photocopy of the forged check.

Interesting.

So that's what she wanted! Janine was afraid that I would use the forged check against her if she bothered me about things. For reasons unknown, she needed to continue bothering me, usually about wanting more money or payment for something, and it was a habit she was either unwilling or unable to give up.

I called the police and reported the break-in. An officer came to the apartment, filed a report, and had a letter, warning her of the consequences of such illegal actions, mailed to Janine. Once again for the sake of my children I chose not to press charges.

When I went to work later that day, I felt the compulsion to open the top drawer of my desk and see with my own eyes the paper that I knew was still in there. Perhaps I did it for some type of reassurance, or simply to validate what I already knew. It was odd, but I just had to see it.

It was another photocopy of the forged check!

Chapter 2

MY THREE BROTHERS ALWAYS used to tease me because I went to college twice. The first time was to get a degree as a math teacher. My second college experience was chiropractic school. My brothers used to call me college boy. One afternoon during the early years of my marriage, Janine and I were stopped at a red light. We were laughing and talking about how my brothers always picked on me about always being in school.

"You know," I can clearly remember saying to her, "if I ever did go back to college again, I would love to go to a Bible school and become a preacher."

A couple of years later we moved to Western New York. One Friday evening my Pastor phoned me and asked if I would be willing to preach in his place because he had to leave town for the weekend. I was a bit hesitant at first, but Janine encouraged me to accept the challenge.

I suppose word got around that I was available to preach, because I got a call a few weeks later to fill in for the Pastor of the Missionary Alliance Church. I accepted and began to prepare another sermon. On Wednesday of that week I received another call.

"Dr. Spencer?" The caller was the same woman who had asked me to preach at the Missionary Alliance Church. "When Pastor Bob was with us," apparently, the guy whose place I was taking was leaving the area, "he also goes and preaches at a small church in the town of Red House. Could you preach there also? Their service begins at 8:30 in the morning."

On Saturday Janine and I searched for the town of Red House. It was an hour from Orchard Park where we lived. Little did we know, but it was the smallest town in the State of New York. The population is certainly less than 50 people! We found the church. Services were held in a building that stored road equipment on one side, and on the other side were the offices of the Town Clerk and Judge. The Red House Union Free Church had their services in the room where the Clerk worked Monday through Friday.

In the early nineties, I preached my first sermon at the Red House Union Free Church. Seventeen years later, I will preach my last when the ninety-year-old congregation closes its doors. Seventeen years! Seventeen years of our tithes and offerings helping and assisting people in need right here in our communities. Seventeen years of financing missions in Kentucky, Mexico, and around the world. Seventeen years of delivering turkeys, Christmas gifts, fruit baskets, or just plain cash to those who had a need. But most importantly, it was seventeen years of sharing the gospel of Jesus Christ to a small group of people whom I was honored to preach to!

The congregation had fifteen to twenty people when I first started preaching there. The total never grew beyond twenty-five to thirty, but I always knew that our size was irrelevant as long as the one person who needed to be there could be counted on. That was Jesus! He showed up every Sunday morning.

Now I suppose that when you're the preacher it's pretty hard to find the service boring! It's like being either the pitcher or the catcher in a baseball game. You're where the action is! At the Red House Union Free Church, one word comes to mind when I describe our time together: Fun! Every Sunday we had fun. Don't get me wrong; we prayed, we cried, and we mourned when the situation warranted, yet we more often than not celebrated answered prayer, enjoyed one another's company, and praised together the God who created us all! The Lord has granted me a multitude of blessings in my life, but allowing me to be Pastor of the Red House Union Free Church was one of the best gifts I've ever received. When the church closes I will miss it. Currently, there are only seven of us left who call the church home. We discuss meeting again, possibly over the summers when one particular couple returns up north to visit. We really don't know if that will happen. God knows! That's good enough for all of us.

One of the really cool things I get to do as a recognized Pastor of a particular church in the State of New York is to marry people. How ironic! Prior to the wedding, the couple and I discuss the purpose of marriage within the plans of God, and it is also my duty to make sure that these two young people understand that their soon-to-be union is for keeps, that it is not a game or a trial period, or some kind of experiment that you test out, to see if you like it! It's an inseparable union formed by the same God who formed your arms, legs, face, and heart. God has appointed me to explain this to people who choose to marry. I repeat: How ironic!

Janine may have initially encouraged me to preach, but as the years went by she actually grew hostile and began to demand that I resign as Pastor of the Red House Church.

"You do not belong behind the pulpit!" She spat out at me more than once. "You can't even love your wife and be the godly leader of this family. How can you expect to be the spiritual leader of a church?"

Janine rarely if ever attended a Sunday service at Red House. The kids came with me on occasion.

"No way I am going to listen to you preach!" She would explain her reason why she would never attend. "You're the biggest hypocrite and phony that I know! I might ever sit and listen to you."

So our Sundays went like this:

I would preach at Red House early and meet Janine and the kids at our family church in Orchard Park later around 11:00. We did that for years. Only on Christmas Day did Janine join me and the kids at Red House and looking back, I'm certain that she did so solely for appearance sake.

When it came to chiropractic, Janine further disrespected me by choosing to go to a chiropractor other than me.

"I don't like the way you adjust." She would always tell me. "You're too rough!"

It was very insulting.

Whenever we were together at a party or a church function and the topic of chiropractic came up, Janine would usually make it a point to let everyone around us know that she went to a different chiropractor, other than her husband.

"I don't like the way Lenny adjusts."

The fact is; she knew that it embarrassed me to hear her tell others that she didn't like me as her chiropractor and that brought her pleasure. Perhaps she did so for the sole purpose of embarrassing me. Janine was always jealous of my love for chiropractic and made it a point to put my practice down at each and every opportunity. By attacking my expertise, she could attack me personally. Yet as a professed Christian woman, she knew that the Bible said, 'respect and support your husband'!

Go figure!

Janine refuses to hear me preach, goes to a different chiropractor, so how does she feel about me being a school teacher?

"Why do you have to act the way you do in class?" She once asked with distain.

Yes, once again, even though she had rarely listened to one of my sermons, and had not been adjusted by me since I was still a chiropractic student, Janine also criticized my teaching ability even though, (you guessed it), she had never once seen me teach!

"What do you know?" I challenged her. "You've never even been in my classroom!"

"I've heard." Janine quickly retorted. "People have told me. You act all crazy and loud. It's a math class, Lenny. Why can't you just teach them math?"

When my brother John asked me to perform his marriage ceremony to Sara, I accepted with delight. I mean, how awesome would it be to marry your own brother! At the time Janine and I were in the midst of our divorce proceedings, but neither of us had told our families about it. I suppose they would see us together as they often did, not talking to one another, Janine being rude and disrespectful to me, or the kids , or anyone else who tried to engage her. In other words, our secret was safe!

A year earlier my youngest brother, Jeff, was married and held his wedding reception at the same restaurant. Jeff was forty-three years old when he finally got married! It was his first time. John was trying marriage again a second time. He already had two grown-up children. Brave man!

Think about the contrast:

My brother Jeff spent the entire first forty-three years of his life living with his parents. He never left and got his own place, and as I recall, he rarely dated or went out at night. We could tell by his demeanor and the daily naps that he took, that he was probably not exactly thrilled with his single life. Jeff is a handsome, athletic, intelligent man, yet he spent a good deal of his time alone. In Genesis, God makes a telling observation: 'It is not good for the man to be alone'.

Let's face it: We were created to be relational. That's what we are. Now I'm not criticizing or pronouncing judgment on people who choose to never marry. God's word addresses that too. I'm talking about my brother Jeff. I believe that my kid brother had something missing from his life. He yearned for and needed a life partner. I don't think he really enjoyed the freedom of the supposedly carefree single life. Jeff wanted someone to love. And when he finally found her, his life had meaning.

I know how he feels.

John, on the other hand, had already been through the pain of a divorce. He married a woman who already had a four-year-old daughter when they first met. The little girl's name was Tara. My brother later adopted Tara and became her Dad. Whenever I witness their relationship I come to the same conclusion: Lucky girl! Two years into his first marriage, God blessed John with a son. They named him Michael. He's an awesome young man. As we prepared for John and Sara's wedding ceremony, I watched Tara and Michael as they looked at their Dad. They were happy for him! I could read the joy in their faces. They both considered him the best father anyone could ask for!

I suppose that in many respects, John was similar to Jeff. They both had met someone special, and they both decided that they couldn't live without her! Divorce had apparently not destroyed his joy, his will to share his life with someone, nor did it create a fear of failure with respect to marriage. He met a woman, fell in love, and as Barry Manilow sings, 'he was ready to take a chance again'!

My brother Rich was also divorced. Married for only a few years, he has not shown any indication that he would ever walk down the aisle again. He tried marriage; it didn't go well, so he is done with it! Rich lives alone, sharing a joint-custody arrangement with his son Dillon. Once again, in spite of having to deal with a divorce at a young age, Dillon is a great kid! I'm very pleased with how both of my nephews and niece have turned out. They've made all of us proud!

I suppose that sums up the trials and tribulations of marriage for the four Spencer brothers! Jeff, never married before, takes the big step. John, divorced father of two grown children, decides to give the institution of marriage another try. Rich, divorced for many years, holds up his hands and says, 'no way am I doing that again'.

Me?

That's a great question!

The night before I was to perform the wedding services for John and Sara, I sat at the kitchen table with my mother. Mostly we talked about Dad's ailing mental health.

"It doesn't seem to be going too well for you and Janine." She put her observation into words. "Are you doing alright?"

Well, actually, no Mom, we're getting a divorce but I haven't told anybody yet, but I'm not about to spoil the festive weekend with bad news.

"The same." Was the only clue I offered.

Then my mother said the thing she always says:

"These girls today don't know how good they have it. You're a good provider, a great father, and you give her everything she wants."

I was not about to argue or concur. My mother was right, even though she left out the most important truth of all: I was also a good husband!

It was with great pleasure that I witnessed John and Sara together the night before the wedding. They seemed so happy, so enamored with one another; it was a joy to see. Tomorrow they would be joined together in holy matrimony. Tomorrow they would each commit themselves to one another and to a new life together. Tomorrow they would be one! I was so happy for them!

You would think that the solidarity of their relationship compared to the crumbling of mine and Janine's, would create a sense of sorrow, or regret, or stimulate the pain of our marriage failure. Nothing could be further from the truth! Just as I did a year ago, witnessing my youngest brother Jeff's marriage, I felt totally consumed with joy for their achievement. Man, I love that kind of stuff! Two people in love with one another: And ready to tell the world that it's for keeps. To witness it, my goodness, to have the honor and privilege of performing this union is the type of thing that makes life worthwhile! For one glorious night, I forgot about Janine and me, and focused my joy on the reality of existence as God intended. All night at the reception as I watched people dance, kept an eye on my own children, and assumed the role of caretaker for my Dad, my mind centered upon a single revelation:

I want to experience this!

Not only that, but I knew in my heart that with the right woman, I could experience and thrive in a successful marriage. I don't want to live like my brother Rich, alone in the country without a life partner and soulmate. He loves his life and Rich is a good father and not only a brother, but a good friend. Only, I realized that as I watched John and Sara on the dance floor, cutting the wedding cake, and kissing to the symphony of clinking glasses, that I wanted what they had! And I wanted it badly! So for the first time in many years I wondered:

Could I ever get married again?

Chapter 3

I woke up Saturday morning at 8:30AM, just like I always do. The first thing I do every morning is pray. While I'm talking to Jesus I take my liquid vitamins along with a piece of fruit, and then I shower. I brush my teeth, just like I always do. Nothing special about the day, in fact, my morning routine is practically anti-special because it's so the same day after day. As I leave the bathroom I always glance at the kids' beds. Sometimes they're empty, meaning that they stayed at their mom's last night. On other mornings I see them lying asleep, so I say a special prayer for God to show them favor on this day. I pack the garbage in my car on this nothing-out-of-the-ordinary Saturday morning and drive to the office. It's just Saturday, no different than any other. My office hours will be ten-to-one just like they always are. Yet unbeknownst to me, this Saturday is about to be special. It will be a day I will remember the rest of my life! Of course, I didn't know that now as I drove to my office but I'll find out. And it's not like I'll find out today or even later this week. No, I'll only regard it as special when I look back at it and realize that on this particular Saturday God had a gift in store for me!

Two or three people were waiting for me outside as I pulled my car into the office parking lot. On many Saturdays the office building is empty except for me. The medical staff and optometrist do not work on the weekends. The psychologist is often there on Saturdays, but on this particular morning he was not present either.

I adjusted my early arrivals and when they left I sat at my desk to read my Bible. My cell phone rang.

"Dr. Spencer." I answered.

The voice on the other end of the line was a woman's.

"Oh, hello Dr. Spencer," she sounded nervous, "my name is Brenda Meyers and I was wondering if you are seeing new patients?"

Am I seeing new patients?

When you pay your ex-wife $700 a week, patients old and new are welcome! Actually, that's not my attitude at all. I like people. Checking their spines is my sole contribution to their health, so I welcome as many as possible into my office.

"I always accept new patients." I told her.

"Can I ask you a few questions first?" She wondered politely.

"Certainly."

"I hurt my back the other night bumping into a wall and now a few days later it's no better. In fact, it seems to be getting worse. I've never been to a chiropractor before. Do you think you can help me?"

I took a deep breath and lightly shook my head. 'Here we go again', I silently said in my mind. People come to me with the misconception that I'm some kind of pain-relief specialist. Backaches, headaches, neck pain, tingling or numbness in the fingers and toes, and everybody thinks that's the role of the chiropractor. Still, I played along.

"I'm here until one o'clock today." I informed her. "Come in any time you like."

"I don't need to make an appointment?" She sounded surprised and glad to learn.

"No," I assured her, "my patients just walk in during my designated hours. On Saturday I work from ten-to-one."

"I can come today?"

"Of course."

"Do you really think you can help me?" She asked a second time.

The answer of course is yes. Only, the help I offer is not always what the patient might have in mind. But that's where it falls upon me to teach them, show them the true value of the chiropractic adjustment, and help them to understand that it's not about backaches or pain relief.

"Yeah, come on down." I invited her. "I look forward to meeting you."

I had a relatively busy morning, but by around noon the action had slowed to a stop, so I sat at my desk to catch up on my paperwork. I work all alone at my chiropractic practice, always have. Besides being the doctor, I am also the receptionist, business manager, and sole member of the custodial staff! As a part-time chiropractor my business is small enough to be handled by me alone. I've always liked it that way. Since I've been divorced, I have opened a second practice out of my apartment. I figured that since I need to pay Janine $700 a week, I'd better do whatever I can to increase my current income. I thought a home practice would be a good way to do that. To this point business at my new office has been rather slow.

As I sat at my desk I heard the front door of the building open and then the footsteps of someone coming my way. I looked through the glass pane of the reception cubicle to see who it was. It was a woman.

My first impression was actually rather unprofessional. I thought she was beautiful, stunning in fact, as she stopped in front of me and introduced herself.

"Hi, I'm Brenda Meyers."

She had short, dark hair, was medium built, and had the prettiest face I think I've ever seen! Her dark eyes pierced my professional demeanor, and I sensed a wave of nervousness on my part as I introduced myself. I've been in practice for fifteen years now, and met many a new patient, but I never before reacted like that to a first hello.

I stood and extended my hand in greeting.

"Dr. Spencer. I'm pleased to meet you."

I say those exact words to all my first-time patients, but this time I really meant it!

"Have a seat," I motioned to a chair in the waiting room, "and I'll give you some paperwork to fill out."

I left her there and walked into my adjusting room where I kept my patient application forms, right to privacy material, terms of acceptance, and a brief chiropractic survey which assesses their personal health philosophy. I put all the papers on a clipboard and was about to return to her when I was struck by a sudden realization: My heart was pounding!

"Here you go." I pronounced calmly, though I knew it was a struggle to sound and appear normal. "Have you ever been to a chiropractor before?"

"No, "she answered, shaking her head, "this is my first time."

"How did you hear about me?"

"A friend told me. You actually come highly recommended."

I've heard that before. Normally, I just accept the compliment and never give it a second thought, but when Brenda Meyers said it, it was exactly what I hoped to hear! Hey, I'm a man! When a beautiful woman tells you that you come highly recommended, it's a good thing!

Just at that moment I once again heard the front door rattle and the sound of footsteps coming this way. It was a regular patient of mine, Michael Day. We smiled at each other and shook hands like we always do.

"Hi Mike." I replied casually. Then as I pointed towards the adjusting room I added, "Go right in."

I followed him.

I'm sorry, but this was really weird! My smile, the handshake, and the tone of my voice towards Mike belied what my heart and mind were really feeling. Was I glad to see my old patient, glad to have an opportunity to adjust him, glad to talk some sports like we usually did, or just glad to make some more money today? No, I wasn't glad to see Mike at all! I wanted to talk to her! I wanted to learn more about what she had heard about me. I wanted to tell her all about straight chiropractic. I wanted to know if she was married!

I forced myself to take my time as I adjusted Mike. We talked a bit about the chiropractic adjustment, its positive effects on his health, and of course, eventually the conversation turned to the Buffalo Bills and what their chances were this coming season. Yet all the while we spoke I couldn't get this new lady off of my mind. Was she too young for an old codger like me?

Now where did that thought come from?

Mike and I walked out of the adjusting room together, but unlike his usual visits I did not walk out to the front door with him. This time the sports talk was cut short. This time I wanted to get rid of Mike as properly and unsuspectingly as possible. Yet before he left he leaned towards me and pronounced quietly:

"Is that a new patient?"

I smiled.

"She's quite a looker!"

She certainly was!

"You'd better be careful." Mike playfully warned me.

He left.

I walked back to the waiting room and saw that Brenda Meyers was still reading and filling out the entrance forms.

"Just give me a holler when you're ready." I told her as I walked by and went into the x-ray area.

Alright: What's going on?

I've seen beautiful women before. I have looked them over, admired their finer points, and moved on with my life totally unaffected. That's the difference; I realized. This woman who I don't even know has affected me. She has penetrated my thoughts and settled herself somewhere in my mind.

Why?

I don't even know who she is, don't know a thing about her, have barely spoken to her yet, but she's giving me a feeling that is vaguely familiar. I'm smitten with her!

I stood in the x-ray room and tried to gather my thoughts and impressions:

Thought number1: I'm done with women! I don't like them. I don't want anything to do with them, and if it weren't for women I wouldn't be in the mess I'm in now!

Thought number 2: I don't even know this lady. She could be a serial killer, or involved in witchcraft, or worse yet; she could be happily married.

Thought 3: Why do I care what or who she is? Why is she affecting me like this? Am I having my mid-life crisis now that I'm divorced?

Thought 4: What if she is interested? Do I really want to get involved with a woman again? Especially after what happened last time!

So there I was. Fifty-six years old and still thinking like a teenager drumming up the courage to approach a pretty girl he just saw! Am I ever going to grow up?

I attempted to gather myself, calm these completely unfounded feelings of romanticism and restore my professional demeanor. I'm a Doctor of Chiropractic; act like it! I reminded myself that this Brenda Meyers is like any other potential chiropractic patient and to knock-off this delusionary daydreaming and get back to work. I just want to be the best chiropractor I can be for her and be done with it. What a bunch of nonsense I allow myself to think!

I left the x-ray room and found her waiting.

"I'm ready!" She cheerfully informed me.

I'm not sure I was!

Brenda followed me into the adjusting room and sat where I motioned to a chair along the rear wall. My x-ray tech was an older man named Dominic. On this particular Saturday morning, Dominic had already left and went home. That was fine, of course, but it meant that Brenda Meyers would not be x-rayed on this day.

"The first thing I want to do," I began to instruct, "is explain the service I offer. There are many misconceptions about chiropractic and I like to clear them up right from the start."

I'd made this introductory presentation for over fifteen years now. I practically knew it all by heart! The first visit is obviously the most important and should also be the most educational. Besides that, I recognized too that on this particular occasion I wished very much to impress this woman with my spiel! Realizing this, and overcome with the need to do so, I chucked my usual systematic explanation of chiropractic, and started off in a more unique direction.

"I was at a party once," I fell into my preacher mode, "and a guy came up to me and asked me what I did for a living. I told him that I worked with the power that created the universe!"

She smiled. It was a beautiful, full set of straight teeth smile that momentarily fogged my train of thought. My mother used to tell me that I had a face only a mother could love. Well, this girl had a face any man could love!

"He asked me how I did that." I resumed my party scenario. "I told him that the human body knows how to run itself as long as there is no interference to the life-sustaining force." I paused to remind myself not to be sharing concepts beyond her comprehension. Now of course I had no clue of just how perceptive this beauty was, but as she gazed back at me, her dark eyes appeared to convey a clear understanding of my introduction thus far.

"I told him that a bone out of place in the spine interferes with the nervous system's ability to coordinate proper function. Then I explained that my job was to restore the proper structure of the body and free-up this life-sustaining force by putting the bones back where they belong! His eyes widened and then he playfully struck my shoulder. He cried out, 'hey, you're a chiropractor'."

She liked that story; I could tell. Still, she said nothing, apparently had no questions to this point, but shifted in her chair and crossed her legs. Nice legs! This woman's looks were striking! I kept reminding myself that I was a professional with a responsibility to temper these wild thoughts and get back to the point of her being here in my office. At the same time, I caught myself thinking, 'boy, I hope nobody else comes through the front door for a while'!

During the awkward silent pause I glanced down at the patient questionnaire.

"It says here," I began a new train of thought, "that you injured your mid-back and that you were also experiencing neck pain."

"Yes," she interrupted, "it was an accident last week, but it seems to be getting worse. Today actually," she giggled as her face brightened, "it feels a little better. Maybe just meeting you already helped."

Was she flirting?

I hope so!

"Well," I said, smiling back, "I really do hope that you feel better, but I want you to understand that how you feel is not my objective." I sat down on my chiropractic table closer to her. "I'm not a pain-relief specialist. I don't diagnose diseases. I simply put bones back in order to promote health. If that's the service you desire," this was the key point of my presentation, "then I'm your guy!"

What a thing to say!

I wanted to be just that: her guy! I wanted her to tell me that that was exactly what she wanted too. She was here to have her spine checked for subluxations, (term for a misaligned vertebrae), and I could tell looking at her that she understood the chiropractic objective.

"So what about my back pain?"

My heart sank. Okay, I thought, my brief explanation and example of a vital approach to health still needed some backup, some support with perhaps further examples, or I needed to present a more clever and clear scenario.

"Often," I picked up where I had left off, "pain is an indication of a problem. That includes back and neck pain. But what if the vertebrae are misaligned, pressuring a nerve, causing an interference to health, and there is no pain? Then what? Do we deal with it? Better yet, does it need to be addressed? Well?" I lifted up both my arms to indicate that this was an important point to consider. "If health is a goal in your life, then I say the bone needs to be restored to its proper place in the spine. If it's left out of place, your health will suffer. Or better put," I told her, "you'll never be everything God intended you to be. You won't realize your health potential."

Brenda was about ready to speak, but my mind was swirling with new ideas. I was on a roll so I introduced a new scenario.

"Imagine that a couple is out on a date. She's thinking to herself, 'is this the guy for me?', but he's wondering, 'why haven't I had my spine checked recently? I like this girl. Shouldn't I be sure that I am functioning at my full health potential?'

Brenda laughed.

I knew that I was being entertaining, but sometimes that's the best way to get your point across. Besides, I wanted to entertain her. I wanted her to find me interesting, clever, creative, intelligent, funny; I wanted Brenda Meyers to like me.

"So did they fall in love?" She suddenly asked, playing along with my story. She leaned forward and pronounced, "Tell me about them."

Is that sexual tension that I'm feeling?

"Well," my voice cracked ever so slightly, "the girl arrived at a point in the relationship where she needed to see some sense of commitment on his part. She thought to herself, 'if I'm going to be happy, I need to know if this is the right man for me.' And she decided that she needed to know tonight! They'd been dating for two months now. It was time to decide."

I'd known Brenda Meyers for approximately fifteen minutes by now, yet to a small degree I wanted to know right now if she's interested in me, not only as her chiropractor, but as a man, a friend, or perhaps even more than that! Incredible! How could I be thinking this in just fifteen minutes?

"Was he right for her?"

Did she just ask if I was right for her?

"So," she continued to encourage my chiropractic scenario, "what was the boyfriend thinking?"

I think my armpits were getting damp.

"The guy was thinking, 'my goodness, it's been two months now since my last chiropractic adjustment! Either I am going to commit myself to regular care, or live at less than my God-given health potential. I need to decide'!"

Brenda laughed again. I sensed that she was enjoying her time with me. I know I was! In fact, later when I reflected on it, I realized that this was the first time in years, since the early days with Janine, that I was relishing the company of a beautiful woman. I remember thinking that I wanted this interview to never end.

"So how did things turn out for both of them?" She asked with a suggestive look of delight.

"Well, the girl asked him what he was thinking and feeling at this moment. His response was not what she expected. He told her that he had come to an important decision. Her heart leaped in her chest! She thought excitedly, 'this is it'! The guy was all excited to tell her about his commitment to regular chiropractic care. When he was finished sharing what was on his mind, she pushed his chest with such a force that he fell roughly to the ground. She stamped off in anger and years later found the man of her dreams and lived happily-ever-after!"

Brenda put her hand to her mouth to suppress a wide grin. She was definitely into the conversation.

"How about the guy?"

I stood up and walked around the table before facing her once again. I needed a moment to make up a good ending to the story.

"After she pushed him down, he noticed the next day that his back hurt a lot so he made an appointment with the chiropractor." I smiled at her. "He spent the rest of his life under regular chiropractic care."

"Did he ever get sick?"

"Certainly, there were periods of lowered resistance, sore throats, colds, and the effects of normal aging, but overall, he experienced an extremely healthy life and lived long enough to see all his grandchildren married."

"Did he live happily-ever-after also?"

Somehow I knew that this question was not playful on her part. I sensed that this was something she wanted to know about me.

"Well," I began, "there were the usual bumps in the road throughout his life, but just as he committed himself to regular chiropractic care, he also made a decision to deal with the regrets and disappointments and dedicate himself to joy, peace, love, and happiness." I kept going. "He chose to see the cup as more than half-filled. So I guess," I smirked, "that we can say that his life turned out to be a happily-ever-after life too!"

It was a true story.

I realized a couple of things at that moment. One, I would live happily-ever-after whether I ever fell in love and married again or not. I am a man who would always choose happiness. Here I was, battered and bruised by an unhappy, horrible marriage to Janine, yet capable of dusting off the debris of heartache and failure and choosing life and joy as my constant companions. The circumstances of life would never scare me, or dictate how I will evaluate the time I have remaining. Instead, I would take to heart the theory that I may never have total control of my circumstances, but I certainly had complete power over my reaction to them. That's a power I can live with.

Secondly, I may never see Breda Meyers again after today, but I needed to feel this very real attraction to a member of the opposite sex. The excitement, sexual tension, and desire to be attractive to a woman had been absent in my life for quite some time. I missed that. No, more than missed it, a part of me craved the attention, the conversation, flirtation, and sexual attraction that a woman brings. I purposely searched this woman's left hand for a ring. There was none!

It was time to shift gears again.

"So what is health to you?" I asked.

She sat up and tapped the fingers of her left hand against her knee.

"I'm not sure I can give you an exact definition," she began, "but I suppose there are things a person can do to be healthy."

"Tell me."

"Well, I like to exercise."

"What do you do?"

"I go to the gym about three times a week to lift weights. I take my dogs on long walks. I try to eat right."

I systematically made two parallel assessments. With respect to health, this Brenda Meyers was making good choices. Like anyone, of course, she still needed her subluxations corrected in order to reach her full health potential, but these are often the type of people who comprehend and eventually embrace the health philosophy of chiropractic.

My parallel assessment to that was that this woman works out regularly and I am attracted to women who care about how their bodies look. And this Brenda Meyers, in my opinion, should be very pleased by the results of her workout routine. She had a great body!

"Those are good health-promoting things that you do, Brenda." That was the first time I pronounced her name. "But think about it: When you lift weights, run, drink plenty of water, eat tofu for dinner," she grimaced at my little playful analogy, "what are you counting on? I mean," My question was obviously rhetorical, "within you resides an inborn wisdom that knows how to run your body in the direction of health. In chiropractic we call that Innate Intelligence."

I could tell that she was impressed. She was staring at me with great interest that appeared to encompass more than just what I was sharing. I know that I could be fooling myself, imagining a lot more than what was really being exchanged between us, but there are times when a man knows that he knows! This woman found me interesting and that awareness was something I had not felt in many years. I thought I heard the front door, but I quickly realized that I was mistaken. Thank God!

"How do you define health?" Brenda asked just the right question. It was quickly becoming apparent that this beautiful woman had more going for her than just her good looks.

"Health," I recited from memory, "is when all the cells, tissues, and organs work together in harmony for the coordinated good of the body."

I seized the moment to expound.

"Misaligned vertebrae, a condition we call a 'subluxation', creates an interference to nerve flow. Now the body doesn't work right. Put the bone back," I demonstrated an adjustment in mid-air, "and now the coordinating system is free to do its best work. It's as simple as that!"

"I think I'm beginning to understand this." Brenda's eyes brightened. "The adjustment is not just to make me feel better, but it improves my overall health at the same time. So," she playfully raised a finger to stop me from interrupting her train of thought, "a person should go to a chiropractor if they want to be healthy, not just because they're in pain."

I couldn't have said it any better myself!

"You get it!" I responded, amazed by her rapid comprehension of the chiropractic principle. "The body is better off with a good nerve supply!"

This woman was a dream! She really understood it!

I think everybody should have a dream. Early in life, mine was to be a major-league baseball player. The only problem was that I couldn't hit the curve ball or any other pitch for that matter. Alright, I stunk as a baseball player, but at least I admitted as much to myself and moved on to other things. When I was a teenager, my dream changed to that of being a rock star! I was the bass player and lead singer of a band called the 'Unknowns'. Good name I suppose, because we stayed that way! Later, I just knew that I would be a famous writer. Before I met Jesus, I wrote a novel about reincarnation. Only one term can adequately describe my mental state during this period of my life: Knucklehead! Years later, I tried my hand at writing again, penning two novels, both with the background theme of chiropractic. I really thought that I would be the literary voice of the profession. In recent years my dream has been more realistic, although just like its predecessors, somewhat unfulfilled.

My dream is to be a successful chiropractor with patients who come to me for the right reason. It's really a simple dream. Problem is: the vast majority of my wonderful patients come to me for relief of pain. Do I welcome them? Of course I do! I have been blessed to service some of the best, kindest, caring and genuinely friendly people that I've ever met. I love my patients! Only, I wish they understood the service that I have to offer. I wish they saw me as a health promoter, someone who can help them realize their full health potential as human beings. I wish they readily understood chiropractic care just the way Brenda did now. She's my dream! Wow, this is really becoming interesting!

Then I asked this beautiful woman the question that led me back to reality and disappointment.

"Do you have insurance?"

She opened her purse and took out a wallet. Leafing through an array of papers, she pulled out a Blue Cross and Blue Shield insurance card. She handed the card to me. I quickly noticed the name Brenda Meyers on the card. Hers was the second name down on the left side. Below it were the names Brandon Meyers, Carl Meyers and Patricia Meyers, no doubt her three children. Above her name was printed, Joseph Meyers. I frowned involuntarily. Brenda must have caught it, because she quickly stated the obvious.

"I'm under my husband's insurance."

Married! Just my luck!

Throughout the tumultuous years with Janine I utilized a technique at such defining moments. I shut down! Janine referred to my defense mechanism as turning into a robot.

"You're a robot!" Janine would tell me. "You turn off all your emotions, all your feelings, all that's genuinely human, and you pretend that nothing matters. Wind you up and you function without a care! It's worse than having multiple personalities."

"Why?" I asked once.

"Because at least a schizophrenic is a person! Your robot isn't even human. He doesn't care; you can't reason with him, because there's no one there to reason with! You're a robot. You're empty!"

I blinked. Then I forced a smile at Brenda Meyers and motioned with my hand to my adjusting table.

"Ready to start?" The robot asked.

I placed the insurance card on my filing cabinet. She moved towards my table, appearing to be a bit unsure of what she was expected to do next.

"Here," the robot spoke politely, "lie face down on the table."

The robot was palpating Brenda Meyers' spine when suddenly a new attitude emerged, as a decision was made without the robot's input or consent. The rising new attitude was this: I don't need the robot anymore! It served its purpose throughout the many years of unfound criticism, and undeserved ridicule. The robot was a necessary wall to protect the innocent man who resided within. Janine and her senseless, cruel, and pompous influence were gone! I was divorced not solely from Janine, but I was now free to be the man I was. I no longer needed a protective shield, or a hedge around me. I could be who God intended me to be. Of course, that was always true. I was guilty of allowing Janine to stop me from my personal destiny. Just like a chiropractic adjustment that enables a body to function at its full potential, divorce has removed an interference to my life! In that split second I said good-bye to the robot, and hello to renewal. Meeting this Brenda Meyers made me realize that I still could be attracted to, still enjoy a conversation with, and still someday hope to be a partner to a woman. Maybe I wasn't done with this female stuff just yet!

So I started flirting again.

Okay, so the woman was married, but I need to practice if I'm ever going to date again, so I figured if I kept things appropriate, then no harm done.

"Your upper back is either really tight or you must be pumping iron!" I teased her as I felt the muscles along her spine.

"Pumping iron!" She replied as she turned her head to look up at me. Then she lifted her left arm and flexed.

"Wow!" I exclaimed observantly. "Those are some nice pipes you got there!"

"I made them myself."

I continued to palpate her spine when suddenly Brenda Meyers winced in pain at my probing.

"You alright?"

"That hurt a little bit." She answered, only this time I detected a change of mood on her part. Whereas all this time she was open, friendly, and even flirtatious, Brenda now seemed to be just the opposite, guarded, secretive, and sheltered. I didn't understand why exactly, but I knew it had something to do with her area of pain. Patients don't often react to palpation that dramatically, and if they do, it would be in the hip or the neck, but rarely the mid-back. I thought her reaction was odd, unless of course, the upper spine was severely bruised.

"How did you hurt yourself?" I asked her, even though such a diagnostic question contradicted my chiropractic philosophy.

"I fell down the stairs."

Now I 'm not a psychologist by any means, in fact, I'm one of the worse discerners of peoples' characters that you'd ever want to meet. I'm the type to search for the good in others, so I usually miss their shortcomings, but I knew then as certainly as I know my own name that this woman was lying! No way did she fall down a flight of stairs. I could also tell by the tone of her voice that she knew that I knew it was a lie.

Boldly, I also sensed that lying to me bothered her. I can't explain it. But I knew that I was right.

I adjusted Brenda's right hip, her neck, and then very carefully applied a light force to the sensitive area of her mid-back. I asked Brenda to turn over onto her back and made an adjustment to her neck again.

"Awesome!" She said as I helped her to her feet. Next, she asked the question I was hoping for:

"When do you want to see me again?"

My first thought was, 'don't play with me'. I sensed that she was aware of my attraction to her, and that it pleased her. When did I want to see her again? How about tonight, dinner somewhere, or perhaps we could walk one of the trails at the Lake? And then I reminded myself that she was married. There would be no time of getting to know each other, no first kiss, no boldly reaching for her hand. Yet try as I might to dispel these romantic notions of grandeur, I still felt that this woman was interested in me. People can tell these things. I don't know her and she didn't know me, but somehow we had made a very real connection this morning, and today was not the end! She would be back and she would be back soon!

"I'm open again on Tuesday."

"What time should I come?"

"My hours on Tuesday are three o'clock until six."

"What time should I come?" She repeated.

I rubbed my fingers into my palm. Just as I suspected they were sweaty.

"How about five-thirty?" I gave her a specific time.

"I'll be here!"

Brenda Meyers paid me her co-pay of ten dollars, thanked me again for helping her, and turned to leave.

"I know you don't care," she pronounced sweetly, "but you did make me feel better."

There was that gorgeous smile.

"Oh," she giggled, "I also can tell that I am now operating at my full health potential. You turned the power on!"

She turned me on!

Brenda waved and left.

Well, I suppose she's correct in saying that I turned the power on with respect to her health potential. Me? I'm not sure what this woman turned on in me, but it's been a long time since any of my masculine dials have been touched. All of my buttons were pushed to the on position! And even though she'd left, I guess she forgot to turn them off, because I could still feel the heat of blood as it raced to my face.

Why Tuesday at five-thirty?

Well, it's the end of my work evening and it's normally a time of few if any patients. She wanted me to choose the time. She knew that I would know best when we could have the most time alone. Just like today. We understood each other completely. There was no denying that something had happened between us on this Saturday morning. A connection was made. What did it mean? I don't know. But I was totally committed to finding out!

My analysis of our short time together was broken by the sound of the front door being opened. I walked towards the footsteps to greet my next patient. I smiled in recognition.

"Hi Rhonda; come on in."

God, I love being a chiropractor!

Chapter 4

I took this Saturday off.

My son Garrett's high school graduation was scheduled for eleven o'clock in the morning. Whew, time flies! Sydney will be a senior in college. The twins enter high school in the fall. My children and their activities are the foundation of my social life. Especially the sports they play.

I remember when Sydney played her final high school soccer game. The girls lost 1-0. I recall the helpless feeling of wanting to stop the clock as the last precious seconds ticked away. Have you ever wanted to stop the clock in your life? When the pressure mounts, when difficulties surround you everywhere, when you feel the need to regroup, start again, and at the same time erase all that's transpired, have you ever felt the urge to shout, time-out! I stood on the sidelines after Sydney's final game, refusing to accept the stark reality that I would never see my oldest daughter play a soccer game again! Three years later, and a part of me still misses the joy of watching her play. You see, on the day she was born, I daydreamed that one day my newborn baby girl would play girls' soccer and that I would be there to watch her. God is good!

When Garrett played his last high school basketball game I was in attendance as always. Often times I would need to change my office hours in order to be there on time. I wasn't missing any of this! I'll make money when the children are grown up and gone. Garrett was Orchard Park High's starting point guard. He and his twin sisters are the athletes I never was. Garrett had an awesome season and the boys finished the year with a winning record. In the words of his coach, Garrett was the quickest kid he'd ever seen! I agree. With less than a minute to go in his final playoff game, Orchard Park was trailing by 5 points. Garrett took a shot from the left corner and missed. Their opponents grabbed the rebound and the season was over. I sat in the stands and held onto the final seconds, knowing the end was soon, yet hoping for more. I knew I would miss it. I have! Still, as all the parents and fans filed out of the gymnasium, one thought permeated my reality: God is good!

I've still got my twin daughters!

The girls will play JV soccer and JV basketball this upcoming school year. Like their older brother, I expect that they will also excel as high school athletes. They're good kids, whose circle of friends, are a fixture at my apartment, playing video games and eating me out of house and home. I wouldn't have it any other way! Lilly, Layla and their sports playing buddies have four years left to play for Orchard Park. I can't wait! There has been no greater joy in my life than to watch my children do their thing, be it sports, the plays they were in, chorus concerts, dance recitals, performing at the Erie County fair, or listening to them sing at the Valley Christian School Christmas plays! Their activities are the joyful source of my social life! My entire schedule revolves around their activities, needs, their accomplishments, and their futures. High School graduation is not the end of my job. I'm still responsible for seeing that Sydney becomes an independent, self-sufficient young woman, who God-willing, will marry a man who will cherish and love my baby girl forever. I need to see that the my son and the twins turn into good God-fearing young people who help support themselves and their families honestly, and who understand the satisfaction of a job well done.

I don't know what I would do with my free time were it not for my children. Janine and I used to go out together occasionally but for the last twenty years my social life has been child-driven. Divorced for over a year-and-a-half now, I still have not gone out on a single date. Not only haven't I met a woman to go out with, but I haven't looked either. I'm not ready, I suppose. It'll happen someday. As I sat at Garrett's high school graduation waiting for the band to strike-up Pomp and Circumstance, and searching the crowd for a friend to acknowledge, my mind was occupied by two thoughts:

One, my life was flying by and there wasn't a thing I could do about it, and secondly, what am I going to do when the kids are gone and the house is empty but for me? I guess finding a woman for companionship was not such a bad idea; it's just that I really hadn't come across anyone who interested me. Well, that was not entirely true. There was a Saturday morning last month when my hopes soared just a bit, but a month later the expectation and scintillating excitement was gone.

Brenda Meyers never did return to my office.

Her appointment was scheduled for Tuesday night at five-thirty. I taught school earlier that day so I was dressed in my usual dress pants, shirt and tie. I've never been an especially handsome man, but as I checked myself out in the mirror, I thought I looked just fine. The night before, right after I shaved, I spent a little extra time trimming nose and ear hairs before going to bed.

Truth is I was looking forward to seeing this Brenda Meyers again. I had her on my mind all weekend. By four-thirty I started looking out to the parking lot in expectation of her arrival. At five o'clock it was all I could think about! Five-thirty came and went. By five-forty-five, and no sign of her, I began to feel a bit stupid about my romantic aspirations. When I left that night I considered myself the village idiot! I remember thinking that maybe she would show up on Thursday instead, but now seven weeks later, and still no sign of Brenda Meyers' much anticipated return. My initial disappointment changed to a frustrated resolve as the days, weeks, and month-and-a-half passed on.

This man and woman thing is an intriguing topic! God gave both sexes much of the same parts. Heart, liver, lungs, spleen, arms, legs, mouth, eyes, ears, skin; we're certainly more similar than we are different, yet the crowning glory of His creation, the woman, affects we males in ways that are simply unexplainable! Okay, so there are some parts we don't share in common, and perhaps there are some distinct differences emotionally, mentally, and psychologically, but how does this explain the magnetic attraction of one sex to the other? What's really interesting is that I'm not drawn to all the members of the opposite sex. Some women, and actually that number is very few, affect me in ways that stir a special interest. I want to get to know them! When that feeling and desire is reciprocated, well watch out, because the entire world takes on a new look and my perspective of life and what is important is totally changed.

It was like that with Janine once.

She may not have ever really been my soul-mate, nor could I ever claim that God made her just for me, but I could still call what we had love for one another. There was an unmistakable attraction and I recall that early in the relationship the thought that this might just be the one, crossed my mind on more than one occasion.

Now we're divorced.

The children are still with me, of course, so a great deal of my time and energy is spent on them, yet it won't be long before they each make choices that will take them into the world and leave me behind. Sydney is already away at college. As I look down the aisle of seats where we sit at Garrett's graduation, I watch my daughter as she playfully laughs with her boyfriend, who is seated beside her. They've been dating for two years now. His name is Brendan and he's a nice boy. I like who he is, but I don't like what he represents! He's messing with my stuff! Sydney still belongs to me, and like the owner of a brand new car; I believe that he needs my permission to borrow it! But I must confess that I like the way he makes her laugh and the way my daughter looks at him when he's around. It's just that I know about the pain of losing a partner, how hard it is to accept the reality, or better yet, the finality of something so precious coming to an end. So I'm afraid for her. I want to protect her, but I know that in this particular arena, a father who once held her hand in the dark, can only sit by and offer a shoulder to cry on if and when the damage is done. I don't want her to experience that type of rejection. Been there, done that! It's that risky, dangerous, man-woman thing again that we dive into adventurously when caution should be noted.

Sitting next to me, the twins appear bored to death! I often wonder if my youngest realizes how awesome it is to be fourteen years old and only at the end of their eighth grade school year. They face July and August without the stress of finances, job responsibilities, relationship traumas, parental duties, or coping with the pain and regrets of previous challenges and choices. Their impending summer vacation consists of playing summer soccer, attending two basketball camps, inviting their gang of friends over to play video games, and I suppose that at fourteen, they will be beginning to develop an interest in the opposite sex.

I will pray for them!

Garrett is standing along the back wall of the gymnasium waiting for the band to play. He's wearing a maroon cap and gown, and oh yeah, he's also wearing a lip ring that looks positively ridiculous! I know I sound like my parents when they criticized my Nehru shirts, bell-bottom pants, and long hair during the 1960's. I suppose it could be worse and really, considering the potentially harmful effects of constant arguing in the home, and finally a divorce, I feel blessed that all four of my children appear to be doing fine with their lives. I'll say it again: God is good!

Down on the other side of Sydney and her boyfriend sat Janine. Camera in hand, she very nonchalantly joined us for the graduation. I can't recall the last time we were together at anything since we rarely associated with each other, but I suppose it was a good idea to form a united front on this special day in our son's life. She was friendly and acting the part of the loving mother. After all, Garrett was our child, together we brought him into the world, and together, even though now separated, and with separate lives and separate parenting skills, we would continue to be his parents. No, we were hardly friends, and we rarely compared notes on our children's lives, but today Janine and I would look the part, and we would do it because all four of them meant the world to us.

I continued to stare at Garrett as my mind returned to his stunning proclamation of earlier this week.

"Dad," he said softly as he sat on his bed with his laptop computer, "I don't think I want to go to Liberty this year."

Huh?

Garrett had been accepted at Liberty University in Lynchburg, Virginia and all the paperwork, financial arrangements, and course selections were completed. Liberty, a Division I University, is the largest Christian college in the world, and Janine and I were both pleased by our son's decision to go there until learning of this change of heart.

"I want to go to Erie Community College for a year." Garrett shared this startling change of educational direction. "I've been thinking about this for a few months now, and I just don't feel like I'm ready to go far away."

"Listen Garrett," it was my turn to give an opinion, "Liberty is a great opportunity for you so I want you to think carefully about this decision.

I really think you'll have a blast there." Then I added my two cents as any father would: "I don't agree with this choice!"

"It's my life, Dad. I just don't want to go to Liberty this year. I'll go next year."

"How do I know that?"

It was time to share my wisdom with him.

"It's over, Garrett." I began. "High school, all the friends you've hung out with, playing ball; it's time to grow up and get on with the next stage in your life. That's college!"

"ECC is college, Dad. I don't want to run up a huge debt by the time I graduate. I can go to ECC practically for nothing."

I couldn't argue with that logic. Garrett would have borrowed sixteen thousand dollars to attend Liberty. He would probably go to ECC for free just as he stated. I respected and even agreed with the wisdom of that choice, only that's not what I considered at issue.

"I think you just want your high school life to continue." I pronounced evenly.

"Yeah," he responded honestly, "I do wish I had another year of high school."

"Did you tell your mother?"

He rolled his eyes.

"She hit the roof!"

I knew immediately that a fierce battle now loomed on the horizon. The very next day Janine was at my apartment ready to defend and fight for her position on this matter. Oh, it's not like we disagreed on the issue at hand; I believe that neither of us was happy about Garrett's decision. It's just that we did not see eye-to-eye on how to handle the situation. For that matter, we've never seen eye-to-eye when it came to raising the kids. It's a wonder they've turned out as well as they have! Janine believed in forcing the children to follow our wishes. Now that may work when they're in grade school, but as young adults I believe that it is a mistake to make them go to the college of our choice. Garrett has his own life to live, including learning from all the mistakes he will make along the way. Is this particular decision a mistake? Well, we don't really know yet, but if you were to ask me, yeah; I think it's the wrong decision and not the best thing for him. Still, it's his life, and though this sudden curve in the road is a bit disconcerting, I will travel along with him and support him regardless of the outcome. Will I say 'I told you so' a year from now? Perhaps. Yet if I do so, it will not be to mock or lord it over him but as a father pointing out and instructing him on the importance of decision-making, especially when those choices involve a bigger picture than we generally can see. In other words, I will not force my son to go where or when I want him to. He's eighteen and he needs to make important choices. I'll support those choices, while at the same time serving as a guide with advice, encouragement, and a love for him that will never end.

Janine is a different story.

When she showed up at my door the next day, I already knew what to expect. For one, the blame for Garrett's decision would fall to me as his father. It was predictable! The funny thing is that Janine has been encouraging both Sydney and Garrett to attend ECC their first two years to ease the financial burden of paying for college, but now that our son was about to do just that, she was enraged.

I never could figure her out.

Of course, back when she wanted them to go to ECC we were married and shared the financial burden of our children's education. Now, since only one of us foots the entire bill, concerns over the money were no longer an issue. Sadly, I'm probably right about that.

"We can't make him go!" I shared my perspective. "I've seen too many kids go away to college and quit after a semester because they weren't ready. Garrett says he's not ready. I think we need to respect the fact that he recognizes that and stand by him as he goes to ECC."

"Garrett has been going downhill for the last couple of years now." Janine replied, apparently ignoring everything I said. "The boy gets whatever he wants, does whatever he wants, and goes wherever he wants! Can't you see how much you've spoiled him? He's totally irresponsible with his money and as his father you let him have his way all the time." Here we go again! "Just like when I thought it was a bad idea for him to take his car to Liberty, we argued and then he told me that he would talk to you about it. He told me that you were a pushover. And that you would let him. I'm on my knees for that boy all the time! My whole family is upset about this and can't believe that his father is standing by doing nothing about it!"

Hmm. Surprise, surprise! Once again the problem is not Garrett's decision, but poor parenting by his father.

"I love my son and would give my very life for him!" Janine declared, now crying and on the verge of hysteria.

That was fast! Usually it takes a while before she reaches for the hysteria card to get her way. So soon! I guess she's out of practice with me being gone and all. Anyway, it struck me that the crying and the attempt to make me the bad guy were old tricks that I used to fall for. No more!

"You never listen." Janine resumed her attack. "You have no concept of what it takes to co-parent these children."

I'd heard enough.

"You quit the team!" I retaliated in anger. "We still had a lot of years left in the season when you selfishly bailed out on us. I kept playing!" I always like to make my point with sport analogies. "When you left I had to keep the team positive, believing in ourselves, and continue to lead us to the finish line! It's been hard, but the kids and I are continuing to make gains, add to our victory total, and unite with confidence even though one of our main stars quit the team! By leaving like this you forfeited your rights to co-captain! You gave up your say in making joint-decisions concerning their welfare. While you went off with other men to Japan, Indonesia and Colorado, I continued to work for the benefit of the team. I give you $350 a week in child support, yet I'm the one who pays their college tuition, their clothing, school activities, car insurance, and whatever else they need. They stay with me most of the time because they feel safe and secure here. There are lots of games still left in this season of raising and providing for our children, but for the last year-and-a-half, I've gone it alone! So don't you dare tell me about my failure to co-parent with you! You left! I'm still here!"

When Janine left that afternoon she departed with her usual threat:

"Wait until the Judge hears about this!"

That has been her little battle cry ever since the divorce. Every time I don't bow to her demands, I'm warned that the Judge is not going to be happy about it! Actually, I don't even know who this Judge is, but if he or she really is preparing some verdict on my post-divorce behavior, I wonder how their decision would be affected if they knew everything!

What would the Judge think about the time Janine broke into my office, took a Medicare check off my desk, opened it, and then cashed it because we had property taxes to pay?

Or what would the Judge say about her right to stand outside of my office door and eavesdrop on my phone calls? Right before we were divorced and still living together, Janine's mother phoned me to tell me that I should let her daughter have her divorce and that I should leave the premises immediately. I was talking to Mrs. Cunningham in the basement of my house when I turned and saw a shadow on the stairway turn and run away when I approached it. Would the Judge be interested in that?

Speaking of my chiropractic office, for two years Janine rented a room across the hall from me for her part-time accounting business. Some of my patients happen to be attractive women. Each time that I spent any time with or chatted with one of these women after adjusting their spines, Janine flipped out on me! A few times, as I was walking a female out of the office, Janine was standing down the hallway, giving a mock interpretation that only I could see of I don't even know what, to show how she felt about the situation. I was routinely called a pervert, a womanizer, and told in no uncertain terms that I needed to tell these attractive women that they need to find another chiropractor for themselves!

"You are practically hitting on them!" She would accuse me. "I see the way you look at them. You like to try and be all funny and you laugh. It's disgusting!"

I suppose the Judge would frown on any doctor who was friendly and laughed with his patients, especially a chiropractor who was friendly and laughed with all of his patients, regardless of their looks or their ability to pay. We don't need guys like that around people in need!

A couple of weeks ago when I balked at paying the full amount of a dentist bill for the kids , Janine changed her threat just a bit from that of the unknown judge to 'I'll see you in family court'. Still, the daily phone calls never stop and the pretense that we somehow should communicate and get along better remains her belief.

Here's an interesting thought.

Janine's parents were separated when she was in college, yet they were always in touch, always trying to reconcile, and of course always fighting over the same issues that caused the problems in the first place. Today they are still married to each other and I would imagine still doing their best to work things out. Truthfully, I admire them for that. I really do! My in-laws both want their future relationship to overcome their past differences and somehow both hope to succeed and live out their final years peacefully together. Like any couple there will be problems. Is it worth all the arguments, pain, insults, re-hashing of old issues, and all the effort it takes to overcome these seemingly insurmountable obstacles? Well, the answer to that is entirely up to them. Me? There is no way on earth that I would even entertain the thought of reconciling with Janine. I'm not going back to that!

Recently, I've begun to consider the possibility that Janine really thinks that the two of us can be friends. After all, she saw her own parents go back and forth and live together after their separation. What she apparently fails to see in her desire for us to co-parent, is that I'm the only person on earth who knows who she is! For many years I too may have wanted a divorce, but I never would have pursued one. That's all on her! So has time erased the resentment, the memories of unjust ridicule, the lies thrown in my face, or the fact that I can't trust her to be fair and honest? No! I will always remember how Janine treated me, and though I will always act friendly for the sake of the kids, or just because behaving civilly is the right thing to do, we will never be friends! Aptly put, you can't treat people that way and expect them to forget about it. Oh, it is certainly my Christian duty to forgive her, but I don't know how to forget it, nor do I plan on learning how!

As I watched Garrett receive his diploma, flip his tassel, toss his cap into the air, and later pose outside for pictures with his buddies, I was struck by the comparison of my life to his. His next step was easy: College! What was mine? I was already a school teacher-chiropractor-preacher, so it wasn't like I needed a career. What I needed was a person. Now that the robot had been destroyed, the internal ache for a partner to share life with reminded me from time-to-time that I was still young enough, and not too ugly or obnoxious to find myself a woman. Truth is: the thought of risking my heart again scared me to death! Besides that, who would want a short, bald, fifty-seven-year-old man who had already failed at this relationship game? There were times when I convinced myself that I was a loser who didn't deserve a second chance. Yet these moments of self-depreciation were short-lived, replaced by the knowledge that I was worthy, that I could be a good husband, and that true beauty is only skin deep. God, through Jesus Christ, proved to me that I was worthy. My steadfast belief that I was not to blame for the demise of my marriage convinced me that I could succeed with the right woman. My mirror told me that, well, two out of three ain't bad!

So here I was, two children finished with high school and two to go, yet as I told Janine last week when we argued, the season is far from over! I was presently celebrating my victory of the second child to graduate high school game, and the next game in life would follow shortly, and just like all the others, preparation, hard work and vision were requirements for success. The realization struck me like a ton of bricks! That's what I was missing! I prepared; I worked hard, but I had no vision, no sense of a desired outcome for what I needed next. I knew at that moment that I wanted to meet my partner, my soul-mate, my best friend, the one person whose very existence would complete me as a human being.

I sensed that God whispered to me:

"She's out there!"

Chapter 5

I HAD A GOOD day at the office. Financially, things have really picked up over the last few months. Old patients have been returning, new patients are being referred by others, and my usual dedicated-to-chiropractic patients continue to come on a regular basis. It was only ten months ago that the second lawyer I visited had informed me that there wasn't a thing I could do about the money amount I paid Janine weekly, so I made a decision right then and there, that what was out of my control was out of my control, but that there was one thing I could do to improve my current financial status. Make more money! So I began to work a little harder at promoting my business, attended more chiropractic seminars, became a participator at health fairs where I adjusted hundreds of people who had never visited a chiropractor before. Many became new patients, most did not. Still, as I watched my business grow the burden of high winter electric bills and other normal expenses became less stressful and I was beginning to settle in with this life as a divorced man screwed by the State of New York.

This particular Tuesday night in early December had been especially prosperous. As the six o'clock hour came around I sat at my desk to try to alleviate as much paperwork as I could in the last few minutes. Before I started I went to the bathroom. While I was in there I heard the front door open and the sound of another patient walking past and into my waiting room. It was probably Maureen. She faithfully comes for an adjustment every Tuesday, although usually she is here by mid-afternoon. Washing my hands, I stepped out to greet whoever it was.

When I saw Brenda Meyers sitting there my heart skipped a beat!

"Tuesday at five-thirty!" She said, smiling.

She was back!

It had been seven months since we first met, yet she smiled so sweetly that it was like we were old friends. I had still thought about her, although by the fall my dashed hopes of seeing her again were replaced by acceptance and the need to force myself to forget about her. I knew that Brenda was from nearby Hamburg so there were times where I went to either Wal-Mart or ate at the Ponderosa that the hope of running into her flickered in my mind. We never did.

I actually thought that I had spotted her once driving around McKinley Mall. The woman I stared at was driving a blue Honda Civic, but as we passed I couldn't be sure that it was really her. I turned my car around and desperately attempted to follow the Honda Civic as it turned down towards the Mall. Another driver cut me off and I cursed softly under my breath. I'd lost track of her. It probably wasn't her anyway. There was a resemblance, but there was one thing I distinctly remember about the woman in the Honda Civic. She looked like she had a black eye.

"Right on time!" I smiled back at her. "Come on in."

When she stood and walked towards the adjusting room I followed. Yes, I'm a man, and yes, I have not been with a woman in that special way for over three years now, so yes, I did take note of her gorgeous figure, and yes, I was turned on by her presence. I don't know what it is about her, but this woman affects me like no other that I have seen in the past few years. As I followed her into the adjusting room I found myself thinking, 'this is the most beautiful woman I've ever seen'!

I started dating at the beginning of last summer as my search for a soul-mate began.

Alecia Hopkins had a son who played basketball with my son Garrett. During the season we sat together on occasion and I found her always very pleasant and easy to talk to. One day, I saw her for the first time in quite a while at the Park and Shop grocery store. We chatted about the boys and then I took a bold step and asked her out to dinner. She was divorced, petite, and I thought we'd enjoy each other's company. Unfortunately, my step of faith turned into a minor embarrassment when she informed me that she was already seeing someone. Actually, the rejection of a dinner date was almost a relief. At least now I didn't have to concern myself with the awkwardness of what to talk about, how funny I should try to be, or whether to kiss her or not at the end of the evening. Nope, rejection has its positive side, I suppose. At least I tried and it wasn't all that bad, so I knew I would try again.

I met a young divorced woman named Lisa Karpenski. She was relatively attractive, forty-three years old, and we shared a common interest in working out at the YMCA. We spoke sparingly a couple of times about weight-lifting, running, and playing tennis. During the U.S. Open tennis tournament in early September, Lisa came up to me and started talking about the upcoming tennis match between Roger Federer and Raphael Nadal. I slipped into my flirtatious tendency to brag a little bit about my tennis playing prowess, when she suddenly challenged me to a match.

"I'll bet I'm better than you." She chided me.

"There's only one way to find out!" I volleyed back.

"I'll tell you what." She challenged. "We'll play and the loser buys dinner afterwards."

I accepted. After all, I like to eat and free food is one of my favorites!

As I drove to meet Lisa at the courts I playfully considered whether I should try to beat her badly or hold back a bit to make the match more fun and compelling. I mean, this was a date, right? There was going to be dinner afterwards and perhaps a little romance. I'd hate to spoil the potential of a nice evening with an attractive young woman just because I whipped her butt in tennis!

Lisa was already on the court practicing her serve when I pulled up to the fence. Hmm, not a bad looking serve. I grabbed my twelve dollar Wal-Mart racket from the trunk and jogged out to my side of the net. We volleyed back-and-forth for a few minutes until my stiff fifty-year-old body loosened up enough to play.

"I'm ready!" I called to her. "You serve first."

Whoosh!

The ball flew off her racket like it was shot out from a cannon. Didn't expect that, did I? Four serves, four misses on my part, and I was already down a game!

Now it was my turn to serve.

I reach back and hit the ball as hard as I could. It landed fairly and Lisa sent it back at me. I hit a forehand shot to the right corner, but she pounced on it and sliced a shot that dropped and died on my side, close to the net. I swore I saw Lisa pumping her fist!

On the next volley I made a spectacular lunging shot, but on the return her ball struck the top of the cord and fell safely on my side for her point.

"Woo!" She yelled out.

This girl was cocky!

Things did not improve for me throughout the first set. Lisa had a monster cross-court backhand, a powerful forehand, and a drop-shot that I just couldn't reach even when I saw it coming! I decided to rush the net. Hitting the ball hard into the right corner again I quickly dashed up to the net, intending to slam home a winner! Yet somehow, with her right arm completely outstretched, Lisa hit a backhand bullet that flew past my racket and landed fairly for yet another point! I dropped my head in resignation and when I looked up, the girl was pumping her right fist again before accentuating her celebration with a body twirl!

A twirl? This obnoxious tennis star was rubbing my nose in it. How big of a jerk do you have to be to twirl in front of your opponent? I'll say it again: She's cocky! Only there wasn't a darn thing I could do about it.

Lisa won the first set 6-0. She beat me in the second set by the same score. Guess who's buying?

Dinner was nice. We talked about coping with our divorces, diet and exercise, and our plans for the future. Lisa was married only seven years and had no children. She told me she was in no hurry to remarry and that she enjoyed her single life. She also told me that at college she played first singles for the tennis team. Oh, did you forget to drop that piece of information before you challenged me to a game? Luckily, the restaurant we ate at accepted Visa because I did not bring any cash. Bringing cash would have been a sign of weakness. I didn't expect to lose. I know; who's the cocky one now?

Since we took separate cars to meet at the tennis court, we departed casually and without much fanfare. There was no pressure of a goodnight kiss, or even the stress of drumming up the courage to ask 'when will I see you again'. It was tennis and dinner. No more than that.

As I drove home a mood of profound sadness, (and for the first time since my divorce), loneliness crept into my being. It had nothing to do with Lisa Karpenski. It was deeper, far more than mentally dissecting a lousy date, but an ache, or rather a void that needed to be filled. Then I had the strangest thought:

I wonder if Brenda Meyers plays tennis?

"Do you play tennis?" I suddenly surprised even myself by asking.

There was that full smile again.

"No, not really," she answered, "but it's so funny that you ask. I've wanted to learn how to play tennis for a long time now, and I've been thinking about it." Then she tossed this zinger. "Would you teach me?"

In my mind I thought 'you bet I will', but I said aloud to her.

"Won't your husband mind?"

"Yeah, he definitely will mind." Next she added: "But it's just tennis, and I would love to learn to play. He can't control everything I do!"

So there was trouble in paradise at the Meyers home.

As I adjusted Brenda I remembered the discomfort she felt in her mid-back the last time she was here. This time, as I palpated the area she showed no reaction. It must have been a bad bruise. While I adjusted her neck I recalled seeing the woman in the blue Honda Civic and thinking that it was Brenda. I remembered the black eye.

"I thought I saw you one day driving by the McKinley Mall." I stated matter-of-factly.

"Could be." She responded.

I tried again to engage her in conversation.

"So what does your husband do for a living?"

Brenda sat up on the adjusting table and looked at me.

"Am I done?"

For some reason the ease with which we spoke on her first visit was missing this time. I sensed that Brenda was nervous, indecisive about how to relate to me, and I must confess that the awkwardness of it all bothered me.

"So when can we play?" She suddenly asked.

"Play what?" I responded, though I knew full well that she was referring to tennis.

Brenda frowned at my deception.

"Where do you want to play?" She asked, ignoring my pretense.

"How about if we play at the fitness center in Hamburg, right next to the hardware store?" I paused. "Do you know where that is?"

"I'll find it."

With that she left. Only this time there were no playful parting remarks, nor any expression of satisfaction about the adjustment. I thought her behavior was rather odd, bordering on unfriendly, especially when you consider that we made plans to play tennis. Still, as Brenda Meyers walked away and out the front door, I secretly followed to see if my suspicion was true. Making sure she didn't see me watching, I stood obscured behind the television set that constantly advertised pharmaceuticals to medical patients on the other side of the building. I listened as her car door shut, the engine start, and heard the whirl of movement as Brenda backed away from the building and pulled out. Sure enough, my intuition was right: It was a blue Honda Civic!

I am so out of practice with women! I told Brenda where we could play, but I forgot to tell her when. This created a bit of a predicament because since she did not reschedule an appointment, I would probably have to call her to set a date and time. Problem with that was: What if he answers?

Okay, it was only tennis. She was obviously a beginner with a normal desire to learn how to play. I was going to be her instructor. She probably couldn't hit the ball over the net so I was there to help her improve. No harm in that, is there? Yet the more I thought about it the more I realized that I couldn't call a married woman and ask her to play tennis with me.

On Saturday morning Brenda returned for another adjustment. Problem solved!

"So when are we going to play?" She asked me right before she left.

"You tell me."

"Well," she replied thoughtfully, "my husband is going skiing with our son and some friends on Sunday, so how about tomorrow?"

There was no hesitancy on my part to agree. She was married, attractive, seemingly interested in me, and all I could do was keep convincing myself that it was no more than a harmless game of tennis. We agreed to meet at the fitness center at two o'clock. The thought that she lived in Hamburg and that people all over the area knew who I was never crossed my mind as something to be careful about. My goodness, it was just tennis! So what if someone sees us playing? What's the big deal?

After church on Sunday I got my gym stuff, a couple of rackets, tennis balls, and drove to the fitness center. I love playing tennis indoors! I had reserved a court for two o'clock. As I pulled up in front I recognized the blue Honda Civic and just as readily spotted Brenda standing inside the glass doorway waiting for me. Her son and husband were at Holiday Valley Ski Resort in Ellicottville, while she was about to play tennis with her chiropractor! What in the world was I thinking?

"Hi!" I greeted her joyfully.

"Hi!" She answered back.

We changed into our tennis playing gear and met out on the court. Brenda wore red shorts and a white top. The woman is a total knockout! I was about to do a mental evaluation of her stunning physique when I appropriately stopped myself and focused only on her face. Problem was, that dark black hair and those dark piercing eyes made her face positively lovely! Where else can I look to avoid being turned on by her?

I was right about one thing: Brenda Meyers stunk at tennis! She had no idea of how to stand, how to best hold the racket, how to swing the racket, and apparently no concept as to why there was a net between her and her opponent! I tried my best to hit the ball in a way to make it as easy as possible for her to return the ball, but more often than not her attempt fell short of the net, or flew over my head to the back wall. Was it really playing tennis? Well, not really. Was it an hour of boredom and putting up with a novice when I could have been playing real tennis with someone else? No way! I loved every minute of it! The entire time we played I thought two things: One, I wish it were spring or summer so we could play outside where nobody would likely see us, and secondly, I couldn't get over just how cute she looked with a tennis racket in her hand!

Afterwards we sat upstairs at the juice bar. We were the only two people there, so it permitted us to talk openly and freely. Brenda works in real estate so we discussed the current problems with the market, which led to my sharing the difficulty I had with selling my home. I told her all about the divorce agreement pertaining to Janine remaining in and being responsible for maintaining our house. Brenda shook her head in empathy on occasion when I related the six-foot-high weeds, or unkempt inside of my former residence.

"Why won't she keep the place clean? Obviously, she doesn't want the house to sell, right?"

"Janine is a movie star." I started to explain sarcastically. "Movie stars don't clean. She has more important things to do with her hair, skin, nails, and stuff like that." Then I said something for no apparent reason except to perhaps promote myself to her. "My wife is a very beautiful woman."

Brenda looked away when I said that.

It was so easy to talk to Brenda Meyers. I shared some of the details of my horrible married life and interesting enough, she spoke of her own marriage and how unhappy she has been through the years. Brenda has been married twenty-three years, has three teenage children, and told me that the only thing that kept her sane was being busy on the job selling real estate. So we talked once more about properties, the present crisis, and every so often we returned to tales concerning our spouses and married life.

"My marriage has been difficult for a long time. I am hoping for the day where I feel like it will be ok if I leave him. But I don't know if that will ever happen. " Brenda openly shared. "I just never, ever would want to do that to my children. When they were younger I would have never been able to be a part-time mom, having them go back and forth from mom's house to dad's house. I need my kids to live with me every day, and I wouldn't have ever taken the chance that they wouldn't if I left him. On the other hand, I don't like my kids seeing how my husband treats me. There isn't a lot of love and caring in our relationship. I hate the fact that my children might think that this is a normal, healthy marriage. You understand what I mean; you've been through it."

How interesting that a Christian man who says he believes in the sanctity of marriage actually feels a sense of hope and joy in learning that someone is unhappily married. A part of me certainly hopes for the best for Brenda and her family. I've been through it and it's no fun! Yet there was this other unmistakable part of me that began to wonder if this was somehow the hand of God on my life. But how could that be? God can't go against his own word. The Bible says that marriage is for a lifetime, yet Janine, a self-professing Christian woman ended ours, and now I'm talking to an unhappily married woman who wants out of hers. On one hand I want to know why staying together forever is so difficult, while at the same time I see friends who are still in love and whom I know will successfully remain together for a lifetime. Are these happily married people better then Brenda and I? Are they more faithful in their Christian walk? Suddenly an important question occurred to me:

"Do you go to church?" I asked Brenda.

"No, not anymore." She confessed. "My husband is Methodist so we used to take the kids when they were younger. I saw an advertisement in the newspaper." She switched gears on the topic of conversation. "You're a preacher, aren't you?"

I certainly wasn't acting like one!

"Yeah, I used to pastor a little church in the town of Red Houses, but we closed down a few months ago."

"How come?"

"Numbers."

I told Brenda how we once had a membership of thirty-five to forty people, but how that number had dwindled to six due to death and younger retirees moving out of state.

"How long did you preach for?"

"Seventeen years." I told her. "Actually I stopped for a few years because my wife thought that I should step down. She told me that I was unfit to be in the pulpit because we were having marriage problems."

"From what you've told me," Brenda correctly observed, "it sounds like she was the one who was unfit!"

I couldn't argue with that. I was really starting to like this girl!

"So how about you?" I changed the subject. "What's the problem with you and your husband?"

She sighed.

"Joe," it was the first time she said his name, "treats me like I'm his disobedient daughter. I always need to ask permission before I spend money or go anywhere with friends. He doesn't trust me, follows me wherever I go, checks up on everything I do, and," she paused self-consciously, "I'm to side with him on all decisions, especially if it concerns the children. I'm sick of it!"

"What do you mean?"

"Well," she explained her complaints with her husband, "I probably make just as much money as he does, but since he pays all the bills, everything I make goes directly to our joint account. I never see any of it, except for the twenty-five dollars spending money he gives me every week. And," she vented, "I have to ask him for that most of the time or I'd have nothing!"

"Man," I interrupted, "how did you ever let that happen?"

Brenda sighed again.

"When the kids were young Joe was the only one working while I stayed at home. I wanted to stay home with the kids so no complaints there. He has always had full control of our money and how it was spent. He has always made it very clear to me that we don't have any money and we struggle to pay our bills each month. So when we talked about buying a new house or simply needing more money, I chose a career to help out. I thought that real estate was perfect because I had control of my own schedule so if the kids were sick I could easily be there. Even though I was making money, our situation never changed. Supposedly we still struggled daily and I still had the same amount of spending money as before. As time went by I began to be pretty successful at selling houses and I know that Joe was real pleased about it too. Only," she shook her head in apparent memory and frustration, "as my hours away from home on showings increased, Joe became more demanding and more suspicious of how I was spending my time."

"That's where the trust problem comes in." I ventured a guess.

"Exactly!" Brenda confirmed. "Joe always accused me of doing other things besides showing people houses to buy. I was especially under severe scrutiny if I showed a house to a single man. And if that same guy wanted to see other houses too, well, you can imagine what my husband thought."

"My God," I thought aloud as Brenda touched a chord of one my own complaints with people in relationships, "why does one person feel like they have to control the other?"

"Joe thinks everything has to be done his way. I know what you're talking about. That's exactly what he does. He tries to control me. It's like I'm not my own separate person, but this thing that belongs to him that he can use to either make money from, or someone to clean and make his meals, or legally have sex with!"

Whoa. That came out of nowhere!

"I hate sex!" Brenda suddenly shared.

"Janine was a control-freak." I seized the moment to get away from how much Brenda hated sex. "She was always trying to re-make me so to speak, mold me into some kind of image of what a real husband should be like. Of course, this image was according to her wants and needs, and hardly the biblical command of how a woman needs to respect her husband for who he is."

"That's a big issue to you, isn't it?"

"What do you mean?" I wondered, not following her line of thought.

"This respect thing." She replied. "That's about the third time you've mentioned how important being respected for who you are is to you."

"It's biblical!"

"I understand that. But what if there were some things about you that could use some change? I would like to think that you're not like Joe, inflexible and set in your ways, and impervious to any change. I believe that in a good relationship people don't control one another, still there are certain expectations to change the way we act and behave because we love our mate so much that we wouldn't have it any other way!"

I really like this girl!

She's right. In a good, loving relationship changes are made by people because they recognize a need to change and have the desire to change. Now their motivation may be to please another, but regardless of why one alters their behavior or modifies their values, the reason for doing so originates from within. They want to change! But when controlling spouses force change, either through manipulation, or withholding love, the result may be the same as a voluntary choice, but it's still fake, unreal, insincere, and most dangerously, a root of resentment has been firmly planted! I know; I spent over twenty years as an object of control. So yeah, being respected for the man I am is very important, if not completely necessary for me in my next relationship, whenever that may be!

"I'm not inflexible!" I responded firmly. "Why is it so much to ask to be accepted for who I am? I've spent the last quarter century with someone who disliked practically everything about me, when most of what she thought about me wasn't even true! I'll make some changes for someone I love, but I don't believe that wholesale changes are necessary!"

"Of course you don't!" Brenda said smiling.

"What does that mean?"

Brenda tapped my arm playfully.

"Somebody thinks that they're pretty awesome just the way they are!"

Hmmm. Very observant woman.

Over the rest of the winter months Brenda Meyers became a regular chiropractic patient. Normally, she came by once a week for an adjustment, yet there were occasions when she showed up twice a week, once claiming that my last adjustment didn't do the trick! She told she was still in some pain.

"I thought you understood chiropractic?" I teased her.

"I do." She claimed right back. "But I also understand something that you apparently don't."

"Go on."

"People are not going to come to your office because they want their subluxations corrected. They're in pain and they expect you to help them. You need to tell them that you just might be the answer to their problem."

I shook my head emphatically.

"I have a dream," I began to share my most private thoughts with Brenda, "that patients will seek care here because they want to function in health, and," I raised my hand to stop her from interrupting, "they understand that only a chiropractor can restore proper nervous system control. This is the only life, this side of Heaven, that I've got, and this is my dream for it!"

In the spring Brenda approached me about playing tennis again. I readily agreed to be her private instructor. Once a week we made plans to meet and play at the outdoor courts.

"I told Joe that I was showing a home." She told me her excuse the first time we played.

After that I didn't ask.

Okay, so I was secretly meeting an extremely attractive woman on the sly to play some tennis. And yes to me, a man with no other romantic interests in his life, they were special times together. I remembered my thought that God somehow had a hand in this, only I changed my spiritual perspective a bit. Brenda Meyers was sent to help me through a difficult healing period. No, the absence of Janine for two years didn't bother me, but being alone and having no special mate to share my thoughts and time with, left a void that Brenda seemed to fill. God did not send a married woman to be my lover. No, I believe what Brenda Meyers became was my closest friend, and someone to talk to about anything on my mind, including my failed marriage.

Only problem was one of those things constantly on my mind was an acute attraction to Brenda Meyers! I wanted her. I couldn't have her. I knew that, but I also recognized that these feelings needed to be suppressed and that an important decision had to be made, or better yet, a self-commitment needed to be established and obeyed! So against the desires of my flesh I made that commitment.

There would be no romantic relationship with Brenda Meyers. Sure, her husband sounded like a controlling, unappreciative, mistrusting jerk who didn't deserve a treasure like Brenda, but none of that had anything to do with me and my feelings towards her. We would be friends, and only friends. I hate to admit it, but that's all there would be to it and now that I've made my commitment, I became more relaxed when I was with her. I even got used to it. We had a great time playing tennis, sharing sandwiches for lunch, and talking together at the office. Talking was what we did more than anything else. Brenda and I talked about everything: our children, our hobbies, the parents who raised us, our careers, our hopes and dreams, and of course our own dysfunctional marriages. I was never happier than when I was with her. There was no denying that I had feelings for her, but as long as I kept those feelings under control there was nothing to fret about. Still I often wondered: Does she have any of those feelings for me?

One night at the office Brenda requested something that practically floored me because it came out of the blue.

"Tell me about this Jesus."

For all the months that we had been friends, the topic of my religious beliefs only came up as some reinforcement of some discussion or to framework a particular point of view. Brenda knew that I used to pastor a small church for many years and of course she was also aware of my claim to be a born-again Christian. On occasion I would purposely force the issue of Jesus just to stoke her interest, but mostly, or so I thought, the subject fell on deaf ears. I guess I was wrong.

"I like the story," I began with a sort of modern-day parable I'd heard, "of the bluebird in the barn who didn't know enough to free itself through the open barn door. A farmer came out and did everything he could to persuade the poor frightened bird to exit the barn, but it continued to fly around scared to death."

I really wanted this to make sense to her.

"If only I could change myself and turn into a bluebird and communicate with it in its own language," the farmer thought to himself, "then I could show him the way!"

I paused for a moment.

"That's what God did." I resumed with the explanation of my parable. "People were living and dying clueless to what mattered, broken, defeated, and at the beck and call of every evil whim. Sin in their lives was destroying them and there was no way out of the barn! The Ten Commandments, the Old Testament promises, and all their religious rituals and practices proved impotent. There was no way out! Or so they thought. Remember the farmer who wished he could be a bird for a short while so he could speak its language and save it? That was God's answer to the downward spiraling plight of man. God Himself got off His Heavenly throne, threw off his majestic robe, and clothed Himself in humanity. God became a man, a human being, one of His very own people, so that He could show us the way in a language of our own that we could understand. That man was Jesus! He came to save us."

"So what exactly did he tell the people?" Brenda asked with sincere interest.

"He told us," I used the pronoun 'us' to denote the inclusion of all mankind, "that we were incapable of saving ourselves. Nobody could live a righteous enough life to be worthy of spending eternity with a Holy God."

"So it's impossible for us," Brenda seemingly also included herself now as part of God's plan, "to live a life well enough to deserve to go to heaven."

"Life has to be lived perfectly!" I countered.

I could tell by looking at Brenda that the wheels in her mind were turning.

"No one can do that!" She remarked correctly. Well, almost correctly.

"Jesus did!" I pronounced with conviction. "He lived a sin-free life on earth and when He was crucified, He died like any other man would have except," I always liked this part of the story the best, "He went to Hell in our place, to pay the price each of us accumulated, and then He rose from the dead, holy, and with a new promise of salvation for all who believe that He did what He did precisely for them!"

"He's the way to heaven." Brenda stated in apparent understanding.

"He's the only way!"

Then Brenda Meyers said the absolute, best, most important, life-changing thing that any person could ever say:

"I want to go to heaven. Will you help me?"

I certainly would!

We prayed together and right there in my office Brenda Meyers gave her heart to Jesus Christ! She would be from this day forth a child of God. She did it! Brenda had made the most important decision of her life and now her name was written in God's book of Life. What an awesome night it was! Yet I must confess that in my imperfect mind there was also the opinion, 'what an awesome woman'!

Oddly enough, after such an intimate encounter as praying together and asking God for her salvation, I did not see Brenda Meyers again for the next three weeks. What was that about? I thought to call her, but I knew I couldn't, not with a husband who could easily be the one to answer the phone if I did. So I did the only thing I could. I waited.

Brenda returned to the office one Saturday morning as if the time elapsed were no big deal. She acted glad to see me, and was her usual friendly self, although I thought she seemed a bit more flirtatious than I remembered.

I liked that!

I'd known Brenda Meyers for little over a year now, and quite frankly, she was the delight of my life! We kept our distance with respect to any romantic advances, yet every time we were together, whether at the office or playing tennis, the chemistry between us was undeniable. I continued to feel something for her, still she never gave me any indication that she felt the same. I wasn't going to worry about it. Our friendship provided me the strength to not only get through my otherwise lonely days, but it was fast becoming the best friendship I'd ever had. I'm not exaggerating! Brenda was a good friend who not only provided fun, stimulating conversation, and some degree of sexual excitement, but she was also not afraid to be open, honest, and downright blunt with me when the occasion presented itself. Over time, she grew to take on the role of my personal psychologist, especially when we played tennis.

Brenda became an honest-to-goodness competitive tennis player! She transformed her game as a one-time inept beginner, to a woman who hit strong forehands, solid backhands, overheads, sometimes rushed the net, and every once in a while got to shots that I at first thought could not be reached. She improved so rapidly that it amazed me. And it was not because she had a good tennis instructor. My role as her teacher lasted only a short time. It wasn't long before Brenda would have none of that! Somehow, as our relationship evolved, Brenda grew to consider me as somewhat of an egotistical, pompous tennis opponent who needed to be shot down a few rungs from his self-made pedestal! Prideful, she refused any instruction from me.

As for her spiritual re-birth, we didn't talk a lot about her conversion that night at my office. Once in a while we entertained the thought of having a Bible study together, but beyond that our shared faith in Christ didn't seem as relevant as we professed. Again, it was Brenda who brought up the topic, only this time she had a well-thought-out objective.

"I was thinking," she introduced her idea, "how you told me that since you stopped preaching you really haven't found a church to call home. Well, I need to go to church too, so how about if we go to the same church somewhere either in Hamburg or Orchard Park? What do you think of that idea?"

I stared blankly at her, registering what she was suggesting, yet too excited to properly respond. Go to church every Sunday with Brenda Meyers! Wow, what an awesome idea! My office, playing tennis, now church together; what would be next?

Then she dropped this bombshell:

"We could see more of each other."

Be careful not to read too much into this, I remember thinking. After all, it's just church. But what did it mean to her that we could see more of each other? Did Brenda feel a little bit of what I felt for her? My mind and heart were swirling. Then she kind of spoiled the excitement by adding:

"Isn't that what best friends do?"

There was that smile again.

Best friends. Brenda Meyers and I were best friends. And it was a wonderful thing to be a man who has such an attractive woman to share his thoughts and feelings with, and relating to a woman brought a great sense of satisfaction and joy. There was no doubt about it: Brenda Meyers was the best thing that had ever happened to me! Huh, the best thing ever? Where did that come from?

"What about your husband?" I asked sheepishly.

"He doesn't like to go to church." She quickly replied. "My kids don't like to go either."

"What will you tell him?"

"I suppose," forming her missing from home on a Sunday morning excuse, "I'll tell him I'm going to church with a girlfriend."

How interesting! Why would she feel the need to lie when the two of us had no romantic involvement? It's not like we were trying to hide an affair. I suddenly realized that I wished that we were. Swiftly, I buried the thought and clothed my mind in denial that I secretly had such feelings for her at all. I was getting good at that as time went by! Any time I sensed a romantic inclination or yearning for Brenda to be more than just my best friend, I suppressed the feeling by making myself think about other things. My mental techniques worked well and I usually felt better quickly. Later of course, I felt lousy!

"I've been going to this church in Orchard Park called the Rock of Revelation." I returned to our conversation. "The pastor is a young fellow named Jericho, and let me tell you, the guy's an awesome teacher and speaker. He's only twenty-five years old, but he is one of the smartest preachers I've ever heard." I stopped and searched her face for some kind of agreement. I didn't detect any so I just continued. "The church is located behind a car dealership so it's not like people will ever see us together." I paused. "What do you think?"

"Are you sure no one will see us?"

"Positive!"

On the following Sunday Brenda and I met outside the Rock of

Revelation Church. The singing and praise time was uplifting as the presence of God filled the house. Many times I looked over at Brenda to gage her reaction.

"This is church?" She leaned over and asked me with some degree of disbelief.

"It sure is!" I responded enthusiastically.

We had a great time.

Brenda had told me earlier that she was raised Catholic, so this experience of upbeat worship hymns, hands lifted in praise, and shouts of amen, were certainly new to her. Pastor Jericho's sermon blew her mind!

Pastor spoke on our position in Christ from the moment we accept the gift of Jesus in our hearts and minds. Next he related the message to the reality of our own day-to-day existence, choices in life, and the constant battle that wages between the flesh and the spirit. Later, he talked about what he referred to as 'progressive sanctification', and how the believer possesses the free will to walk in the spirit and invite more of God into their hearts. As always, Pastor's sermon was well-presented, relevant, and chock-full of biblical truths to base our lives upon.

"He's always good!" I said to Brenda in the parking lot outside afterwards.

"It was so relevant!" She agreed. "That's what I like. I want the preacher to teach me things that I can use in my daily life to help me sort out and sort through all the issues and pain that I live with. You said he's only twenty-five years old?" Then she added. "I really like him. Can we come back again next week?"

"Of course." I answered.

My mind had left the moment to concentrate on two things Brenda had said. One was her words, or was it a confession, of issues and pain that she claims to live with. Lives with! So it was not some general sense of life's regrets, but an underlying specific ailment or cause of pain that was part of her always. It was as if by saying little, Brenda had revealed much. Secondly, my spirit recorded her statement that she really liked Pastor Jericho so she wanted to return next week. Perhaps my past church experiences have made me a bit cynical, but I immediately felt like we needed to talk about who pastor is, and who Jesus is, and why we came to church in the first place.

"I really like and respect Pastor Jericho," I began," but we always have to be careful to remember that the preacher is just an instrument used by God to speak to his people. Don't get me wrong; I'm not jealous of Pastor Jericho. I told you that I think he's a brilliant young man. God has gifted him with brains, insight, organizational skills, enthusiasm, and speaking ability, but all those tools are useless unless Pastor himself develops, hones, and eventually puts these skills into practice. Here's my point: The stories, the relevant examples, analogies, humor, and whatever other things Pastor uses to pull in his audience are all his, yet the message, the truth about to be shared, and the ultimate goal of this morning's instruction comes from God."

"What's your point?" Brenda wondered sincerely.

"My point is this: Next Sunday Pastor Jericho has to prepare another sermon for the people of his church. His reputation doesn't matter to God, neither does it matter how well Jericho delivered last week's sermon. He has to do it all over again. Pastors have to remind themselves that 'it is not about me', but that it's about a God who will once again invite them to be used for His divine purpose."

"You think," Brenda interrupted, "that I want to come back next week because Jericho is such a dynamic speaker, and because what he spoke about made sense to me, don't you?"

I nodded my head.

"Remember," she proclaimed, "it was my idea to go to church together. I know why I'm here."

Somehow I think I just got told off!

For the remainder of the summer we added church to our usual tennis matches and chiropractic adjustments. Except that on one particular Sunday morning Brenda failed to meet me at church. I found out why later when I read the Buffalo News.

When I read the newspaper I always look through the obituaries and the hospital reports. I am intrigued by the lives of the deceased. I note whether or not they were married, how many children they had, and if they were members of a certain church. It's cool when you read about someone's life and you discover that they were married to the same person for over fifty years. I admire that type of commitment. I should have been able to do that!

I browse the hospital reports to see if anyone I know has been admitted or discharged. I was shocked to find Brenda Meyers name there. Yesterday she was both admitted and discharged. What was that about? There was no way I could call her so I knew that I would just have to be patient and wait for her to contact me. She had already been discharged so how serious could it be? Then it hit me! The bruised back the day she first came to my office, the black eye of the lady driving the Honda Civic, and now a hospital emergency room report. I had a feeling that she was leaving out some important events of her life story.

He abuses her!

The realization made me physically sick! My stomach was churning and for the first time in my life I knew what a headache felt like. My mind screamed out in anguish for this dear lady whose friendship meant so much to me. I began to torment myself, imagining the things he probably does to her. Push her into walls, twist her arms, slap her face, (my God, how could anybody slap that beautiful face?), and all this time she remains the dearest, most upbeat, and positive friend I've ever known. My God, he hits her! How could he possibly do that to a sweetheart like Brenda?

A couple of days passed by and still no word from Brenda. On the following Tuesday night as I prepared to leave the office, I saw her blue Honda Civic pull up to the building. I watched her get out of the car and noted nothing physically different about her. No black eye, no limp, no antalgic lean, but only a slow deliberate stroll up the sidewalk and through the front door. Our eyes met.

No smile either.

I couldn't help myself as I rushed towards her and put my arms around her.

"Why didn't you tell me?"

Pulling back from my embrace Brenda tapped my shoulder, and only then did I get to see that magnificent smile.

"I've left him."

She then released herself and walked into my reception area.

"You coming?" She asked, turning around to look at me. "I really need an adjustment."

I remained at the office and talked to Brenda about the horror of her emotionally and sometimes even physically abusive marriage. This time, she did not hold back. She told me stories of frightful episodes of violence throughout the years and how for the sake of her three children she remained in a union that was life-threatening. There was never any rhyme or reason, no predictable patterns of behavior that seemed to explain the nature of this man, Joseph Meyers. He was not an alcoholic, nor did his past seem to excuse or foster his erratic behavior. He was a business man, well-off financially, an involved member of the Hamburg community, and a man whose treatment of his family would have stunned his closest friends, associates, and other extended family members. Only Brenda and the children knew of the fear that reigned in their household.

"Where are you staying?" I asked.

"For now, I'm staying with my sister and her family in Williamsville. Eventually, I'll get a place of my own."

"The kids?"

"They're with me." Brenda informed me. "Joe wanted it that way too. He says he's going to seek help for his issues and for the time being we agreed that it is best to keep him away from the kids too. They've seen and suffered enough!"

The man abuses his own children?

For a brief instant my mind turned to my own children. Dear God, I adore them! I would never strike them in any abusive manner because I treasure their lives and I can't help but seek the best for them. When they were younger there were occasions when their little rumps needed a good swat, but not their faces or their extremities! My thoughts returned to Brenda's children. I've never met them and know little to nothing about them, yet aside from the physical abuse suffered, how do you measure the mental, emotional, and psychological effects of such treatment? They probably love their poor, sick father very much. I'm sorry, but a man who strikes and bullies his dear wife and own children is a sick person! There is no other logical explanation. Perhaps there's hope for a man like Joe Meyers. Maybe even a chance of reconciliation and restoration with his wife and kids. I could never understand how Brenda would even consider returning to the potential for that treatment, but relationships are so complex, so psychologically-charged, that I suppose anything is possible. Brenda herself just used the words, 'for the time being', to describe the present state of her family's predicament. For the time being? What did that mean?

"I'll never go back to him." Brenda suddenly spoke as though reading my mind. "I know you're thinking that with all the mistrust, the controlling, and the constant following of me everywhere I go, and that I still stayed all these years, that I won't make this final. But you're wrong! Joe has been physically abusive on occasion, but it was rarely in front of the kids, and we also had long stretches of calmness in our marriage where things were ok. Still, that's way too much for me. I'm done with it!"

"Do you love him?" I wanted to know.

"I haven't loved Joe for years now." She lamented. "In the beginning we had feelings for each other, but from the time we were married I wanted out of the relationship."

Boy, that sounds familiar.

"I remember," Brenda resumed, "during the first year of our marriage how hard it was, how much I just wanted to run away, and start my life all over again somewhere else and with someone else. Joe always thought things were fine. He had his career, a wife at home, three kids, a house, and he could have lived the way we lived forever."

"What do you mean by the way we lived?"

"We have lived like strangers!" Brenda confessed. "Oh, not really strangers, but hardly like two people who are supposed to be best friends and share a level of intimacy with each other. Our sex life was horrible! It was non-existent, really, and I avoided every encounter at every turn. I told you once before; I hated sex with Joe! Sure, I let him have me from time-to-time just to keep the peace around the house, but I avoided sex more often than not. When we did it, I would try not to think about it, and hope that it would be over soon. I know that's a horrible attitude and I tried to enjoy it at first, but I never could. "

Been there, done that!

Sex, or as I prefer to call it, making love is a gift from God to we humans. It is a physical expression of our love for the other person. It involves not only our bodies, but it incorporates our mind, our heart, and our spirit, every facet of our being as the two become one. Sex is intended to be a pleasurable experience. Unfortunately, for Brenda, it was not.

I just realized something.

A part of me, that selfish life is all about me part of me, was actually glad to learn that Brenda hated her sex life with her husband.

Is it any wonder Jesus had to come?

Brenda stayed and talked at my office until almost ten o'clock. We mostly discussed the difficulties of her marriage and her current plans. Living with her sister in Williamsville was only about a fifteen minute move from Hamburg so when September arrived, she could drive her daughter to Hamburg High School, while her son continued to attend Erie Community College.

There were an astounding number of similarities between Brenda's marital woes and my own past dealings with Janine. Her husband and my wife sounded like clones at times! Both were controlling, manipulative, insecure, bullies, and blamers of their spouse for their marital unhappiness. How do people get like that? Or better yet, why do they choose to remain that way? Brenda would share how Joe would hide their finances from her, and I marveled at how Janine did the same. Her husband always accused her of flirting with other men and preferring to go out with her girlfriends instead of being with him. Jealous, he assumed that she went out with her friends to meet other men. Janine was just like him! Brenda told me that the majority of their big arguments concerned how they raised the children. Joe was overly authoritative. So was Janine!

"He always accuses me of never supporting him when it comes to the kids." Brenda explained.

Those were practically Janine's exact words on the same issue.

Now I'm all for supporting my spouse when it comes to discipline, family rules, expectations and the like, but there's a problem when these demands are completely unreasonable. Then what does a sensible, caring husband do? How do I support what I can never agree with? Obviously the answer is to sit down with Janine, discuss the decisions amiably, and form realistic expectations in order to reach an agreement.

Yeah, right!

For one, it grew increasingly impossible to talk with Janine about anything! You see: She talks to me! She tells me what is best. She knows. My job is to listen. And as always, God agrees with her. Or so she claims.

Give me a break!

As I listened to Brenda tell the tales of their joint-child rearing, the similarities between her husband and Janine were striking. I always like to keep things as simple as possible when attempting to understand disagreements. A friend asked me once what I thought were the foundational issues between Janine and me.

"We both want to be the man!" I answered.

That wasn't God's plan.

The obvious question, I suppose, is what is God's plan then? What is the marriage relationship supposed to look like? When I make the point to Janine that only one of us can be the man, my understanding is that we were created differently for a purpose. Men and women are different! One is certainly not better than the other, or more valuable, or more significant. Different, that's all.

Not everyone believes that the Bible is the infallible word of God. I can respect that. As people we come from different backgrounds, viewpoints, philosophies, and belief systems. What we all have of course is free will. Having said that, of my personal free will I have chosen to accept and believe that the Bible contains the truth as God presents it to us. The Bible contains a lot of information about a lot of topics, such as the creation of the earth, the history of early mankind, the Jewish Nation, and ultimately the Lord's plan for salvation through belief in Jesus Christ. But this book also deals with a wide range of topics such as finances, child-rearing, respect for others, generosity, health and hygiene, and marriage. So according to the Bible, God has a blueprint for the relationship between a man and a woman. Admittedly, I failed to do my part. Apparently, Brenda Meyers and her husband are guilty of doing the same. Some couples live out the biblical blueprint without ever reading a word about it, completely oblivious to its existence. I, on the other hand, knew all about it before I was married yet couldn't, or wouldn't carry it out!

Here goes:

The Bible tells the man to love his wife. In other words, treat her like gold, lift her up, be generous to her, show her daily how valuable she is to you, and that you would die for her if need be. The woman is told to respect her husband. I suppose that implies supporting his decisions, appreciating his hard work, believing him when he tells you things, and trusting his ability to lead. Yes, I know it's controversial but God expects the man to love and cherish his wife while at the same time serving as a strong leader for his family. Note: serving! It's not all about him. He lives for her and the children. He treats them well. But note also: Only one of them is designated to be the leader. I repeat: This leadership role does not mean better! It only suggests a difference. No more, no less, simply different!

In my house Janine wanted to be the leader. I did too. Only one of us was called to be, while the other was not. That's a recipe for a disaster!

An obvious question though would be, what if the so-called designated leader doesn't live up to his billing? Then what? Or an even more interesting concern would be the very real likelihood that the wife is better suited to lead in many areas. I don't have an answer that will soothe or please everybody. I'm a Bible guy. It says that I'm to be the leader of my family so I try to do the very best I can to lead well. In reality, decisions should be jointly agreed upon, sensible, realistic, and made after great debate and discussion with your wife. Her input on all issues is equal to the husband. No one is better, and no one's opinion is more valuable than anyone else. People are people! My point is this: Both spouses cannot be the man. One of you, when agreement is hard, needs to step forward and have the final say when a decision is necessary. The Bible says that that falls upon the man!

It became very obvious as I listened to Brenda share her personal drama of life with Joseph Meyers, that he was not following biblical principles. Was he the boss? Sure sounds like it, owing to the way Brenda claims he likes to have full control of finances, her time and whereabouts, and that he makes all the important decisions without seeking her input. Question is: is that a definition of leadership? I don't think so.

I'm a middle school math teacher. One of the topics I teach every year is called inequalities. Here's an example: Leader does not equal boss! In a business the boss calls the shots, and if you don't like it, go get another job! You should be treated well and there are laws to protect people from abuse of power. A boss can be a leader, but the title of president, or vice-president, or chairman of the board, doesn't make it so!

A leader sets an example.

He is there for everyone else. He accepts the responsibility of setting the tone, showing how it's done, encouraging others, loving no matter what, and taking the initiative of making sure that everyone is included, feels wanted and needed, and is making their contribution to the big picture. A successful husband doesn't lord power over his family. That's what an insecure man does. And if things aren't working as well as they should, well, he's the one who always has to step up and accept a good portion of the blame.

I'm a big fan of the New York Mets. Last year their manager and leader, Willie Randolph, was fired. The team had blown a big lead down the stretch the previous fall, and when the next season started the losing continued. Randolph was the recognized designated leader of the Mets. When the team didn't perform up to expectations he was held responsible. Now I'm not a biblical scholar by any means, but if I read my Bible correctly, God does not want to hear excuses from me about how difficult a wife Janine was to live with. And she was difficult! No, I'm the appointed leader. I set the example. If the team is losing, I need to accept my portion of the blame.

Alright, so I never once hit Janine, nor did I hide finances from her. I did not attempt to control her or monitor her every move, just the opposite was true in fact; I let her do whatever she wanted. I probably sound like a better husband than Joe Meyers. Problem is: God doesn't make those types of comparisons. I have my own unique circumstances to be held accountable for. He still expects me to do my best to lead my family. In many ways I would tout myself as very successful. I have witnessed the fruit of raising good kids. Only it is very likely that I have failed them in some ways by divorcing their mother. Did I try my best? Yeah, at times, I suppose. Will the Lord someday give me another chance to be a good husband for a different woman?

I hope so!

In fact, as I listen to Brenda Meyers talk about her marriage, I can't help but wonder if the hand of God is at work in my life right at this moment. Wouldn't that be something! Me and this beautiful best friend of mine, Brenda Meyers!

Could you imagine that?

Chapter 6

DURING THE LAST FEW weeks of August I spent more time than I ever had with Brenda. We played tennis nearly every day. She stopped by my office even when she didn't want an adjustment, coming over just to say hello or staying and having dinner with me when we ordered out. One time she surprised me with a turkey-and-cheese wrap that she made at home. It was delicious! Still, we both kept our relationship low-key, avoiding any romantic overtures, while our friendship blossomed daily. My children knew nothing about her, and Brenda's kids had yet to meet me. We talked once about bring everybody together for a picnic at Delaware Park, but we decided it wasn't really such a good idea. Brenda's husband was still very much in the picture and continued to check up on her comings and goings in his usual suspicious manner. Joe was attending counseling for his anger and control issues, yet during the few times that Brenda interacted with him she noted no real change.

"He wants me to come home." She told me one afternoon as we rested after a game of tennis.

"What did you tell him?"

"I told him that I was never going back with him." She replied, matter-of-factly. "I told him that things were just not working and that it's been that way for a long time now."

I was gaining hope!

"He says that," she resumed, "it's not that bad and that all couples have their rough spots. But I asked him why he would to continue in a relationship that's 'not bad'. Then he says to me that I never try, and that if I would just try to make it work, we could be happy together."

"So what did you tell him?"

"I told him that I don't want to try anymore. I don't want to be with a person for the rest of my life, just trying over and over to make it work!"

"And?"

"Of course, he was upset, so he stormed off and went to talk to the kids."

When Brenda would leave, my mood was usually a mixture of joy and sorrow. Joy because the time spent together was a shot of hope, a glimpse into what life could be like with a woman who liked and respected me. After all these years with Janine, I had forgotten how nice it was to be with a member of the opposite sex. I missed it.

Brenda and I also got involved at the Rock of Revelation Church. We went to a church picnic together, played in a church volleyball league, and regularly attended a small Bible study. I was divorced and Brenda was separated, yet we were greeted and welcomed with open arms by the wonderfully kind people of the church. Afterwards, Brenda and I would go out to a Friendly's or a Perkins Restaurant and talk about our evening or just simply enjoy one another's company. On occasion, Pastor Jericho, or his brother, Jerome, or other people from the church would join us. We stayed for hours sometimes discussing the goodness of God and the many blessings we were each grateful for. There was always plenty of humor, stories, and sometimes even tears. Prayers were made, spirits were lifted, hearts were mended, and new friendships were forged.

Still, part of my joy was tempered by the frustration of knowing that I felt much more than just a friendship for Brenda Meyers. It was hard to stop myself at a certain point in a discussion, or to pause when my hand wanted to reach for hers across the restaurant booth. Our friendship was awesome! But I yearned for it to be much more!

There were nights when I would return to my apartment, practically unglued because of my growing fear that Brenda would eventually return home to her husband. What if the counseling helps? What if he proved to her that he was restored and changed and that he was ready to be the good husband he was intended to be? What if Brenda herself sensed that it could be true, and grew to realize deep down in her heart this was why she married Joseph in the first place. Of course the biggest question that concerned me was: What happens to me then?

Some people say that it is impossible to be best friends with someone of the opposite sex. Add my name to the list! Brenda is a great lady, and I really like who she is, how she handles and presents herself, and I especially like the way she thinks. What's not to like? Intelligent, kind, friendly, good sense of humor, athletic, caring, hard-working, and oh yeah, a physical knockout! I realized one night as I was out walking that I couldn't do it! There was no way that I could be 'just friends' with Brenda Meyers. From the moment I first met her at my office over a year ago, I was smitten by her. Now that separation from her husband made her relatively available to date, I was downright nuts about her!

So what do I do?

On this warm August night I knew that I had reached a crossroads. I had to tell her how I felt. There was no way around it. To continue on like this, pretending that all I felt was a friendship for her, was not only killing me, but it was deceptive, misleading, and frankly, dishonest.

I had to tell Brenda how I felt!

She came to my office for an adjustment like she often does right before I'm about to close. She was still living in Williamsville with her sister, but she made the drive to my office because she told me once, 'I like spending time with you'. There was never any pretense with Brenda. She always told me exactly what she thought, or why she did the things she did. Tonight, I would be the open book!

Following her adjustment, Brenda sat on the chair next to the chiropractic table. I sat straddling the table looking at the wall to her right. Neither of us spoke for a minute.

"What are you thinking?" She broke our silence.

I turned to her and smiled sadly.

"We've got to talk!"

Brenda gave me a look of surprise. I could tell that she recognized that this talk was going to be a lot different than our previous ones.

Here goes:

"Brenda," I began by saying her name, which I rarely do, "I can't begin to tell you how much I enjoy our relationship. This is probably the best friendship I've ever had."

"Probably?" She teased to ease the mounting tension.

"Okay," I smiled, "this is the best friendship ever! Only," I reestablished the seriousness of the moment, "I need for you to know something else that is true about this relationship."

She leaned forward with interest. It was crunch time!

"I'm really infatuated with you!" I blurted out. "I can't continue any longer without you knowing how I feel about you. You're more than just my best friend, and incredibly, you really are that: my best friend! But I feel so much more, that is well beyond the boundaries of a platonic friendship. I can't help it! You're a gorgeous woman, and even though I acknowledge what a wonderful, kind, intelligent person you are, I can't deny that I'm affected by the way you move, the way you toss your hair when we talk, your eyes, your breasts, and that awesome butt!"

Brenda actually smiled broadly.

"I am so smitten with you." I continued what was paramount to totally embarrassing myself. " I think about you all the time! When I wake up in the morning, you're the first thing on my mind and my last thought when I go to bed. I know it sounds corny but you affect me in ways that are new to me, in ways that make me glad that I'm alive and that I'm a man who can admire a woman such as yourself. You make me feel totally relaxed and I am completely myself when I am with you. No other woman has ever done that! I just think that if we are going to continue to be friends then you deserve to know the reality of how I think about you, how I dream about you, and how more than anything on earth I want you to be my own!"

My God, what a loser I must seem like to her! But I had to tell her; she deserved to know, but now I was afraid that I may have ruined the friendship we did have, and that there was no going back. We would never be what we were ever again! I had either destroyed it, or what? I stared at Brenda as she sat there, subconsciously hoping that she could deal with this new information, sift through it, and remain the dear friend she had become to me.

She was simply looking at me as if she too were struggling with the awkwardness of the moment. Then she pursed her lips nervously and shook her head ever so slightly.

"Didn't you know I felt the same way?"

What?

Honestly, never in a million years did I expect that response from her. No matter how many times I wondered to myself if she had feelings for me too, no matter how comfortable she seemed with me, and dare I say, happy when we were together, I could never bring myself to actually believe that Brenda could feel the way I did! This was incredibly awesome news!

"I'm infatuated with you too!" She pronounced firmly. "Why do you think I come here so often, or asked you to be my tennis instructor, or wanted you to take me to church? How could I not be? You tell me tonight how deeply you feel about me, holding nothing back, risking the very real possibility that I may not feel the same, and you do it because you believe that I need to know. Everything you said just now, you confessed for my sake, because you're a man who cares deeply about me as a person, not the sex object that as a man you also take note of, but as a person with needs, dreams, visions, and past hurts. You have always been great to me, did you know that? And my feelings for you are probably just as strong as yours are for me!"

I sat and listened, stunned, and too thrilled to utter a single word in return.

"I think you're a beautiful person." She said out of the blue. "I really do. I am as physically attracted to you as you are to me, but what I really think is beautiful is who you are!" Brenda paused. "You're a beautiful person."

In a split second my mind spiraled into the past. I remembered Betty King telling me the ten things that were wrong with me, and Janine echoing a similar mantra of complaint. I recalled that I resolved once to change who I was, improve my character and qualities, and just like I used to make up nicknames for myself like, 'white lightning', or the 'sunshine kid', I gave my goal a name. I told myself that I wanted to be a beautiful person! Now here today, a woman whom I admired and thought the world of, was pronouncing out loud what I'd long time hoped would be true. Someone would see me as a beautiful person!

The contrast between this moment and all the years with Janine was too striking to overlook. Even though I knew that my wife's accusations of pervert, selfish, self-absorbed, coward and the like were not true, nevertheless, a need to be encouraged, uplifted, revered, and respected never left me. I never fell for Janine's lies, but at the same time, my desire to be recognized as a good, caring, and loving man always remained. I was not about to feign embarrassment or rebuke Brenda for her comments because a part of me agreed. There is beauty in me! I do have value. I can help make the world a better place. I was worthy of God to die for, and the beauty of this life within me is capable of positively affecting those around me who, in need of a lift, a pat on the back, an encouraging word, or a point in the right direction, I can help. No one had ever called me a beautiful person before. And who better to hear it from than my best friend!

I'll never be able to understand how the human mind can ponder all of that in a split second, perhaps it's more deeply subconscious, but I quickly recovered myself to the present moment and was glad to simply know that I was here in my office with Brenda Meyers and that we had something going!

"So," I picked up where we left off, "does this mean that I can ask you out on a date?"

"I've been waiting!"

"Will there be a goodnight kiss?" I asked playfully, trying to be cool at fifty-eight years old.

"If you're lucky!" She answered smiling. Next she added, "If you're really lucky, there may be more than that!"

Whew!

I was ready, excited, and looking forward to our first date with great anticipation, but mostly I felt grateful. What an odd reaction to experience at a moment like this. To who, to what, and of all things, why that? Obviously, there are no guarantees when a man dates a woman, but all I could ever hope for at this stage of my life is a chance. For that matter, a second chance, with a woman who I already cared deeply about, and whom I had dreamed about having this opportunity with!

"Can I take you out to dinner?" I proposed an idea for our first date.

"You've already done that many times." Brenda correctly pointed out.

"Yeah, but this time I'll pay." I countered.

"You always pay."

"That's true."

Brenda held out her hand to me so I took it into my own and rubbed my thumb across the back of it.

Electricity!

"We've never done that before." I noted.

"Yes we did." She shot back. "At the church picnic we all held hands and prayed together for a blessing on the meal. I held your hand and you rubbed the back of mine just like you did now." She stopped speaking for just a moment. "I remember," she looked right into my eyes, "it sent shivers all through me."

"Me too!" I said, remembering the moment as clearly as if it were happening now. "When Pastor Jericho finished the prayer we both turned to each other and smiled. And," I recalled excitedly, "we even held our hands together a few more seconds before letting go."

I don't know how I knew, but I was suddenly positive that I was rubbing the back of the hand of the woman I had searched my entire life for. Then I remembered something:

"I want very badly to kiss you." I openly confessed. "But we can't until you've resolved issues with your husband. If we're going to do this, then I need to know that I'm not some stop-gap boyfriend who comforted you during a trial separation from Joe. I'm not asking you for a promise of permanency, but at least I want to be certain that I'm someone special to you, someone possibly worth giving up your marriage for, because, well," I was experiencing difficulty expressing myself clearly, "because what I feel for you is really a lot more than infatuation . I can't get you off my mind. I've been hurt before, and quite honestly, if I let myself go with this the way I know I want to, well, I'll be putting myself in position to be hurt all over again!" I smiled faintly. "I really like you!"

I must watch too many movies!

Brenda and I were so open, so honest, and making ourselves so vulnerable to each other, that this level of intimacy seemed like it came from some carefully written script from a romantic movie. Only, this wasn't a movie, and there were no cleverly construed lines of dialogue to add interest or suspense to a romantic tale. This was real life, my real life, and I knew that I was about to plunge headlong with no guarantee of a happy ending. Today was the beginning. Today I would take my first step, and I was not the least bit afraid of where I may be going, nor frightened by the memory of past disappointments that could easily have changed my mind. No, there were no signs of risk here. It was going to be full speed ahead. The throttle was wide open and I had the accelerator to the floor! That's how to live life! We live only once and then we die. That's definite. What happens in between is up to us and how we decide to travel. Take no chances, create no fruit! That's biblical.

All the while as I sat on my adjusting table Brenda was watching me. She could probably tell that I was thinking about things, and once she nodded her head as if to share her understanding of what was going on in my mind. We were that close.

She scooted forward on the chair, and with her elbows on her knees, she cupped her face in her hands. All I could think of was how beautiful she looked!

"Are you in love with me yet?" She asked me, and I knew that she was serious.

"You bet I am!" I quickly and truthfully replied.

"Good!" Brenda answered back as she shifted in the chair. "Because I'm in love with you!"

Then as if the power of self-control were temporarily dissolved, we both leaned towards each other and kissed. Her lips were soft and sensual, just as I imagined and it took my breath away. It was a great kiss! When she pulled her head back she smiled broadly.

Well, so much for my commitment not to kiss her until matters with her husband are resolved. My God, please forgive me, I've just kissed another man's wife!

Over the next few weeks Brenda Meyers and I kissed a lot! She stopped by the office every night that I worked and stayed until ten o'clock or later. Janine had the kids on nights that I worked, so I had all the time in the world to spend with Brenda.

I was so very happy!

We went out to dinner a couple of times, always with friends from church because we feared suspicion of the true reality of our relationship, since Brenda was still married. After some relentless persuasion on my part, Brenda came to my apartment to meet my children. Sydney was still with me now that she had graduated from Riley College and Garrett and the twins joined us for a meal that Garrett actually cooked himself. It was one of his specialties, hot Italian sausage, macaroni and garlic bread. We had a wonderful evening.

Interestingly enough, my kids liked Brenda and appeared to be glad that Dad, after nearly three years of being divorced, brought a woman into the house. Their mother had introduced them to more than a few men over the past three years, yet they never spoke to me about them. I would ask questions on occasion though not out of jealousy, but curiosity. Quite honestly, I hoped that Janine would re-marry so I could stop the alimony payments. I continue to look forward to that day!

Even though my kids never said a word about Mom's boyfriends, I could tell that they didn't like it one bit! Sydney once remarked that she thought it was stupid for her mother to date. A part of me was a little flattered by their non-reaction because I believed that I knew what it meant: They loved their Dad and considered Janine the bad guy because she's the one who sought the divorce. I suppose that in their young minds the unresolved question mark loomed: How could Mom divorce Dad? There was no reason to, and as they grew older they were capable of figuring things out for themselves, and no doubt arrived at the conclusion that the only real reason was that their mother was unappreciative, wildly selfish, and either unable or unwilling to keep a commitment. I think that to this day, three years later, my children maintain a level of anger at their mother for her unjustified act against me. What do I think? Well, I look like the good guy!

Since the divorce, Garrett rarely if ever stays with Janine overnight. I'm not even sure if he ever visits her. I don't ask him any questions, nor do I gloat about him choosing me as his primary caretaker. I do remember Garrett telling his sister once, 'he's the only parent I've got', and pointing at me! I recall thinking later on how Janine lives in a six-bedroom house, receives thirty-six` thousand dollars a year to use as she pleases, although rarely spending even a dime on the kids even though a portion of the money is specifically for child support. She's got all that! But I have the kids! They stay with me practically all the time. When Sydney came home for summer vacation she also lived with me. Awesome! I wouldn't change a thing about how it all came down just because I got them!

The same night that Garrett made his 'only parent I've got' comment, I told him that his mother said that he called me a pushover because I supposedly always give in on disciplinary issues.

"What's a pushover?" Garrett asked me.

Just as I thought.

If the truth be known, there are probably many factors as to why the kids stay with me that have nothing to do with parental preference. The big house on the hill that Janine and I had built is in the country. My apartment is located in town where the kids can move more freely about, see their friends more easily, or run to the store or Subway for something to eat. Speaking of having something to eat, the kids especially complain that there is little or no food at their mother's house. Janine is into health food. I applaud her discipline, but the kids want their food to have some flavor! That issue has also influenced their decision to stay mostly with me. I bought the kids a PS-3 video game system for the first Christmas we spent together. That tends to keep them occupied. They complain of boredom when they stay up on the hill. So in all fairness to Janine, it's not like they just like me better. They just like where I live better!

Another thing is that my apartment is their home. It's where they live, and they have a true sense of belonging there because I leave the house unlocked, allowing them to come and go as they please, bring friends over, and eat when they're hungry. Janine keeps the big house locked at all times! Yes, locked! Now I've lived in a number of different homes with my ex-wife for over twenty-five years, and during that time there was never a day that any of our places were locked. Not a day! So just who is she trying to keep out? I never go up there unless it's to clean up the mess she's made to prepare the place for a prospective buyer. And besides: The realtor never shows the house anyway! The children are unable to enter the house that I paid for and had built for all of us, unless Janine is there to open it for them. She has refused to give them a key! Garrett has asked her many times for one. Since the divorce, Janine has yet to allow her children free access to the same home that they entered unlocked for many years, when we were still married! Figure that one out!

One time Garrett's car died in her driveway. A couple of days later I returned with a mechanic to see if we could get the thing started. Garrett informed me that his mother had just left on a vacation with her latest boyfriend. While we were looking at the engine, a neighborhood girl, about nine or ten years old, came up the driveway and with the garage remote in her hand, opened the garage door. The ten-year-old walked into the house and a few minutes later came out with Janine's two dogs on leashes. After walking them she brought them back into the house, used the remote once again to shut the garage door, and left!

The full picture of what I had just witnessed made me angry. Janine refused to give her own children free access to the house, denying them a key, yet hands over the garage door remote control opener to permit a ten-year-old neighbor in to walk and feed the dogs. Garrett has a car. Why couldn't she trust her own son to do it? I've wondered often: What's she hiding in that house that is so secretive that no one is allowed to enter when she is not there? Bewildering! No wonder they prefer to live with me.

Falling in love with Brenda was so easy to do. No bizarre behavior, no high maintenance emotional needs, but simply a woman who was not only beautiful, but normal! For years as I dealt with Janine's selfish peculiarities, I used to always repeat a simple mantra to myself: I just wanted to be with someone normal!

Brenda was just that.

One day we were sitting by the tennis courts and an attractive woman rode by on her bicycle.

"She's really cute, don't you think?" Brenda suddenly pointed out to me.

Wait a second! Was this woman actually inviting me to share what I thought about another woman's looks? With Janine, if I had even accidently glanced the bike rider's way I would have been called a pervert.

"Yeah," I spoke softly and even a little guiltily, "she was attractive. Why do you ask me like that?"

"I want to see what you find pretty. You always tell me how beautiful I am, so I'm trying to figure out why you say that."

What?

As we were sitting in bed at night, Janine used to ask me to draw caricatures of female body parts so that she could compare and analyze my artistic preferences. She would shove a pad and pencil right in front of me and demand that I sketch the type and size of breasts that I liked, or draw the shape of a woman's butt the way I liked it.

"Show me!" Janine would cry out.

I always refused.

With no recourse left to her, Janine would then sketch different female shapes and sizes of breasts, butts, legs, and shoulders and demand that I share my evaluation. She was actually very artistic. Janine would draw pictures of all types of butt sizes, shapes, and create them from all angles. Her breast caricatures were equally detailed.

"Are these the kind of breasts that you like?'

"Are the butt cheeks more rounded or flat?

"How do you like the butt to look from the side?"

"Do you prefer these legs to be longer?"

I told Brenda how Janine used to draw these pictures and become more frustrated by my lack of cooperation.

"Weird! I don't care what you think about other women." Brenda explained. "I know that you think I'm beautiful. Why would I care about anyone else?"

Normal. Brenda Meyers is normal.

Once we were out with some friends from church and we started singing some of our old favorite rock songs from our youth. At one point I sang a song by the Turtles, 'She's My Girl', and a few of the older crew joined in. We had a fun night.

One summer afternoon we were driving in my car when Brenda asked me to sing to her.

"I want you to sing loud." She requested. "I want to hear your voice. Sing like you did that night at Friendly's"

Reaching down into my glove compartment, she pulled out a CD of Barry Manilow's greatest hits.

"I love Barry Manilow!' She exclaimed. "Here: sing 'Looks Like We Made It' for me."

So I did.

Later, Brenda told me that she loved my singing to her and that I had a very sexy voice.

"Someday," she boldly stated, "when we make love for the first time, I want you to sing to me before we do!"

"Sing to you?"

"Yeah," she stated seductively, "I want you to sing to me first. I think it's really sexy!"

Once again the contrast between Brenda and Janine was striking. Janine hated me listening to Barry Manilow and often accused me of harboring some secret past lover who the songs supposedly reminded me of. I told Brenda how Janine felt about my singing Manilow songs in the house while doing the dishes.

"It's a song." She replied. "Who cares about the words? You either like the song or you don't!"

Normal. Brenda Meyers is normal.

When Janine and I first started dating, we used to go out to Chinese restaurants, Pizza Hut, and occasionally to all-you-can-eat buffets. She ate with me at my parents' house during the summers. Somewhere along the line though, Janine's eating habits changed drastically. She became a vegetarian. Now there's certainly nothing wrong with that, many people refrain from eating meat, but my ex-wife took it to the extreme. Only organically grown fruit and vegetables were fit for consumption. Tofu was served three to four times a week for dinner. Special food items that could only be purchased at the local co-op became the source of our family diet. Veggie-burgers, Not-dogs, soy milk, rice dream bars, and other healthy alternatives were not just added to our diets, but became the only foods permitted to all of us! While other children ate pizza at school, my kids feasted on wheat-free, dairy-free, preservative-free, and especially taste-free substitutes. While other kids snacked on tasty desserts, my three children chewed an all-natural fruit strip that they brought from home.

One Thanksgiving Janine decided that instead of the traditional turkey that American families normally eat, we would feast on stuffed squash for the holiday! It was horrible! There was the usual football game on Thanksgiving Day so I told Janine that I was going next door to a neighbor's house to watch it. We didn't have the game on our TV because we were limited to only three channels. Janine strongly felt that the evil of contemporary programming would adversely affect the kid's minds and spirits, so we were not allowed to have cable. When the movie, Toy Story, came out on video, my kids had to leave the room when the mean, toy-destroying, bad kid Sid was smashing toys. Disney portrayed him as an evil, sadistic child, full of hatred, and obviously destructive; so Janine did not want our kids exposed to such behavior. This Thanksgiving Day was probably the only time I was actually glad we didn't get the game on TV. It gave me the opportunity to, not only get away from her for awhile, but I got to eat turkey, mashed potatoes, stuffing, gravy, and pumpkin pie next door! My kids had stuffed squash!

Why didn't I put my foot down and protest her extreme and odd dietary restrictions? I guess I just didn't want to start another fight. Janine had all the facts, figures, and research at her fingertips to support the importance of eating healthy. On the other hand, I had nothing to back up my side, except a desire to eat something that had flavor. I often mused at what Janine would consider a greater sin for our children: that they grow up to be thieves, murderers, or worse of all, fast-food junkies!

One time we left church and I noticed that we were probably one of the only families not remaining for an after service party.

"Why aren't we staying?" I asked her.

"They're having pizza, hot wings, ice cream and soda." Janine responded. "I don't want the kids to see that and not be allowed to have any."

"Isn't there also," I attempted to explain another side, "going to be games, contests, singing, plays, and other things for the kids to enjoy?"

"We're not going!" She pronounced authoritatively.

I can't even begin to recount how many times a similar scenario was repeated through the years. Today, now that we're divorced, Janine's diet has apparently made a U-turn.

"So what's Mom feeding you?" I asked my son once out of normal curiosity.

"Nothing!" Garrett replied.

Then he grew very lively as he began to explain the latest culinary development.

"Mom has a whole freezer filled with steaks She eats steak and salad every night."

Huh?

"Well," I interjected with some surprise, "you guys must like that! Steak every night sounds great to me."

"We're not allowed to have any." Garrett informed me. "They're only for her." Then he laughed. "She says they're too expensive for all of us to have. They're for her new diet."

My money is paying for her to eat steak while the kids claim to eat next to nothing! No surprise there.

Brenda and I go out for a bite to eat fairly often. Dinner together seems benign, harmless, and though we sometimes invite other friends to join us, there are times when it's just the two of us.

Now for a woman with a fantastic figure, Brenda Meyers can eat! She's always hungry, and since she's my princess, I'm always buying her food somewhere to satisfy her hearty appetite. We can't play tennis unless she has food in her tummy! Breakfast is a must! Lunch is usually restricted to the same turkey and Swiss cheese sandwich every day along with a diet Mountain Dew. Occasionally she desires a chocolate chip muffin, slice of pizza, or a salad. Basically, Brenda likes to eat the same things and she likes to eat them often! Still she never puts on a pound and looks gorgeous all the time! Now I haven't seen it all yet, but from what I have observed so far, I think that Brenda Meyers has the best female body I've ever laid my eyes upon. Still, what is most appealing to me is that she eats regular food, watches regular TV, and we can talk together like two people who share a common attraction, respect, and interest with and towards each other.

Normal. Brenda Meyers is normal!

On the Friday before Labor Day, Brenda had divorce papers served to her husband, Joe. The ball was rolling!

Even though I have never seen nor met Joseph Meyers, I can't deny that I feel for the man. I've been through the experience of a stranger coming to my home and handing me papers declaring my wife's intent to divorce me. Your world comes crashing down around you! You wonder how the children will fare, where you will live, but mostly you can't believe that this is really happening.

I need to keep reminding myself that Brenda's divorce is not about me. I am certainly a new piece in the puzzle, but there were many years of disharmony before she first came to my office. So if I'm not to blame, then what is the true source of my guilt? I am in love with another man's wife! Brenda is still married to him. Yet here I am sitting across a restaurant table from her, gazing into her dark brown eyes, and perhaps later this evening kissing once again her soft pink lips. They're getting divorced, right? I'm not the reason. I love this woman deeply and consider her the absolute best thing that has ever happened to me! The real question is: What does God think? Am I being blessed, or am I acting sinfully outside of His will for my life? It feels so right!

This Joe Meyers guy did not appreciate what he had in Brenda. I do! He did not treat her well and did not lift her up as someone special, unique, worthy, or as a treasure to be adored. I do! Throughout their years of marriage, according to Brenda, she and her husband rarely talked openly about their goals, thoughts, dreams, visions, or professed the immensity of their unfailing love. We do!

In God's Word, the Israelites are instructed that the choice between good and evil is constantly placed before them. Choose what's right and reap the blessings. Choose what's wrong and endure the curses. I am in love with another man's wife. Is that okay? Does God take into consideration that I've already spent over twenty-five years of my life with a woman who did not love me and treated me poorly? Does that really matter? Does the past somehow entitle me to some kind of special reprieve? All I know is that I love this woman and that I could never give her up no matter what!

I have never been in love like this! Our physical relationship aside, Brenda and I talk, have fun, and are totally enamored with each other.

We talked openly and freely about spending the rest of our lives together. I wasn't afraid of being hurt. I trusted Brenda. She was not only my lover, tennis partner, and best friend, but she grew to become someone I knew I could rely upon to be truthful and always honest with.

Brenda Meyers is the closest thing to perfection in a human being that I've ever experienced. Okay, perhaps I'm a bit over the line with my evaluation, since nobody's perfect and we all have our flaws and character blemishes. As I got to know Brenda better, two things became pretty obvious: For one, we were meant for each other. This highly romantic relationship was growing leaps and bounds in intimacy, as we grew closer physically, emotionally, and spiritually. I repeat: We are soul-mates! Secondly, as time went by, and as we spent a good deal of that time together, I discovered something else about Brenda Meyers: She's not perfect!

During the fall, the tennis court became the psychological laboratory for the study of human behavior tendencies. Namely, mine! I was a case study to evaluate, analyze, and eventually prescribe counsel of change to. Brenda evolved into my personal psychologist, while I became her difficult patient! Our sessions mostly were centered upon Brenda's astute theory that Lenny Spencer thinks way too much of himself.

One day I hit a hard return that struck the top white cord of the net and then dropped over on her side of the court. My point!

"Woo!" I shouted triumphantly.

Brenda dropped her racket, placed her hands on her hips, and slowly moved towards the net.

"Why did you do that?" She asked, and dare I add, she did not look like she thought it was funny.

"Do what?"

"Why do you have to celebrate every good shot that you make?"

Huh?

"You do." She continued. "You act like you're such an awesome tennis player and that everyone should just stop and applaud your victories."

Everyone? We were the only two people there!

"You have to pump your fist, yell out 'woo', and one time last week you actually twirled your body around after a good shot!"

"I never twirled my body around!" I protested.

"I watched you. It was a twirl!"

Another time we were playing and I raced over into the corner to retrieve a hard hit ball by Brenda. I hit a nice backhand return that sliced across the court as Brenda could only stand there and watch it land fairly.

"Un-returnable!" I cried out.

She stopped dead in her tracks.

I suspected that another psychology lesson was impending.

"Un-returnable? Un-returnable?" She repeated with apparent exasperation. "Why?"

"Why what?" I asked, smiling at her reprimand.

"Why do you have to say things that make you sound like you are the most awesome tennis player in the world? You're so proud of yourself"

"That's tennis lingo." I defended my choice of terminology. "When a player hits a shot that is so good that his opponent can only stand there and watch it; it's called un-returnable."

Another time Brenda dropped her racket to the ground and stormed away from her side of the court.

"I'm not playing!" She said in disgust.

"What did I do now?"

She went over to the cooler, took out a bottle of water, and sat down on the blanket we had put there. When I joined her, she shook her head at me, although I thought I also noticed a little smile.

"Why do you have to have a name for everything?"

I didn't have a clue as to what she was talking about.

"What did you just call that shot you made a second ago?" She elaborated.

"A back-hand slide." I answered. Now I felt a need to better explain my choice of words. "I'm going to my back-hand side, and since I have to reach for it, my feet are sort of sliding along the court, so I call it a …"

"I don't care what you call it! Do you understand that? Why does everything have to have a name?"

One day she really got to the root of my issues!

Following two consecutive missed serves into the net, I yelled out, "I've never missed three serves in a row!"

Brenda immediately dropped her racket to the ground.

"Are you kidding me? Just last week you missed three or four in a row. I was there. I saw it. Why do you lie?"

I acted dumb. Of course I knew that I had missed three in a row before, but claiming that I didn't was my way of having a little fun with her.

"Here's what you do." She began to explain to me. "You tell yourself that something is true, and then after saying it enough times you start to believe it. You do! It's like your mind erases everything that you don't like or want to forget, and then after a while it's like it never really happened. You're like that with your wife. All the terrible things she did, you choose to forget as though she were really a nice person. You keep telling yourself that she wasn't really all that bad and then you actually start to believe it. Well she was that bad!" There was a definite note of exasperation in her tone. "She stole your money, took the house and trust me; she's not going to get married any time soon. See if I'm right. Your wife is going to milk this thing until the very end."

One day as I was riding my bike, I got to thinking about my relationship with Brenda and suddenly had a profound realization. All my life I've searched for purpose, reason, joy, trying to fill a need to understand existence, myself, my goals, desires, and exactly what I seek to make it all meaningful. Now I knew. Brenda Meyers was the culmination of all I've ever really wanted out of life. She embodies in her being all that I have searched for. Obviously, I am referring to my purpose and joy here on earth. I am certainly not about to lift her above my Lord and Savior, Jesus Christ. Yet life on earth does matter. It does count for something, and I believe that when God creates us, it is part of his intent that we each enjoy our lives and be happy. I've always thought of myself as happy. But not like this! At no time in my life have I felt this level of joy and happiness!

"I wouldn't have missed this for the world!" I told Brenda once.

"Me neither." My soul-mate agreed.

Surprisingly, as time went by a portion of our romantic bliss was tempered by Brenda's mild complaints about little things that I either did or failed to do to her liking. I suppose there's nothing surprising about that! Throughout my journeys with women I have discovered that our differences often create dissatisfaction and conflict. Brenda and I were awesome together, but I'm still a man who is occasionally oblivious to a woman's needs, and Brenda is certainly a woman who expects answers and explanations for why her man lives and acts the way he does.

But here's what I really like about our wonderful relationship. Unlike Janine, Brenda doesn't resort to outrageous accusations or displays of emotional drama to get her message across. Brenda tells me what she thinks, and tells me quite directly and emphatically what changes she would like to see me make. Does it bother me that she shares some dissatisfaction with me? A little, I suppose, but what has really enhanced our relationship is that she shares her concerns with respect, dignity, and a foundational love for a man she truly adores.

I don't leave our disagreements wounded or emotionally scarred by unfair abuse. Most of the time, our little arguments leave me thinking, actually considering the plausibility of her complaints and whether I can act quickly to change. The bottom line is that I desire to do everything I can to make Brenda Meyers happy. I really do! I want her to feel good about herself, and I hope that part of the reason why she feels good about who she is, is because she sees herself the way I see her. I always believed that a woman's happiness is a reflection of how her man loves and treats her. Obviously, that is a statement of how I failed Janine. I have never claimed total innocence for the demise of my marriage. I want what I feel for Brenda to shine through so that she can't help but see herself as loved, valued, cherished, and held in the highest regard. So when I hear complaints of how I am failing to prioritize her, I certainly take them seriously. I hate to make her even slightly unhappy.

We both carry cell phones. I enjoy talking on the phone with Brenda because it gives us a solid connection throughout our busy days. Only problem is, I sometimes get tired while I'm on the phone, or I've got other chores or responsibilities and can't talk as freely as I would like. Brenda does not sympathize with my phone dilemmas.

"I called you five times!" She scolded me. "Why don't you answer your phone?"

"I didn't hear it."

"Do patients need to reach you?"

I've heard this one from Brenda before.

"If patients need to get a hold of you," she resumed her minor tirade, "you need to answer your phone. What if I was a patient? Do you want your business to grow? A patient is not going to call you five times! If you don't answer your phone they are going to find another chiropractor."

Back in the spring, before Brenda and I became romantically linked, she asked me questions about my current financial status. She knew all about the amount of money I paid Janine weekly, and the bills I paid monthly to live on. It always bothered her when I shared how I bought things for the kids when Janine refused to help out.

"She's such a loser!" She would comment.

No argument there!

On this particular spring day, our conversation about my finances took a different turn.

"Are you saving any money?" She asked me.

"I wish I could." I began defensively. "But it's impossible. I make enough to pay Janine, pay my bills and do a few things for the kids. It's impossible!"

"It's not impossible!" She shot back at me. "Why do you always say that things are impossible? Let me ask you: Have you ever tried to put some money away?"

"How?" I countered. "You tell me how I can do that? If I could I would."

"Ten dollars a week." She offered an idea. "Can you afford to put ten dollars a week into savings?"

"Wow! Ten dollars a week." I was obviously not thrilled by the idea. "By the end of the year, I'll have a whole five-hundred-and-twenty dollars in savings!"

We argued for well over an hour, Brenda simply trying to give some reasonable, sensible, financial advice, and me stubborn, difficult, and unreasonable to accept change in how I might better manage my money.

As my business continued to grow I adopted a practice of putting aside extra cash each day at the office. The amount was much more than ten bucks a week and today I have seventeen hundred dollars in a separate savings account. I like that! It's nice to have some savings of my own. Thanks to Brenda!

A couple of weeks ago we had a small spat about what we were going to do during Christmas Vacation.

"The kids want to go to New Jersey to see their cousins." I said as I quickly cut-off any holiday suggestions about to be made by Brenda.

The moment I said it, I knew that an old argument was about to resurface. We'd been through this issue before.

"So once again," she started, "it's whatever your kids want. I wish you wouldn't make decisions like this without my input. I am a part of your life too. I thought that maybe this Christmas your wife could take them and we could go away somewhere. I'll get Joe to watch mine; wouldn't you like to do the same?"

A new romantic relationship, even one as awesome as Brenda and I, still had obstacles to overcome. We are both parents, with our own separate families, and our obligations can often be torn between the love of our children and the love for our new mate. Brenda and I were no different and often struggled with our personal priorities.

I broke my right leg tobogganing during my sophomore year at Saint Francis College. A group of friends encouraged me to cut class and join them at the golf course for some winter fun. Easily persuaded, I went along. The second time down the hill a bump jarred my right leg off the toboggan, and when we landed in a bunker my leg snapped. Less than six months later I was out running and playing ball again, but I was never again as fast as I used to be, even though I was only twenty-years-old at the time.

Divorce is like that. I'm still young enough to love, be loved, feel love, and make love, but there are scars from a failed relationship with Janine and I am no longer who I used to be! My broken leg only slowed me physically. Divorce has affected me physically, mentally, emotionally, and psychologically.

Brenda has to deal with the reality of this: Simply put: I'm damaged goods!

Think about purchasing a new car. Never been driven, new brakes, engine, tires, and completely rust-free. Personally, I almost always buy a used car with low mileage because I feel like it's getting a new car in many respects. Used is much less expensive. Well, I'm hardly brand new to the game of love. To use an old expression: I've been around the block a few times! I'm still a good deal, but now Brenda gets me after the heartache, insecurities, and verbal and emotional abuse have taken their toll. Let's face it: I've got miles on me! Okay, I've been repaired, and in my opinion, running better than ever, still my tolerance level for criticism, or even loving suggestions about how I could improve my part in the relationship, is very low. There is now a very real part of me that just wants to be left alone to do whatever I want. And above all things, I don't ever want anyone to tell me what to do! Brenda has learned this about me. She has to deal with it just the buyer of a used car deals with the imperfections of an automobile that was once driven by someone else.

"Every time I say something to you that you don't like, you tell me that I don't respect you." Brenda started in. "This respect thing is very annoying! You would think that it's the most important thing in your life."

It is.

Janine showed little to no respect for my work ethic, preaching, the way I ran my business, how I disciplined the kids, treated her, or even how I valued people and God. Her attitude was completely uncalled for. True, throughout the majority of our years together I highly regarded her opinion, and at times did my best to change. At her request I even attended four sessions of marital counseling with a Christian psychologist in Buffalo. My health insurance covered it, so I figured: why not? There were two rather odd conditions to my going though. One was that I would see the psychologist alone. Janine refused to join me.

"Why don't we both go?" I asked several times.

"I'm not the one with the issues." She would always reply.

"But we're married." I tried my best to explain my point of view. "He needs to see us together, hear from both of us, if he's going to be of any help."

"I'm not going!" Janine declared as if the matter were closed. "I know that I can be a good wife to a mature man. You're the one who doesn't value me and just takes me for granted. You're the pervert who looks at other women!"

It was an issue for her that never died.

"But here's what I want you to do."

Janine revealed the second oddity in her plan.

"Here's a tape recorder. While you're talking to the psychologist I want you to keep this running so I can listen later to what you tell him."

"What?"

If you think it's odd that Janine would make such a request to have me record my counseling sessions, what is even odder, or worse, is that I did what she asked! Two questions: Why did she want to play back and hear everything we talked about, and why in the world would I agree?

Here's the answer to the second question. I always did what Janine asked. I figured I had nothing to hide and maybe it would help the marriage. After all, that's why I went to counseling, to help the marriage.

I walked into the counseling session in Buffalo, tape recorder in hand, looking forward to telling some psychologist all about my crazy married life with Janine. I did exactly what my wife asked.

So why did she ask? Janine balked at my attempt to have her attend with me, yet she still wanted to listen to a tape as if she were present. Hmm! After returning from my first counseling visit, I handed the tape recorder over to her just like a good boy! The next day the fireworks began.

"You told him that I'm jealous of other women?"

"You are." I defended my point of view. "You always think that I'm out looking for somebody prettier than you."

"In one part," she was obviously ignoring my reply, "you tell the psychologist that you are happy with your life and that you have no regrets. Do you remember how he answered that?"

I didn't.

"He explained to you that all the men who seek his counsel are broken, seeking forgiveness, and ready to do just about anything to make amends." Janine was steadily raising her voice. "You sit there talking as if you haven't a care in the world, like everything is just fine between us. Why are you even there?"

"You asked me to go."

"Yeah,' she replied, "but I expect you to take it seriously and make some changes."

By the end of the fourth session the psychologist requested that I shut-off the tape recorder.

"Why are you here?" He wanted to know.

I shrugged my shoulders and smiled.

"My wife wanted me to."

"And where is she?"

"She said she doesn't need counseling. Only I do!"

I could not suppress a knowing smile.

"So," he was choosing his words carefully, "what do you believe your issues are?"

I gave him the most honest answer I could come up with.

"I don't know."

"There's really no point of you coming if you don't have any particular issues that you want to deal with."

"What about looking at other women?" I interjected, making it purposely sound as though I knew I really didn't have a problem in that area.

"It's normal. All men do that. That's how we're wired." He twisted around in his chair. "I believe that this area of concern is your wife's issue, not yours. Obviously, she's a bit of an insecure woman who thinks you are not completely satisfied with her and her appearance."

"I think she's a beautiful woman!"

"That may be true, but for some reason she doesn't believe you. It's her issue. Tell her that I would be willing to talk to her about it."

"Should I turn on the tape recorder?" I asked, half-trying to be funny and half-trying to put him on the spot.

"Why does she want these sessions recorded?"

Now it was my turn to shuffle in my seat.

"It gives her a reason to start an argument, or make a point of some kind, or show me how I'm to blame for her unhappiness. Quite frankly," I spoke very casually, "Janine is a user. She is using both of us to satisfy her agenda."

"And what exactly is her agenda?"

"She wants a divorce." I answered briskly. "But she needs reasons, and since no legitimate ones exist, she has to fabricate issues, create situations that somehow support her right to disobey God's commandment concerning divorce."

I paused momentarily as a realization stuck me.

"Janine is using us and this tape to build her case against me." I concluded. "She needs evidence. That's why I'm here alone, to make it look like I'm the problem child who needs psychiatric care, and she's the poor woman unfairly yoked to me. Your credentials validate that I've been under counseling. That's why she made me come here. She doesn't care if I change or become a better husband; she wants proof, a recording if you will, to demonstrate that she has the right to divorce a man who has emotional and psychological issues."

"Why do you think she got to this point in your marriage?"

I paused again to give it some thought.

"She fell out of love with me, I guess. Janine was young when we met and perhaps became infatuated with an older man. As she grew to become a woman, she saw herself stuck with a guy who was really a boy in a man's body!" I smirked at my own self-analogy. "I like to have fun, play ball, and sometimes I can be a bit immature. Janine probably woke up one day and realized to her dismay that she did not love me. Being a Christian woman and knowing the commands of God, she knew she would be disobeying the Lord if she left the marriage. So instead, she concocted a plan. She deliberately created scenarios, and formed accusations to try and make me see that I was the one who didn't love her, and she cleverly backed up these suppositions with cunning, skewed logic, and seizing every digression on my part to prove her point."

I sounded like I was the psychologist!

"I think you may be right!"

I was right. Janine simply didn't love her husband. She used to tell me all the time that no woman could ever love me, that I didn't know what love is, and that I was totally incapable of being part of a healthy relationship.

Boy was she wrong!

Brenda Meyers loved me. True, she was still legally married to another man, and even we had our little issues, but she loved me and I knew now for the first time in my life what it means to completely give of myself and to love another person! Certainly, I've felt that way in some respect about my own children, but this kind of love is different. What I felt for Brenda was unprecedented. This woman was the love of my life! My wife was oh, so wrong about me. The only reason that Janine could claim that I didn't know what love is, is because to that point, I had never experienced it. Now I had!

"I just wish you would make me the one you consider when you make your plans." Brenda complained on occasion. "I want to see you sacrifice something for me the way you sacrifice for your kids."

I could only gaze at her and smile. It wasn't a smile finding humor at her comments, nor was it a smirk to show distain for her opinion. I was smiling because I have a special someone who is first, second, and third in my life, and though I do make fatherly sacrifices for my children, the one sacrifice I will never make is giving up my relationship with Brenda Meyers! Never!

I'm in love with a beautiful woman. And Praise God, this beautiful woman is in love with me!

Chapter 7

BRENDA AND I HAVE been having this little spat for over a week now. You see: I wanted to go to my thirty-fifth college reunion to be with my old fraternity brothers, and she asked me to compromise the time of my departure from her.

Really a lot of the problem goes back to me being damaged goods. My college friends spend a weekend together every year in October, calling themselves the Columbus Day Campers. Over thirty years ago when we were younger, we did meet over Columbus Day weekend and we did camp outdoors. Through the last twenty years though, the guys stay in motels or beach houses and the choice of weekend is arbitrary depending upon the busyness of their lives. In thirty-three years I've joined them only three times. Before I married Janine, I missed many a weekend outing because I was in South Carolina at Chiropractic school. For the twenty-five years that I was married to Janine, the reason why I didn't join my friends was simple: Janine did not allow me to go.

Oh, I know that she is not my mother and I'm not a child who needs permission, but as a husband, father, and family man, I did seek her blessing. I wanted badly to see my college friends, but every time I brought the topic up my wife flipped out! The reasons for why she didn't want me to go varied through the years, but the theme was usually the same.

"You promised when we got married that you would always be here for me."

I would be gone for a weekend.

"What about how you said you would sleep in the same bed with me every night?"

Janine had already on numerous occasions asked me to sleep on the couch following an argument.

"How can you leave me alone with the kids?"

Or:

"Your friends are alcoholics! Why do you want to associate with them?"

And of course:

"You're always trying to get away from me. Why don't you love me?"

During our twenty-five years together I got to join my fraternity brothers just once. Looking back, I'm not even sure how that happened. But I do remember this about that time: There was hell to pay for a long period afterwards. Janine made her point! If you go away like this when I don't want you to, I will make you suffer long and hard so that you'll think twice about ever going again!

I never did take that chance.

Shame on me!

So here I am today free of the unjust shackles placed on me by my wife, and all prepared to go see my friends at a class reunion, and Brenda is not happy about the time I'm choosing to leave! My reaction is part, 'oh no, here we go again', and part, 'from now on I will do exactly as I please with my life'. The conflict with Brenda is not her fault. I'm the problem! I'm the damaged goods. Brenda is an awesome woman who truly wants me to enjoy a good time with my friends. She appreciates and understands that this is important to me, so she supports my desire to go. Only she wants to spend time with me and play some tennis before I leave. All she asks is that I depart a little later than planned. She wants to see that I value our time together. She's a female. That's how they are! I know this, but the damaged part of me rebels because it senses a bad memory, and the damaged part of me refuses to have anything to do with ever returning to a place I've left behind for good. I struggle with my unwillingness to give up total control of my life, yet at the same time I know that Brenda is not like Janine, and that she loves me and supports me and has no desire to tame or control me for her own purposes. I know all this. If I hadn't spent so many years leashed to a control-freak like Janine, I would handle these conflicts much better. I will improve. I will heal. I won't always be damaged goods.

"You are the most stubborn, difficult, and unreasonable man I've ever met!" Brenda tells me. "All I'm asking is that instead of leaving at ten-thirty, you wait until after noon."

"It won't be worth it!" I try to explain. "The reunion starts at one o'clock and I don't want to miss seeing people I haven't seen in thirty-five years."

Now of course I've never been to a Saint Francis reunion before but I'm talking like I know exactly what is going to go on when I get there.

"I haven't seen my friends in years!" I complain. "I just want your blessing that it's okay to do this. I've waited a long time. Please don't try to stop me."

"You think I'm your wife!" Brenda fired back. "You think I'm just like her, that I'm not going to let you do the things you like. I hate when you compare me to her! It's not fair that I have to take the brunt of all your past issues with her. This is a new relationship. I'm somebody different. I really wish you would treat me that way! You're going for three days to see your friends and that's great. I'm just asking for a couple hours of your time before you leave."

She was right.

I am stubborn. I get things set in my mind that I'm going to do this a certain way, and nobody is going to stop me! It's as though I've escaped the bondage of Janine, only to imprison myself to my own rebellious cell of stubbornness and unreasonableness. I allowed Janine to intimidate and control me, so now no one is even going to come close to having any say in what I do! I can understand my reaction because I'm damaged, still I cannot pander to it because it is not a trait conducive to making a healthy relationship with Brenda. I will improve. I will heal. I will not always be damaged goods.

"I'm not Janine!" Brenda continues to remind me. "I love you for who you are. I respect you and I want you to enjoy the things you like. Yes, there are areas I want to see you improve. I don't always want to play second-fiddle to your kids. I don't want you to think that not seeing me today is not such a big deal because you can always see me tomorrow. There is no guarantee of tomorrow. We need to make the most of today!"

I love everything about this woman!

"You don't know what can happen to us at any time. Sure, I believe that you and me are going to spend the next thirty or forty years together. We plan to go on lots of vacations, play tennis, ride horses, and a whole bunch of stuff. It's okay to plan, to dream, to hope and even believe that these things will happen. But don't count on it like it's a done deal! We don't even know if both of us will be here tomorrow. You always talk to me about how God has given us a free will. You said, 'anything can happen at any time to anybody'. I want you to spend more time with me on Friday. Our time together is so precious! Please don't be so stubborn, and locked into your plans that you won't even consider waiting a bit longer before you leave. I want you to go. I hope you have a great time with your friends. I just want more time with you before you go."

Who could argue with that?

Well, for a few days I did. On that Friday though, I came to my senses and Brenda and I played tennis early in the morning and later we ate lunch. It was the most intimate, romantic lunch date we've ever had. I wouldn't have missed it for the world! Yet I almost did due to my stubbornness and unreasonableness.

On the drive down to Saint Francis I couldn't stop thinking about Brenda. The past year of my life has been the most wonderful experience ever. So different than Janine, Brenda cares about me, roots for me, respects my decisions even when she doesn't necessarily agree, and never stands in the way of my desires. We certainly have our disagreements and I do need to accept her whining from time-to-time, but Brenda is so easy to love, so easy to spend time with, and such a perfect complement to me as my partner. As I drove, my thoughts wandered back to that Saturday morning well over a year ago, when she walked into my office for the first time. It was an ordinary morning, yet unbeknownst to me, God had prepared a gift, the greatest gift next to His Son Jesus, that I've ever received. I recalled how I had once given up on women and romance, and now here I was living a dream. I smiled to myself as I mused over the words of basketball coach, Jim Valvano, who as he was dying, told a crowd, 'never give up, never give up, never give up'!

Life is so strange. At one time I was committed to a relationship with my wife that had a great deal of regret, sorrow, pain, and most tragically, was a daily futility of living without love. God created us to love and to be loved. God is the one who created this whole male-female arrangement. We were meant to complement each other. He gave us the opportunity to reproduce, work together, and His idea of marriage is for the purpose of stability not only within a single family unit, but for the society at large. Can you imagine what our world would be like if all of us jumped from one partner to another routinely? Yet in my personal circumstance the marriage relationship was a failure. I could make excuses, I suppose, but instead, how about if I just accept my part of the blame and move on?

I have done just that.

Brenda is still married to Joe. They've been legally separated for months but Joe is stalling. There is a very real part of me that thinks I should halt the nature of our relationship where it is now, and wait until her impending divorce is final. I have no legitimate argument against that recourse. Honestly, I want Brenda and I want her now, and may God forgive me for my selfish transgression. I can't give her up and I do not want to put a halt to the incredible blossoming of this relationship. If anything, I desire more of her. I want to spend more time with Brenda, have her here with me in my car as I drive to visit old college friends so they can meet the love of my life. I want to sleep with her every night. I believe that our love will grow deeper as the years go by. How can I know such a thing? Well, I'm unable to present any proof of what I believe, except my feeling that when a man meets his soul-mate, he knows it, and it is a special relationship that lasts a lifetime! Aptly put, we were made for each other! Oh, I know I sound overly romantic and perhaps a bit out of mind in love, but Brenda Meyers is far different than any woman I've ever been with. She belongs to me. I belong to her. We are forever!

I arrived at Saint Francis University by mid-afternoon. After a short stroll around campus, I entered the JFK Center to reunite with my old classmates. What a great time! Later a small group of us went into the town of Loretto for dinner. As I sat there with Bill, John, Ed and Jane, I was struck by the reality that our many years apart were quickly washed away by the intimacy of the present moment. It was like we always saw each other on a regular basis. Good friendships are like that. Time apart is not really a factor when the legitimacy of a solid relationship is evaluated. Do I wish I had made more of an effort to see them over the years? Of course! Has that absence altered the bond of friendship? Not in my opinion.

The meal itself was comprised of cheeseburgers, fries, and cokes, but the fellowship was a relational buffet! It was a time to catch up on one another's lives.

"You really met your soul-mate, didn't you?" I asked Bill when we first sat at the table.

"I really did." He responded. "She's great! In fact, tomorrow night we have a date planned and I am really looking forward to it."

Bill's wife, Kathy, has MS. They've been married for close to thirty years, children are grown up, and still he excitedly tells me about a date they have planned for tomorrow night. I love hearing that kind of stuff! I haven't seen Bill in fourteen years. I've always prayed for his family and I imagine that her illness has been difficult not only for her physically, but has also placed a strain on their relationship at times. Yet as soul-mates, they have persevered and even thrived in their love for one another. Through the years I've only been with Bill and Kathy a few times, yet when I asked Bill about Kathy being his soul-mate, I already knew the answer. During those few times I saw them together I could tell. Soul-mates are like that. Their love for one another is so obvious that everyone can see it.

Jane and Ed Karpenski also seem to be soul-mates. They have been together for nearly forty years! I admire that! Ed's a lucky guy and Jane is like one of the guys. They go together like peanut butter and jelly. In all the years that I've known them, I have never noticed an occasion when they were either miffed at each other, or even a little bit snippy. Remember, they're married, and married people have issues with each other, feelings are hurt, tempers flare, and solitude is often sought. I'm sure Ed and Jane have had their moments! Still, they remain happy with one another and apparently content to spend a lifetime together. Soul-mates are like that. I suppose that couples like Ed and Jane or Bill and Kathy are representative of what God had in mind when He said that the 'two shall become one'.

So how do I feel about the good marital fortune of my friends? Am I jealous? Well, if I am, it is only in the most loving and admirable way. I am happy for them. They are an inspiration to people like me who have failed in their marriage, yet believe in their hearts that soul-mates do exist and that life is worth the wait to find yours!

I don't know John's wife well at all. Like me, my old fraternity brother has been through a divorce. We've never really talked about it, but from what I've gathered through the years the cause was a basic fundamental issue that ripples through many an unsuccessful relationship. Put simply: John married the wrong person! He married someone who was not his soul-mate. I did the same.

"So how's it going with you?" Jane asked me.

"I'm doing great!" I replied truthfully. "In fact, I'm writing a novel about my divorce."

"You're still writing?" Ed laughed.

"Yeah, this is my fourth novel," I grinned, "and I think this time I may just publish one."

"Is it about your marriage and divorce to Janine?" John interjected.

"Yeah," I answered again, "I'm going to write a story about a man who is divorced against his will."

"Wow!" Jane exclaimed smiling. "You must have quite a lot of experiences to draw from judging by what you've told us."

I certainly did!

At a reception later that night held at the JFK center again, John and I talked a little about our relationships.

"I've learned not to be defensive." He shared his personal formula for keeping peace around the house. "My wife gets pretty upset when I do that."

"So how is it going the second time around?" I wondered, so I asked him.

"It's good. We have a good relationship; we're best friends and the kids are awesome."

Good for you!

John and his first wife were married for only a short time and did not have any children together. I've never asked, but I imagine that he doesn't even know where she is today. Unfortunately, I'll probably always know where Janine is. Even after the kids are grown up and out on their own, and the house on the hill is sold, she will be phoning, complaining, and expecting me to provide her money for some reason. Still when I think about my friend John's second opportunity at love, I think about Brenda and my own second chance to get it right this second time around.

I left around nine o'clock to head back to New York. So much to think about! It was an absolute treat to visit with old friends, walk around the campus, and laugh about those days when we were still young. There were no jobs to cause stress, unmarried, no children, and a young healthy body that ran and jumped with reckless abandon. Yet as my mind filled with memories of the past, I quickly realized that I could not refer to those college years as the good old days. No, as I drove now thirty-five years later, I knew that I was living in the best days of my life right now! I can think how I like my work, and I'm nuts about my kids, and even though my body can't do what it used to, I've still maintained my health and fitness and I can still play ball. I can think about all of that and weigh it as reasons why I enjoy my life today, but none of those blessings on their own, or even collectively, tells the whole story.

It's Brenda.

From the time I was a teenager, playing all sorts of sports, I looked for her and wished that she was there watching. Like the Moody Blues sing, 'I know You're Out There Somewhere'. On walks through the woods, or reading novels at the foot of waterfalls, I kept this dream of her in my mind. My daughter always teases me about how I like to watch what she refers to as chick flicks. Apparently, what she means is movies that may have some action or comedy, but are really about romance between a man and a woman. I think I've seen "Shakespeare in Love' half-a-dozen times already. The movie couple has a highly charged sexual and deeply intimate relationship that is forbidden by the era in which they live. They are portrayed as soul-mates who tragically cannot be a forever thing. I guess I enjoy watching movies about soul-mates. Now praise God, I'm living out a dream of my own! The old cliché that, 'I have to pinch myself to see if this is really true', fits. At times I still can't believe that this wonderful relationship has happened to me!

Back in the mid-seventies, my friend Jack Jeffries got married. I don't recall much about the ceremony or the reception, but I can vividly remember going for a walk afterwards and thinking about my life. I was not a Christian at the time and knew little to nothing about the God of the Bible, yet I prayed that night, and looking back I realized now as I drove, that my prayer was about Brenda. It was thirty years ago and it went something like this:

"God, I'm really happy for Jack. I'm glad he's met someone and I hope it turns out well for him and Denise."

It didn't. They divorced a short time later.

"I know my special someone is out there somewhere. I know she exists. I don't know where she is or where to look, but I want more than anything to find her. It's what I live for, God. I'm grateful for all the things you've already done for me. I thank you for my health, my parents and brothers, my teaching job, and everything else you've provided. I don't know if I'll ever find her, but I want you to know that it's the most important thing in the world to me, and I just need to ask for your help. It will be a good life even if I never do meet her. But it will never be enough unless I do. Please God, bring her to me. It's all I've ever wanted."

At a Wednesday night church service a few weeks back, Pastor Jericho's brother Jerome delivered a sermon that really hit home. He talked about how the Lord wishes to develop patience, steadfastness, and endurance in each of us. He related an episode in his own life, sharing his personal devastation at a job opportunity that did not work out. He spoke of how angry he was at God and how difficult it was to return to his old job again, knowing that there was something better out there, yet had escaped his grasp. Jerome concluded his message with how a second job opportunity presented itself and how it was not only more conducive to his lifestyle, but paid a higher salary. The point of the sermon was this: God is always good! He hears our prayers and He wants to give us the desires of our heart. Yet more importantly, God wants us to develop character, be people who trust Him during the hard times, and choose to persevere even when we can't see any evidence of impending success. God wants to develop patience, steadfastness, and endurance in us, so that we will be ready when the prayer is about to be answered.

I took Jerome's message to heart.

Thirty years ago I would not have been ready for someone like Brenda.

It took me an extra year at Saint Francis to graduate. I was immature and uninterested in studying. I did not treat my college girlfriend very well either. I was not ready to treasure and value any young woman, let alone a god-given future soul-mate. Had I met Brenda during my college years, I'd have missed it by a mile! I didn't have a clue as to how a man treats a woman, how he is to lift her up, treasure her, or regard her as the most precious gift in the world. Back then I would have blown it and missed out on the greatest thing in my life. God knew that. He would make me wait until I was ready.

Even as I prayed on my walk that night following Jack's wedding, I still wasn't ready. I was over my poor treatment of women, but I was too independent, too focused on my own desires and plans, and hardly prepared to love someone deeply and fully. Women were still like trophies to me, a possession to show-off to my friends and family, and even then only on occasions or at certain times when it was convenient to my agenda. I wasn't ready for a woman to be my best friend, a truly intimate lover, or a life-time companion. Intimacy scared me to death! I didn't know how to let a woman know the real me, the 'me' no one else sees, the 'me' cleverly hidden behind a façade of jokes, bravado, and ego. Even then I was not ready for a soul-mate. God knew that. He wanted for me what I wanted. But He knew that the timing wasn't right. There was still much character to develop and lessons about relationships to learn.

When Janine came along, I believed for a while that she might be the one I'd been waiting for. She was pretty, athletic, fun to be with, cared about others, generous, and committed to her relationship with me. She was a catch! So I reeled her in, married her, and promised to love her for the rest of our lives. The only problem was that Janine changed. Drastically! Oh, she's still pretty and athletic, but I don't know what happened to the girl who cared about others, and whose generosity and commitment disappeared. The last time I saw the original Janine was in the early nineteen-eighties. I haven't seen her since!

Here's an example of how much she changed:

When Garrett graduated high school Janine wanted to have a graduation party for him. We had a big party for Sydney three years earlier when she graduated, but now that Janine and I were divorced, planning a party together was uncomfortable to say the least. I told Garrett to tell his mother that my family was going to throw him a graduation party when we visited in New Jersey later in the summer. That way, my parents, brothers, and other relatives wouldn't have to travel up to Western New York like they did for Sydney. Besides, I was not planning to do anything ever again that involved Janine!

Garrett informed me that his mother wanted to have a party here also. She left a message on my cell phone about her desire to do this, so for a change I decided to call her back.

"I want to have a party here." Janine explained. "I want to invite some of my friends. Garrett can tell his classmates to come. I told him to pick a day and let me know."

Janine and Garrett agreed on a day in July.

Now this was her idea, her desire, and the party was to be at the house where she lived, but a week before the designated date, Janine announced that she would be gone for the entire week to go on a vacation. I can respect that, but what transpired I cannot accept as anything but selfish and totally self-centered on her part.

She told Garrett that she was making hot dogs. My son was miffed!

"Hot dogs!" He complained. "This is supposed to be a graduation party, not a picnic!"

Garrett asked me to lend him some money so he could buy meatballs, chicken wings, and pizza. He decided that he would cook all the food himself at the restaurant where he works part-time.

"We can buy the meatballs, hot wings and rolls at cost." Garrett explained to me. "I'll get up early Sunday morning, go to Pizza-land, and cook it all myself."

"How long will that take?"

"One hour, tops." He assured me.

So that's what Garrett did. Nothing about his mother was spoken between us, but it was readily understood that Janine would have practically nothing prepared for her son's graduation party. It was all her idea, yet she did nothing to make it happen.

By eleven o'clock Sunday morning, Garrett was at his mother's house cooking meatballs and sauce in a portable roaster that he borrowed from his boss. When I arrived around noon I was quickly approached by an angry Janine.

What now?

"I want you to know," she started raving, "that your son broke into the house through the side garage door. He probably did a hundred dollars worth of damage."

The instant Janine informed me of this apparent break-in, I knew exactly what had happened. She had been away for a week without a concern about the party that was her idea, and Garrett, seeing that the lawn needed mowing, took action. He discovered the house locked as usual, but managed to enter the garage through a side door. Once inside, Garrett could open the garage, take out the rider mower, and make the lawn look a little more respectable for the party. I knew that this is what had happened, because a couple of days earlier he expressed his concern about the high weeds along the unkempt pool.

"Can you borrow a weed-whacker?" Garrett asked me then. "The outside looks like the house is abandoned."

"I don't know." Was all I could say at the time.

So now here was my ex-wife visibly upset because Garrett forced his way into his own house that is perpetually locked for reasons unknown.

"Give him a key." I shrugged, suggesting my lack of concern.

"He doesn't need a key. I'm the adult here and I have the right to keep the house locked if I so please."

"He needed to mow the lawn." I responded casually.

"You're his father!" She fired back. "Are you going to punish him for the damage he's done? I could call the police, you know! That would teach him a lesson."

Call the police on your own son for entering his own house? I shook my head and did the only sensible thing I could think of. I walked away from her.

Unfortunately, not a lot of people came to the party. I don't know the reasons, perhaps because it was Sunday, or because Garrett was late sending out invitations, but whatever the cause the turnout was less than expected.

I was very proud of Garrett. He made it a point to greet everyone who came, and chatted with each of them. Quite a number of his high school friends showed up so they played football, hit golf balls, and did things that teenagers do at graduation parties. I know my son was hoping for a larger adult turnout, since they're the ones who bring the envelopes filled with money!

Garrett mowed the lawn, prepared all the food, set up the tables and chairs, so it was a little disconcerting to see a smaller turnout than anticipated. I felt for him. I knew it bothered him.

Meanwhile, I curiously noted that every time I talked with a guest, Janine would stroll over and join our conversation. She apparently thought nothing of standing beside me, her former husband and mate of twenty-five years who she had decided to get rid of, as if we got along just smoothly. I don't know what Janine thinks about me or the present state of our relationship, and frankly I don't care! I don't want to be friends. Oh, I've forgiven her alright, but Janine is not the type of person I trust, or like, or even remotely would choose to spend time with. No thank you, but I have no desire to go back there!

The party ended around five o'clock. As the last of the people were leaving, a couple friends of Janine, arrived. They were the only friends of Janine to come to the party, and they didn't show up until the party was over.

Let me try to understand this:

Janine insists that there be a graduation party at her house for Garrett. The same son, mind you, who she threatens to have arrested for entering his own home. She only prepares hot dogs and a small cake. Then she invites two people! Quite honestly, I was infuriated. Janine demands a party and does absolutely nothing to make the party a good one for her own son. What was that all about? Why this charade?

Later that evening as my anger subsided I spoke on the phone to Brenda.

"This is not the girl I married." I protested. "Janine didn't want a party for Garrett. It was for herself, and then when other things came up that interested her more, she discarded her responsibility in the matter. Once again," I echoed an old mantra, "she demonstrates that she doesn't care about anyone else but herself. Two people! She invited two people to a party that was completely her idea alone. The old Janine Cunningham would never have done that!" I said using my wife's maiden name. "This woman is a stranger. This is not the woman I fell in love with. I don't like this woman at all!"

Afterwards as I sat on my porch the same thought returned to me. What happened to her? Was I fooled by Janine right from the start? Did I only imagine that she was a kind, thoughtful, and caring young woman? Or did her deception take root while we first started dating? Did infatuation cloud my judgment? I've always had this rather hokey theory about what may have happened.

We had been dating for about two years when early in the summer Janine phoned me from New Jersey while I was taking final exams in South Carolina. She had been in a motorcycle accident and hit her head on the ground when she was tossed from the bike. I remember what she told me about that night.

"I blacked out for a second." Janine said as she related all the details of her accident. "But right before that I felt pressure against my chest as if arms were holding me back to prevent me from hitting the ground too hard. I should have died, but something held me back and protected me. Something softened the blow." I could tell over the phone that she was about to cry. "That pressure saved my life!"

I believed her.

Angels?

The Bible talks about the very real existence of angels and since I believe every word of the Bible, I believe in angels too! Now I wasn't there of course when Janine's car veered over to the side of the road that night, but her college friends were. They were driving right behind Janine, returning from a trip to Pennsylvania to visit other friends. They witnessed the entire accident. For the sake of argument, let's agree that what Janine felt that night was true. Arms held her back and protected her from dying. Question: Why would God spare Janine Cunningham, when as we all know, countless others have not been so fortunate? Possible answer: Her time was not up! And where do I enter the picture in God's future plans for the two of us? I suppose that I could theorize that God, since the creation of the world and man, had decided upon Sydney, Garrett, Lily and Layla to be His very own. And I suppose that I could further assume that since Janine and I are the only two people capable of taking part in their formation, that the Lord required both of us to fulfill His desire for our children. I know this all sounds like a bunch of theological hogwash, but if the protective pressure that Janine felt that night was real, then there must be some purposeful explanation behind it! I believe her, but to this day I don't understand it! I guess I'll find out someday when I arrive on the other side.

Anyway, the real point of my memory is this: Janine hit her head on something. Right after that, beginning with summer vacation that year, my once pleasant, cheerful, fun-loving girlfriend started to change.

She grew argumentative, quick-tempered, suspicious, impatient with my behavior, and no longer a joy to be around. As we continued to date and subsequently married, her ravings, jealousies, and outbursts got worse. Was there a relationship between the head injury and this new forming personality? It was just a theory. I really don't know.

One evening as I was palpating the muscles of Brenda's neck, a thought occurred to me.

"Have you ever been in a car accident or had any type of head injury?" I asked her out of the blue.

Lying on her back with her head in my hands, she moved her eyes back towards the top of her head and smiled.

"Never!" She answered sternly. "And don't think I don't know why you're asking me." She added.

I remembered instantly that I had shared my 'why Janine is so crazy' theory with her once before.

"It wasn't a car accident that made her such a loser." Brenda pronounced evenly. "Your wife chose to take advantage of you, steal your money weekly, cheat you out of all your belongings, and deceive you as badly as she did. Don't make excuses for her! She's a loser who didn't deserve a wonderful man like you in the first place. You made a mistake. You never should have married her." Then she smiled again. "Get over it!"

I was over it. Janine could not be counted as a loss in my life. She was never really my soul-mate. I don't believe that we were ever meant to be.

Now Brenda's a totally different story!

Chapter 8

IN THE SPRING, PASTOR Derrick Myles returned to Orchard Park and preached at the Rock of Revelation Church. By return, I mean that Pastor Derrick had left Orchard Park, New York six years before. In the mid-nineteen nineties, Janine and I were invited by a friend to join her at a Sunday service at Assembly Christian Fellowship. Our friend raved about the preacher, Derrick Myles. We were floored that first Sunday by the praise and worship music, and the incredible sharing of the word of God by the obviously anointed Pastor Derrick. Janine and I returned the following Sunday and remained a part of Assembly Christian Fellowship for many years.

When the church held a fiftieth birthday party for Derrick, it was fascinating to witness the immense outpouring of love and adoration people felt for this man. Many love him so, because in a very real sense, they owed him their lives! Pastor had been instrumental in transforming their lives from the darkness of what was for some a life of prostitution, drug abuse, alcoholism, generational poverty, financial ruin, divorce, homosexuality, and other forms of oppression which drown people's spirits in regret, pain, and mostly a sense of hopelessness. Aptly put, Derrick Myles and his ministry made a positive difference in the lives of many here in the Orchard Park, New York area.

During the party I leaned towards Janine and felt compelled to share what I was thinking.

"If people loved and adored me like that, I wouldn't be able to handle it! I would mess it up. I would fall. It would be too lofty a standard for me to maintain."

Well, as it turned out, Derrick couldn't handle it either!

Pastor Myles announced that he was resigning as leader of the church and that his family had been called by God to relocate in Miami, Florida to start a new ministry there. The congregation was shocked. We couldn't believe that Derrick would not be our shepherd any longer. Oh, we gave our blessing to him, but we knew a void would be left by his absence. All we could do was accept his calling from God and continue on. After all, we were at Assembly Christian Fellowship because Jesus was there; we were not there to worship the man, Derrick Myles.

We had a going away party, wished them well, and hoped to see the Myles family again when they returned up north for a visit. Only, it wasn't long before the rumors started, and soon became fact, and our collective hearts were broken by the news.

Pastor Derrick and his wife were getting a divorce. The cause was infidelity on the part of Pastor Derrick. Later we learned of financial improprieties, church funds being extorted to support his affluent lifestyle. Some of that money was mine! I gave it to the church in faith. I heard through the grapevine that he was no longer involved in ministry and was working at a Sears somewhere down in Miami.

He fell. Just as surely as I stated that night at his birthday party how I would never be able to deal with that much adoration, Pastor couldn't either. I'm not making excuses for him. He's just a man with frailties and weaknesses like the rest of us. His fall from grace was sudden, dramatic, and complete.

Just like a divorce.

When I walked out of the courtroom following my divorce, my life with Janine was suddenly, dramatically, completely, and I might add, legally over with. There was no embarrassment, no one to apologize to, no reputation to rebuild, nor any explanation to give.

Pastor Derrick was not so fortunate.

When Pastor Jericho first told me that he had invited Derrick to preach at our church, my initial reaction was welcoming. I loved Pastor Derrick. He was my spiritual leader, a friend, and a mentor that I once greatly respected. Certainly, I held reservations about his honesty and integrity owing to all that had transpired, yet with little thought or effort on my part I did what I believe a man of God is expected to do. I forgave him!

Who was I not to?

I'm divorced myself and I am currently dating a woman who is only recently divorced. During my lifetime, I have lied, stolen, coveted, disrespected my parents, and worshipped items like cars, clothes, sports, chiropractic, and other such idols instead of placing my Lord first and foremost.

I am a guilty man!

That's why Jesus came.

Pastor Derrick is no better or worse than the rest of us. He needs the forgiveness of God also. But there's another command the Lord gives in His Word, and it's contained in the popular prayer that most of us have uttered from time-to-time. 'Forgive us our trespasses as we forgive others!' So I forgave him. Now keep in mind I know little or nothing about what really happened in his life. I am not privy to his marriage relationship, just as no one knows the reality of mine and Janine's. I'm in no position to judge and neither is anyone else in any position to judge my marriage to Janine and our subsequent divorce.

As I listened to my former Pastor deliver his sermon I was struck by two thoughts: One was my recognition of the obvious anointing of God on this man. Derrick talked about transforming lives, being aware of the times we're living in, and preparing ourselves for such a time as this to be used mightily by God. I understand preaching. It's God's way of speaking to his people. I knew too that God was speaking to me on this morning. As a Christian there are things for me to do, to be prepared for, and I am to provide spiritual nourishment to those in need right here in the community in which I live. I may be divorced, but my work is not done! I'm no longer a preacher, but I'm still a Christian on assignment to assist the Kingdom of God in any way I can.

The other thought I had concerned those of us in attendance that morning who for many years sat under Pastor Derrick's instruction. The Assembly Christian Fellowship had reached a membership of nearly 500 worshippers during Derrick's time there. On the morning of his return there was only handful of us present. Who were we? Why were we the only ones who came? And what was it about us that caused us to be there that morning? We had the same information and heard the same rumors as all the others. We learned of the same stories, and knew of the many disturbing facts. Yet we were there to listen to Pastor Derrick, perhaps expecting to hear an apology, or just out of curiosity. Or maybe we were there because we knew in our hearts that God would speak to us through this man.

I wondered: Has anyone felt the need to forgive me for my transgressions leading up to my divorce? A divorce involves a lot of people. Do our children forgive us for the turmoil they were forced to listen to? One day I took a peek in my daughter's journal and read. She wrote: "I have a secret. My parents are going to get divorced." Actually, we didn't get divorced until years later, yet to what extent did my children live in fear of the inevitable?

Do they forgive me?

I haven't seen Janine's parents or siblings and their families in over four years now. When I consider what they must be thinking, my concern is tempered by the reality that they know little to nothing of the truth. Naturally, they have stuck by and supported Janine. What if they knew? Through the years we spent lots of time together during the holidays. They saw the two of us together. How could they not see?

I hope that they, too, can forgive me.

I drove home from the church service that night assured of two very important things: God had certainly forgiven me, and because of that I have forgiven others, such as Pastor Derrick and Janine. I feel no bitterness, harbor no hatred, nor do I need to repress any anger towards the woman I married. It didn't work out, so in the words of Brenda Meyers, 'get over it'!

Speaking of Brenda, I reflect from time-to-time what her ex-spouse Joe and their three children must be feeling about this radical change in their lives. Can her children ever begin to understand how difficult, if not impossible it was for their mother to remain in such a physically-threatening relationship? And now that their mother is divorced, are they and Joe able to forgive Brenda and me for our love for each other? Does God?

Forgivenness…

We all make mistakes, errors of judgment, unwise decisions, and on occasion we purposely sin because we want our way! This is a common thread that runs through the heart of all mankind. Janine, Brenda and I are no exception. We need the forgiveness of others to continue on this incredible journey of life. And we'll always need to be forgiven until the ride is over!

I had a dream one night.

Apparently, I had died, and it was my time to stand before the judgment seat of God. I was scared to death!

"So you're Lenny Spencer!" Someone pronounced with a hint of distain. "This is quite a list of things here."

Then I heard a voice read aloud:

"Divorced, lustful, self-centered, adulterer."

I began to protest that last one.

"She was still married, wasn't she?"

I made no reply, but simply acknowledged that what was written was true.

"When you were married why didn't you do your best?"

Was I supposed to answer?

"So what do you have to say about all this?"

This time I was about to speak, when all of a sudden a voice behind me spoke.

"I'm here on his behalf." I heard the voice but did not look back to see who it was. Besides, I already knew who it was!

This guy came forward and stood right next to me. He hardly looked like the Jesus we've all seen pictures of, but I knew it was Him. And I knew why He was here! My gosh, it's true, I remember thinking; Jesus really is going to step in and take my place!

"So it's you again." The first voice acknowledged.

"It's me." Jesus replied.

"This Spencer fellow needs to pay the piper." The first voice resumed. "Have you seen the list?"

"I have." Jesus sighed. "And I have every intention of paying this penalty in full."

There was silence for a moment.

"This is serious stuff." The first voice continued. "These are not simple mistakes, or oversights, or look at this example here where he claims that he was unable to love his wife because he didn't know how. What a load of nonsense! He knew. He simply chose not to. What I see here is purposeful, intentional, and at times downright sinful, knowing full well that what he was doing was against the Word of God! But he did it anyway. It's a disgrace! This man was given extraordinary health, an abundance of talents and skills, and more opportunities to serve the Kingdom of God than you can shake a stick at, and look at how far short his fruit is from what could have been."

I was crestfallen because it was all true.

"This has to be paid for!" The first voice concluded, before it noticeably softened and stated knowingly. "And you're willing to take his place? Pay this bill yourself? Suffer for him? Is that the deal?"

My Jesus, who didn't look anything like the Jesus I saw in pictures, nodded.

"Yes, that's the deal." Then he looked at me and smiled. "I will trade places with him."

Forgiven!

When I woke up the next morning I discovered that I had an extra bounce in my step. It was one of those dreams that stick with you for awhile. Now I've heard countless times the story of how Jesus is going to stand in the believer's place on judgment day and pay the penalty for our sins. Nothing about my dream was original. Yet it was certainly a nice reminder about forgiveness in its truest sense. So as I made my way towards Brenda's apartment, prepared to do what was once unthinkable, I took stock of my most recent journey.

I'd married Janine Cunningham with the full intention of honoring my vows forever. Early in the marriage it became quite evident that this woman was not my soul-mate, and that this was not going to turn out well. Still, as good Bible-believing Christians, we persevered. Things got worse. Yet along the way some wonderful things happened: Three daughters and a son, meeting and enjoying new friends, and building our dream home. God was always good to us, even when we weren't exactly so good to each other.

I had the opportunity to teach school, to encourage and provide needed discipline to hundreds of young people, many of whom are today hard-working business people, doctors, lawyers, laborers, and of course, parents to the next up-and-coming generation. It wasn't always easy , and it certainly wasn't always fun, but I welcomed each school day as a chance to make a difference, a choice to be a light for these young hearts and minds in an often dark and dangerous environment.

I started my own chiropractic business where I have had the pleasure to service some of the nicest, kindest people I have ever met. As a result of these two simultaneous professions, my bills have always been paid and my debts have been kept low. Once again, I praise God for my good fortune.

I was honored to pastor a small church for seventeen years. God used me, an imperfect vessel, when no doubt countless other men would have served Him better, to shepherd friends who would love and support me, even through my divorce, and show their faith in me by standing at my side during the most difficult times. Can you believe it? God is not only good, but I guess He has an uncanny knack for choosing the least likely, in my case, the least qualified to further His Kingdom.

Yet despite all the many blessings, there was always something very real and significant missing from my life. The blessings I counted were never enough. My joy was never quite complete. My quest for happiness seemed to go only so far.

Until Brenda.

On my way to her apartment I thought back to Pastor Derrick and the infidelity that led to his stunning divorce. He had notoriety, adoration, the anointing of the Lord on his ministry, health, money, personality, and seemingly everything a man could ever ask for. I was jealous of him. Yet for all he had, he was willing to risk it all, his fame, his reputation, his good standing in the community, his integrity, and even his own family to be in the arms of another woman! Today he is remarried to this same woman he apparently had to have.

Why?

Is there something more important than fame, recognition, reputation, even our own families that causes us to search for it, dream about it, and chase it down because it's the one thing on earth we cannot live without? The Bible talks about Jesus that way. He is a treasure that once we have found it, we can do away with all other things in life as long as His residence in our hearts is preserved.

Can the same thing be said for finding your soul-mate? And for that matter, is it a universal desire, or only something some people need to make their lives complete?

My mind was still swirling as I knocked on Brenda's door. She opened it wearing a tank top and shorts, and she was the most beautiful woman I'd ever seen. I just stood there staring, unable to take a single step towards her, totally focused on the matter at hand as I reached into my left pocket and pulled out a small box containing the ring I had purchased just yesterday.

Our eyes met and we both smiled.

"Will you marry me?"

Epilogue

I STOOD ALONG THE wall behind the curtain waiting to be called out on stage. This was unbelievable! The sale of my novel, 'Mental Cruelty: One Side of the Story', had been growing steadily over the past six months. It was now number 3 on the New York Times best seller list, but more than that, it had become the hot topic of many a marriage psychologist or talk show host. My novel was having its fifteen minutes of fame and admittedly, I was soaking it all in.

People were actually reading my book, men especially. While I had been writing, I knew that there was an audience of men like myself who had also been screwed by the unjust divorce laws of their respective states. Men were angry about their situation and it seemed like nobody cared about how they felt. I had been there and done that, so I knew. I cared!

A man standing next to me was holding a clipboard, and motioned to me that I had ten more seconds. Was this really happening? Me, a small-time chiropractor and school teacher, and I suppose I should add, budding novelist, was about to walk out on stage before a packed audience and millions watching on TV at home. The success of my novel about the trials and perils of divorced men was beyond my wildest dreams. I wrote because I enjoy writing, and I write because I believe I have something positive to share with other men who have found themselves in the same boat as me!

Women read my book too.

The initial response from the feminine front was not exactly welcoming. My stance and opinions on the inequities of current divorce laws, and their bias against men was hardly embraced by women who feel that they need to be financially protected since a large number are not the main provider in their former household. I can understand their fury. Only I must make it clear that my novel represents a single case. My book chronicles my wife and me and is not intended to reflect society at large. Certainly, my goal was to warn future about-to-be-divorced men of what to expect in an impending divorce. I made lots of mistakes. I allowed myself as the expression goes, to be taken to the cleaners. I have no one to blame for that but myself. Still, if my novel can serve as an alarm, a wakeup call to other men, and help prevent them from making similar mistakes, then I would consider what I had to share effective and worthwhile.

The Christian audience had mixed reviews. All believers were supportive of seeing a mainstream novel containing scripture, a biblical perspective on marriage, and God's eternal plan for salvation. The evangelical aspect of my novel was a welcome change from what many of today's contemporary authors share as their philosophy of life. Still, there were issues taken by the church against my story because of the adultery that occurred between Brenda and me. I can accept and even sympathize with these legitimate concerns about a novel that is authored by a man who calls himself a born-again Christian, while some aspects of his life are disobedient to the commands of God.

The Straight Chiropractic audience loved seeing a good portion of the pure chiropractic philosophy explained within the confines of a novel. Of all the different groups of people who enjoyed my novel, I think I received more congratulatory phone calls and e-mails from the straight chiropractic community than any other. Few patients are ever really taught the true health value of the chiropractic adjustment. It was my honor to be able to share whatever little instruction I could on the pages of my book.

Obviously, my family and friends were thrilled to see close facsimiles of their characters represented, and were no doubt proud to point out to others that, 'hey, that's me he's talking about'! Yet like a large portion of the reading audience they too shared a criticism that was expressed by many.

Why does the book have to be so religious?

People liked reading about the trials and tribulations of my marriage and divorce, yet were often turned off by references to Jesus, the Bible, and anything else spiritual in nature. I'm sure that many a potential reader put my novel down when the religious connotations became too much for them. But that's who I am! Jesus is real to me in my everyday life. He's not someone I put up on a shelf and just pull out on Sunday or when I need to pray. And most notably, He's not someone to be kept secret, a topic of conversation better off avoided, or representative of a philosophy of life that one should just keep to church on Sundays. He's the author of life! I'm just a plain, old author. I can't write a book without mentioning Him. He's the one who gifted me with my writing ability. He's my main man!

My children:

From the time I first started writing my novel I worried about what they would think. It's fiction. The characters are not real. This is a story that I made up. I hope that the four of them can see that. I pray that they will forgive their father if I wrote anything that might offend them. My novel is only based upon the experiences of my own life. Fiction! It's just a story about a guy who got the short end of the stick in marriage and in the financial arrangement of a divorce.

It's also a novel about one man's redemption. How he never gave up, never succumbed to hopelessness, and subsequently was rewarded for his attitude by meeting his soul-mate. I hope my children, extended family, friends, and the millions of readers who bought my book recognize that Lenny Spencer triumphs in the end. His story is a story of victory! Divorce is like death, and I went through it. Psalm 23 reminded me to fear no evil, God was with me, and that if I trusted Him, and looked to Him, then everything would be okay. I want the men who are about to go through a divorce to know that that's what happened to me. As Barry Manilow sings: 'I Made It Through the Rain; I kept my world protected. I kept my point of view. And I found myself respected by the others who got rained on too and made it through.'

Through the curtain I could see Oprah standing in front of her chair, and waving to the large crowd.

"We have as our guest today," Oprah was introducing the topic of the program, "the author of the novel about divorce from the man's perspective, Dr. Lenny Spencer. His book," I could see Oprah holding my novel in her hand, "is titled, 'Mental Cruelty: One Side of the Story'. Would you please welcome with me today, chiropractor, teacher, and best-selling author, Dr. Lenny Spencer!"

As I walked on stage to shake hands and greet Oprah Winfrey, I noted that the welcoming applause were polite and strained. I thought I sensed a cold reception from a part of the audience.

I sat next to Oprah and smiled.

I'm just a chiropractor, a teacher, and the father of four healthy, awesome children. I went through a difficult marriage and finally a divorce. I wrote about it. People are now buying my book and at least for the time-being, I'm semi-famous. I'm today's news. It's just a season that I'm in. Fame will be fleeting, my name will soon be forgotten, my children are going to grow up and move away. I thought all this as I allowed my eyes to scan the huge audience in front of me. Nothing lasts. Everything is so temporary.

Then my eyes locked onto the eyes of someone in the crowd. I'm sitting next to Oprah Winfrey, for goodness sakes, but all I could really focus on was the reality that I was wrong! Things can last. Some things don't have to be just temporary, and besides Jesus, there is someone else I can depend upon, count on to be there forever, and trust with my very life.

I gave the most beautiful woman I've ever seen the broadest smile I could muster.

Brenda smiled back.